FOR LAURIE
I HOPE YOU

Austin Thomas (signature)

JUN 3 0 2014

LOGAN

AUSTIN THOMAS

ISBN: 1466391669
ISBN 13: 9781466391666

Library of Congress Control Number: 2011918004
CreateSpace, North Charleston, SC

Acknowledgements

I would like to thank the following people, who are just a few among many that provided support and assistance during the writing of this story.

First; my father in law Russ who encouraged me often to keep at it, but mostly because he appreciated it just because it's a good story.

Second; my good friend Charlie Castleberry who provided the picture of the Ranger badge on the cover (and so much more over the years).

Third; Joel Purkerson of JP Custom Knives in Lebanon, OR for allowing me to use a picture of one of his knives (without even asking for recognition).

Fourth; Videll Yackeschi of the Comanche Nation College in Lawton, OK for the translation of the Comanche names.

Last, but certainly not least to Linda, without whom I would be so much less than I am today and would likely never have written anything.

AUTHOR'S NOTE

Throughout the course of American history, many heroes have captured our attention and received our praise. However, none has been more deserving of our attention and praise than Logan Vandeveer, adventurer, soldier, Texas Ranger, and entrepreneur. His many accomplishments are the things legends are made of.

He was awarded a 1,700-acre parcel of land for his bravery at the Battle of San Jacinto, and yet he offered to give it back when asked by the newly formed Republic of Texas for land on which to build the new capital of Austin.

He served for ten years as a Texas Ranger during one of the most dangerous and troubled times in Texas' history, a tenure almost unheard of at that time.

He was the first Postmaster of Burnet County, where he established the first Free Masons charter in the area and built the county's first bank, church, and school, and where he hired an Oxford graduate to teach the children of this tough frontier area subjects usually offered at only the best of schools in the nation.

He was a loving husband and father as well as a staunch supporter of the Comanche and Kiowa people, finally developing friendly terms with them, even trading openly.

Logan built one of the first cattle ranches in the area and secured numerous contracts with the U.S. Army and other private individuals.

Sadly, for Texas and America, Logan Vandeveer's life was cut short; not by bandits, Comanches, or even Santa Ana himself, but by something much more insidious.

Many Texas historians agree that Logan would have become Governor of the great State of Texas if he had lived just ten or twenty more years.

Unfortunately, few people have heard the name of Logan Vandeveer, yet he is certainly one of the most indelible characters in our earlier history, and one I'm sure American history would be much poorer without. This is his story.

TABLE OF CONTENTS

LOGAN

Written by

AUSTIN THOMAS

FOREWORD

As I sit down to write the story of one of the truly great unsung heroes of the old west, I realize how painfully inadequate any storyteller might feel writing about such an incredible character. In that light, let me say a few things about what I have written, how and why. I spent many hours doing research, but didn't want to write a documentary style novel. As with all history, accounts can vary from one source to another, unless the witnesses to an act took the time to record its events in detail. This is where fictionalization comes into play. This book is a fictionalized account based upon a true story. I do not claim this is a purely historical novel. There are many real characters and events in this book whose stories I read in historical documents, and there are many fictional characters and events that have come from the depths of my mind. Sometimes the names of fictional characters overlap with real characters of the era. It is possible, even likely, that this has happened in this book. For the descendants of any of these real characters that bear the same name as one of my fictional characters,

I offer my humblest apology. Please bear in mind it is a fictional story based on some true events.

Throughout this book, I have tried to respect the different characters, both real and fictional, as much as possible. The Comanches, Kiowas, and Apaches were not mindless killers as they have often been portrayed in our history. They were intelligent, happy, loving people who simply lived in an environment that wouldn't allow for physical or emotional weakness. Although semi nomadic, they were territorial, regardless of their location at the time. The Comanches of this era were, by their own description and historical evidence, the 'Lords of the Southern Plains'. As such they defended their territory aggressively, thus appearing to the white man as ruthless, unsympathetic killers. I have included Comanche names for the respective characters found throughout this story, but because Comanche is a very complex language and difficult for the non-Comanche speaker to read, I have used the English translations of their names.

I have done a large amount of research, but, as with any subject, there is always more that can be done. Often times I found contradicting eyewitness accounts of some of the events. This is very common throughout history.

I hope the reader will keep this in mind and enjoy this story about an incredible man who has been too long forgotten.

Thank you very much, and I hope you enjoy it.

Austin Thomas

CHAPTER 1

SAN JACINTO

April 21, 1836

Logan saw the flash of the exploding cannon round. The sound assailed his ears, deafening him. Its impact hit his tall muscular body with such force that it drove him backward by at least twenty feet. He lay still for a long moment in shock, confused by what had happened. He tried to see and hear what was going on around him. He knew he was in danger and that he should get up and get moving, but he was unable to do so. His eyes had been blinded by the flash, and he only heard silence. After several tries, he made it to his feet. He stumbled, but kept his balance. He was able to make out blurred forms rushing past him as his eyes began to clear, so he moved along with them. His eyes kept watering in an attempt to flush out the dirt that felt like sandpaper against his eyelids. He wondered why it was so quiet. All he could hear was his own pounding heartbeat. Was war always this quiet? He wouldn't have thought so. He felt light, as though he might float away, so he held on tight to his rifle. Surely it would hold him down. He staggered forward through the blurred haze, gripped by shock, fear, and confusion. Images suddenly flooded his mind, each one telling a story from his past. Memories rushed through the silence as if they were happening all over again.

He thought of William Harrison Magill, his best friend and cousin from his mother's side, and their decision to leave their homes and families behind. They had come out from Kentucky together to make something of themselves in this Texas frontier.

Will was the one man Logan loved and admired above all others. He was older by just three years, but had looked after Logan since they were youngsters. Will had taught him to hunt and track game, and together they had run all over the hills of Kentucky, until Logan had begun to hear tales of a new land being settled out west; a land called Texas. When Logan told Will of these tales, he had listened intently, and advised him as a father would.

"What about your Ma and Pa? What about your brother and sisters?" Will had said, pausing for effect. "What about them? Would they take to these tales so easily?"

Logan knew he was right. His family wouldn't want him to go. After all, he was only seventeen, and Texas was a wild country a thousand miles away and filled with dangers unheard of in Casey County, Kentucky, where he'd been born and raised. Will let him ponder this decision for more than two months without saying another word about it. When Logan finally decided to go see this fabled land of Texas, he went to Will to tell him goodbye.

But before Logan could say a word, Will looked him in the eye very seriously and asked, "Are you sure you're ready for this? What if we get there and don't like it?" His expression hardened as he spoke. "These tales are usually blown up bigger than real life."

Logan was taken by complete surprise. He had never suggested that Will go with him, and his cousin had never shown any inclination to go to Texas. He had listened patiently to Logan for months and never said a word about going along. Logan wondered if Will had decided to go along just to protect him, to look after him as he'd always done. Then he saw the mischievous look on Will's face.

"Whadda'ya mean we? You got a frog in your pocket or somethin'? " Logan finally asked, grinning.

"You didn't really think I'd just sit by and let you go off and get yourself lost half way to Texas did you?" Will asked, with the slightest grin on his face. "Why, you'd be wanderin' around within a week cryin' for your mammy." Mischief sparkled in his grey eyes again. "Prob'ly get yourself scalped by wild Injuns."

"What makes you think I'd want you to go along anyway?" Logan said with a look of mock irritation on his face. "Probably have to carry you most of the way. Not sure I'm up for it."

"Well, the way you was dilly dallyin' around, decidin' whether to go or not, I was about to give up on you and just go my own self," Will said, as he punched Logan in the shoulder.

Logan's face lit up. "How long would it take you to get your gear together?" he asked, excitement flooding his face.

Will looked sidelong at Logan and said, "Hell boy, I've had my gear packed and ready to go for near six weeks. You shore' are slow at makin' up your mind." Logan just grinned and shook his head slowly.

They left the next day amid tears and pleading from Logan's mother not to go. As Logan turned and walked off to the west, Will put his arms around his Aunt Emily and promised he'd look after her boy. She wasn't comforted.

Now here they were in Texas fighting for its independence and their very lives.

Suddenly a blue clad figure rose up in front of him. He saw the flash of a bayonet through the blurry haze of smoke and blindness. Fear lashed out in him and he struck the figure down with the butt of his rifle. He lunged forward slashing with the big knife Will had given him just two weeks earlier, claiming that the knife was even bigger than the one Jim Bowie had made famous. Will had said that it just might save his life, adding with a chuckle, "even in a sword fight."

Logan hoped he wouldn't let Will down. He began to feel tired. They had marched many miles with little food or sleep and he was weary, but he pushed on through the silent haze, slashing and stabbing until he could go no further, the darkness folding around him, the silence complete. He thought he saw a blurry face hovering over him as he hit the muddy ground. It seemed familiar, but he couldn't hold on to it. As the blackness covered him like a warm blanket, he wondered if he was dying, or was he already dead? He began to dream about the days that had brought him to this point of life or death. The images seemed so real, as if he were going through it all again. He could hear the sounds of the night marches running through his head hypnotically: the endless rattle and clink of men trudging wearily through the darkness. Sometimes the men were so quiet they almost escaped notice, but sometimes they were so loud that Logan was sure they could be heard for miles. It was at this moment that Logan had felt fear for the first time, fear that Santa Ana himself would hear the sounds and come to kill them all, right down to the last man, as he had done at the Alamo and Goliad. But, the sounds were always there, driving them onward. There was no stopping for rest or refreshment from the constant marching and the aching fatigue, day and night. More than seven hundred men continued marching through yet another night under the command of General Sam Houston, the tramp, clink and rattle driving them on without mercy. When one of the seven hundred would falter and give in to the merciless toil of the forced march, others around him would bolster his spirits by calling out quietly, "Remember the Alamo! Remember Goliad!" and then the hypnotic tramp, clink and rattle would begin again, pushing their weary legs onward.

They had marched, fought and trained for the last six weeks, ever since they'd reached Gonzales on March 11, 1836, when word had come to them that the Alamo had fallen and all two hundred fifty seven men inside had been killed. No quarter asked by them, and none was given. This had started a general panic in the area, and with good reason. The settlers knew that Santa Ana would come and kill them without mercy if they were caught west of the Sabine River and a frantic rush from the area commenced. General Sam Houston knew that the only chance many of these settlers had would be if he and his troops could delay Santa Ana long enough for them to get across the Sabine. Houston himself had the town of Gonzales burned to keep Santa Ana from using any part of it for supplies. Then Houston began what became known as the 'runaway scrape', with his troops and all the settlers running and fighting their way either north or east. On March 31, 1836, Houston's army of seven hundred stopped running and camped on the banks of the Brazos, opposite Groce's Plantation. Here they heard of the slaughter at Goliad, where Colonel Fannin and three hundred forty-two unarmed men were marched out onto the prairie then shot, stabbed, and clubbed to death. Even the ones that lay wounded and helpless were killed without mercy. Santa Ana's brutality again steeled their resolve. At Groce's, they rested and trained for the next two weeks, then were off again in search of Santa Ana, the self-proclaimed 'Napoleon of the West' who was in search of them, or so it seemed. The march was slow, but continued until they reached Harrisburg and captured a Mexican courier that gave them information about Santa Ana's location.

They had marched for more than two days and nights without stop, covering well over fifty miles through the brush, trees, and hills that made up this country they called Texas—country they would fight for and very likely die in.

During the past two brutal days Logan found himself faltering, as they all likely did. He wondered why he was even here. What was it that was making them drive on through the blistering days and freezing, dark nights? But when he looked around and saw the determination on the faces of these men, marching beside him at this breakneck pace, it steeled his resolve. There was comfort in the brotherhood of these tough men rushing out to kill, and possibly die for, what they knew to be a threat to their freedom and their very lives. Finally, just after midday on April 18, 1836, the two-day forced march of fifty-five miles ended at the bottom of a small rise, and when they stopped to make camp, the seven hundred men fell to the ground, exhausted. Some slept where they dropped; others began to make coffee or cook what little food was left.

Captain Billingsley came around to all his men and spoke what little words of comfort he could muster.

General Sam Houston was seen and heard throughout, giving encouragement and praise to all the men for what they had done. But what was it they had done? Marching non-stop to the point of near death didn't seem such a great deed. Rather, it seemed foolhardy. If Santa Ana came at them now, they would all die, as surely as those poor bastards had on the plains at Goliad, or the ones trapped inside the Alamo. But, Santa Ana didn't come that day. He and his army were nowhere to be found. Early in the evening another courier was captured and it was determined that Santa Ana had pressed on, burning the town of Harrisburg on the way. The men were told to rest and prepare for another march in the early morning.

Long before first light, the rag-tag group of hardened men moved out without a word. There was justice to be meted out and every one of them was determined to fight in the name of liberty. They made it across the Buffalo Bayou on the San Jacinto River that day and discovered the resolve of Santa Ana. He was still pushing his fifteen hundred men as hard as these Texas men were pushing themselves. Houston's army was closing in, but they would still have to march again. On April 21, Houston's men closed on Santa Ana, undetected. General Houston used Lynch's Ferry to move his troops across the San Jacinto River, then sank the ferry and burned Vince's Bridge, the only bridge in the area. Now they would fight to the end, for there was no way back, no retreat. The fate of Texas rested on their weary shoulders. If they won, Texas would be born; if they died, Texas would die with them. At around one thirty in the afternoon, in what seemed like a blur of fatigue, Santa Ana's troops were sighted behind bulwarks hastily thrown up at the top of the rise. The seven hundred took up their positions in a grove of trees at the bottom, hidden from view. Every man there sloughed off his fatigue, renewed by the looming battle ahead.

Captain Billingsley came and informed his men that they would have the honor of being in the first wave to charge the encampment and deliver payment for the good men lost at Goliad and the Alamo. The excitement at finally meeting what many considered the devil on earth did more for the morale of these hard, determined men than a full week's rest could have done. They were on their feet refreshed and ready to have at him. From where Billingsley was ordered to take up the line, they were front and center, marching straight, so it seemed, into the belly of the beast. They were ready, and when the order was given, they rushed up the rise and into history.

"Logan… Logan…" He could hear the voice in the back of his mind, but it seemed many miles away. How could he hear it from that far?

"Logan! Come on boy, come back to me!" The voice, a little louder now, was insistent and seemed to be driving back the dark warm blanket that enveloped him. He didn't want to answer; he just wanted to sleep.

"LOGAN VANDEVEER!"

Suddenly the voice was very loud and seemed for all the world to be stinging his face.

"DAMMIT LOGAN, YOU WAKE UP BOY!"

He sat bolt upright, pain searing his side from armpit to hipbone, and oddly across his left cheek. Will's face appeared not two inches from his own. A grin spread across it and then a look of anguish as he grabbed at Logan and helped him lie back onto the cot.

"Careful son! You'll open up that cut on your side again, and I don't think the Doc's got enough catgut to re-do 'er," he said as he gently deposited Logan against the roll of dirty canvas that was used as a pillow. The look of relief and concern was genuine and showed in the moistness of his eyes.

Logan tried to speak, but found the effort too much.

"Just relax, but you stay awake for a minute now," Will said as he sat on the side of the cot. It creaked under their combined weight. "You been gone from us for quite a while now. It's good to have you back."

Logan tried to speak again, but the searing pain shot up his side once again, taking his breath.

"I reckon you want to know what happened, eh boy?" Logan's eyes said yes. "Seems I was right back in Kentuck', cause you musta got lost. Someone said you went down under a cannon round, and before I could get to you we was overwhelmed. A retreat was called and they was drivin' us back when the Cap'n yelled for us to look yonder… Seemed Santa Ana's men was running in all directions, and there you was, way back yonder, behind us, at the top of the ridge, surrounded by half the Mex'can army. You was screamin' at the top of your lungs and slashin' Mex'cans as quick as you could get to 'em. Couldn't tell if they was more scared of your screamin' or that dang big knife. Either way they musta thought you was some kinda demon or something, 'cause they couldn't seem to get away from you fast enough." Will's eyes flashed with joy and pride at being able to recount the story to Logan himself, rather than to his pallbearers. "Why, when Cap'n Billingsley seen you up there a'killin' 'em by the dozen, he turned us around and we fought our way back to where you was, and then you went down. By then, them Mex'cans was runnin' so fast we could hardly catch 'em, but we did. Ever damn one of 'em, even caught that devil Santa Ana himself hidin' by the river dressed in a private's uniform. We routed the entire Mex'can army. Killed near six hundred of 'em, captured the rest, *and* all their guns, ammo and livestock, all without losing hardly a man. If ever one man turned the tide of a battle, it was you, then and there. General Houston's been here every day since you come in, seein' if you was awake yet. He took a rifle ball in the leg and had to be carried the first three days."

There was a question in Logan's eyes he couldn't put to words because of the wound in his side, but Will understood.

"You been here five days now, boy. Seems that explodin' cannon round near cut you in half. Doc used more'n two hundred stitches of catgut to hold you together till you could heal. He says you're knittin' up real fine though, but we was afraid you might not wake up. I tried to tell 'im you just needed some roustin' being the heavy sleeper you always was." Will reached out and gently patted Logan's stinging left cheek. "I knew a couple a smacks on the face'd probably do it. Reckon if you wasn't so damned ornery you probably wouldn't have come back to us." Will stopped and became serious. "Don't know that I could ever face your Ma again if you didn't pull through. But it looks like you're gonna, so you get well and let's get on with what we started. This here war is over, boy!" Logan looked puzzled, but sleep began to drag him back down again and he couldn't keep his eyes open any longer. He heard Will's voice one last time before succumbing to the comforting warmth of the blanket.

"It's okay boy, you go on and sleep awhile now and just get well. When you're better, we'll…"

And that was the last thing Logan heard.

Logan was rousted from the warm blanket once more, this time by voices he didn't recognize. One was gravelly and old.

"Why, he's about the toughest fella I've ever put knife or needle to, General. That cannon round cut him from armpit clear down to his hip. Opened him as neat as ever I could've with my sharpest knife. I'm sure that's why he never putrefied. Cleanest battle cut I ever seen, and cauterized to boot. Don't know how he survived the day let alone these last five. The question is will he wake up. Five days is a long time to be unconscious. Many a man has found that trip too long to endure and have gone on, if you know what I mean."

The other voice was silky smooth, but there was an unmistakable hardness to it.

"Well, Doc, this young fella doesn't seem the type to give up. I've been told he not only took the wound, but got back on his feet while the rest were starting to retreat, and he fought his way to the top of the rise with only that big knife there under his pillow. His friend, Sgt. Magill, put it there and warned everyone to leave it be. Said it would comfort him if ever he woke up again. Captain Billingsley claims he killed twenty-two armed Mexican Regulars with it in hand-to-hand combat before they could get away from him," said the hard silky voice.

Logan's eyes fluttered open. His blurred vision slowly cleared. There was a short balding man in a long gray coat talking to General Sam Houston. They both stopped talking and looked over at Logan. His eyes wandered the small tent. He seemed to be alone, save for a small table littered with a few bottles and a canteen.

"It's good to see you awake son," said General Houston. "We surely didn't want to lose you," he said, a big smile spreading across his face.

The smaller man moved to Logan's side. He placed one hand over Logan's eyes and then pulled it away quickly while peering into them.

"Eye reflexes are good, probably no bleeding inside his skull." He loosened the bandage around Logan's torso. Logan felt the cool air on his skin and twitched.

"Sorry if I hurt you son, I surely don't mean to. I've got a little laudanum if the pain is too bad," he said, as he examined the long wound. Logan didn't know what laudanum was, but it only hurt whenever he tried to move, so he figured he didn't need it.

He spoke then, being careful to move only his lips. "Reckon there might be others need it worse 'n me," he croaked. His throat was so parched that he didn't recognize the rasp of his own voice.

General Houston picked up the canteen and, cradling Logan's head, helped him drink. Logan was thirsty and drank big gulps of the cool water. General Houston quickly pulled the canteen from his lips.

He wanted more, but General Houston said he should wait a bit, adding with a grin, "It's not good to drink too fast...it could founder you."

Logan lay back on the cot as the doctor finished examining his wound and put on a fresh bandage.

"Yes sir, healing better than any battle wound I've ever seen. Maybe three or four more days and he can try to walk," the doctor said as he finished tying the last knot on the bandage. "Always found it better to get 'em on their feet as soon as possible. Helps speed the healing and helps 'em get over the pain. Seen men hurt much less than this die from layin' a-bed too long, allowing themselves to suffer."

General Houston looked down at Logan. "We owe you a debt, Private, and I'm not entirely sure we'll ever be able to repay you for what you did. I've never heard of anything like what you did. I hate to think where we'd be now if Billingsley hadn't seen you and turned the men to charge again. I fear we'd all be dead on the prairie like those poor devils in Goliad."

Logan didn't know what to say; the last thing he remembered was stumbling up the rise. It was as if they were talking about someone else. So he just said the one thing that he knew. "Sure would like another drink of water, sir. I'm mighty thirsty," he croaked.

The general and the doctor looked at one another. Houston laughed as he uncorked the canteen.

"Well I swear!" exclaimed the doctor shaking his head.

"I'd appreciate it if you wouldn't let it get around that I'm waiting on a private; might not look good to the rest of the men," General Houston said, still chuckling. "They all might begin to feel…slighted."

Logan swallowed several more gulps of the water, looking a little sheepish at the thought of the general waiting on him.

Three days later, Logan awoke in the early morning and struggled from the cot amid a torrent of pain. He gritted his teeth and forced himself to his feet. He felt as weak as a new kitten and stood for a long while next to the cot before he tried to move anything else. Nausea and dizziness swept over him as he stood there. When it had passed, he felt stronger. He was as determined as ever. Focusing on the flap of the tent, he fought forward. The pain brought the nausea back, but he struggled on through it. Six small steps and he caught hold of the tent's center pole and steadied himself. He lifted the flap slowly and stepped out into the morning. There, spread before him was the most beautiful sunrise he could ever remember seeing. Maybe it was because he had come so close to death, or maybe it was because he felt himself to be a truly free man with a great future ahead. Either way, it was with a look of rapture and tears streaming down his face that Will found him.

"Whoa, there son!" Will exclaimed as he ran to support Logan. "You gotta' be careful awhile yet. Don't overdo it."

Logan held up his hand and stopped Will in his tracks. "I'm okay. So far," he said weakly. "Doc says I should walk as soon as I can, and, well, I guess I can. Right now I just want to look at that sunrise." They stood side by side gazing happily into the east.

"Well, where do we go and what do we do now?" Will asked, looking over at his best friend, this tough young man with more grit than he had ever imagined. He felt humbled next to Logan, even though he had played the part of older compatriot and advisor all of their lives. Logan was clearly the one to call the next shot. He'd earned it.

"I was thinkin' maybe we should go back to Mina," Logan said without taking his eyes off the sunrise. Mina was the small settlement started by Moses Austin and his son Stephen F. Austin, who would later become known as the Father of Texas. "I was noticin' all those wild beeves runnin' around and I figure now that this war's over, folks'll be flockin' in here. A couple of fellas like us might try gatherin' some of 'em up and sellin' 'em to the folks when they get here." He took his eyes off the sunrise and glanced over at Will.

When their eyes met, Will smiled. "Brother, if you think it might be a good idea then I'd bet my bottom dollar on it."

Logan looked troubled "Will, I heard some things when I was comin' round the other day. Things General Houston said, and they been botherin' me." Logan looked straight into Will's face. "I didn't do anything like everybody is making me out to have done, leastwise, not that I remember. I don't feel brave or smart or anything; except lucky..." He touched his bandaged side gingerly then added, "...and sore." Logan turned slowly to face Will, searching his eyes for answers. "I was gone in the head, I guess, back during the fight. I remember a bright flash and then I remember thinkin' it seemed awful quiet, but that's all. I don't remember nothin' else." There was the questioning look on his face that Will had never seen on anyone before. Logan was truly puzzled and bothered by what had happened.

"You mean you can't remember none of it?" Will asked, hesitantly. Logan just shook his head. "Well, trust my words now, Brother, 'cause I'm speakin' gospel. When Cap'n Billingsley turned us back up the rise, I watched you kill at least seven or eight Mex'cans clean, and fast, then I got busy with 'em my own self and don't know how many more you took, but if they say it was twenty two then by Almighty God I believe it." He had his hand on Logan's hard, muscular shoulder, and the two men just stood looking at each other. Logan looked distressed. "One other thing I should tell you; I just don't want you getting' a big head and lordin' it over me," Will said with a funny look on his face. "I was the first to get to you, and when you started to go down I reached for you and you lunged toward me with your knife, and Brother, I want to tell you, that thing looks mighty big when it's coming at you point first."

Logan jumped as if he'd been slapped, then just stood staring at Will for a moment in disbelief. "No, Will, don't say it. Don't tell me I tried to…kill you too!" He was now truly anguished.

"Yes sir, I surely thought so…at first. That big ol' blade slipped under my arm just as slick and clean as could be…" Will said, turning from the sunrise to look into Logan's eyes again, "…and into the belly of a Mex'can Regular. He was comin' at me from the side, and when you fell into my arms, I turned a might. His bayonet missed, and when he fell, that big ol' knife was stickin' clean out his backbone. He was as dead as stone before he hit the ground," Will said, putting his hand on Logan's shoulder. "You just grinned that goofy grin of yours, and then you was out." Logan didn't want to believe him, but he was sure Will wouldn't josh him about such a thing. "You saved our lives, Brother, and I'm surely grateful to you, for both of 'em."

Logan realized that Will had called him 'Brother' again and no longer called him 'boy' or 'son'. His heart seemed to swell so big in his chest, he thought it might just burst out on its own.

They turned to the sunrise again.

"Mina, beeves, suttlers…that's the ticket," Will said, without looking away from the east and the magnificent sunrise.

Four days later, with the Doc's okay, Logan left the infirmary tent and went to the tent he shared with Will. They settled in and waited for orders. Except for some minor patrols to make sure the area was clear of any Mexican sympathizers, little happened after Logan's recovery until May 3rd. They were ordered back to Mina and departed early the next day with a patrol made up of the First Regiment of the Texas Militia.

CHAPTER 2

YELLOW WOLF

His name was Oha Isa, which in the Comanche language, means Yellow Wolf. He was respected and feared by many as one of the great war chiefs of his time. He awoke that morning to the sound of horses galloping into camp. He arose and went out into the dim morning light to see his two scouts, Tuwikaa Wahati (Two Crows) and Wasape Nikʉ Tunehtsʉ (Runs Like a Bear), coming in. He had sent them out to the east to watch the Mexican Army and steal horses from them if they could. Yellow Wolf hated these white men, who dig in the dirt, these Tosapi̱ Tohkonaru'. They called themselves Texians, but to him they were simply White Diggers. Yellow Wolf hated the Mexican Army even more. He was glad that the Mexicans and Texians were enemies. Maybe they would kill each other until none of them were left, or at least until there were so few left that Yellow Wolf and his sizable band of Comanches, called the Kutsutʉʉka, or Buffalo Eaters, could come in and finish off the rest. He would like to see that; then he and all the tribes around could go back to the way of life they'd known before either of these hated enemies had trampled their land. He would like to kill as many Whites and Mexicans as he could. As he walked out to meet Two Crows and Runs Like a Bear, he felt irritation at them, especially Runs Like a Bear. He did not like this big lumbering warrior.

Hmph, some warrior, he thought. *He barely killed one enemy, and an old man at that.* Runs Like a Bear knew Yellow Wolf did not like him. He sat on his skinny, tired, old horse (his only horse) and tried to look indifferent, but made sure he did not look directly at Yellow Wolf. He could never tell what would set Yellow Wolf off. "Why are you here?" Yellow Wolf asked, looking straight at Two Crows. "It is hard to steal horses from the Mexican Army, far to the east, if you are here." He stood looking up at both warriors. Two Crows had grown up with Yellow Wolf and did not fear him like many of the others in camp. They had been friends as children and had gone on their first raid together. They had counted coup together, and were lifelong friends. Two Crows had proven time and again that he was equal to Yellow Wolf at many things. Many things, but not at being the war chief of this fierce group of Comanches. Two Crows had neither the ambition nor the blood lust of Yellow Wolf. He would rather stick to stealing horses, something he knew well and was very good at.

Runs Like a Bear didn't like it when Yellow Wolf made him go with Two Crows, because he wanted to steal horses for himself, but Two Crows always made him wait, and hold their own horses. He said Runs Like a Bear was too noisy and would get them caught. Two Crows always kept all the horses he stole for himself. Runs Like a Bear decided he wouldn't go with Two Crows anymore.

Two Crows sat looking down at Yellow Wolf passively, the two black feathers he wore braided into his hair to honor his namesake waving slightly. "The Mexican, Santa Ana, has gone east to kill more of the White Diggers," Two Crows said. Yellow Wolf thought about this for a moment. That was good. It would be better if the White Diggers killed Santa Ana and all of his men. "An army of the White Diggers chases him, but he does not know it." Two Crows said, still looking down at Yellow Wolf. "They may catch him soon, but I think there aren't enough to kill him. He is twice as many."

Yellow Wolf rubbed his chin. "I would like to see the White Diggers try to kill him," he said thoughtfully. "They will probably die, but I will go and see for myself." Two Crows and Runs Like a Bear sat awhile longer watching Yellow Wolf, and then turned to ride away. "Two Crows will go with me to see them die, but Runs Like a Bear will stay here." Yellow Wolf said, as he turned back toward his lodge.

Yellow Wolf was ready to go and sat on his horse, waiting impatiently. Two Crows put the rest of his food in a pouch to eat on the way. He and Runs Like a Bear had hurried back to camp to tell Yellow Wolf about the Mexican Army and had not stopped to eat or rest, something that had made Runs Like a Bear very surly. Two Crows decided he would take one of the younger boys with him to steal horses from now on. They would probably not be so noisy.

Yellow Wolf was getting very irritated, sitting, waiting for Two Crows with the whole camp watching.

"Stop moving like an old woman. We should be leaving, now!" Yellow Wolf snapped. Two Crows finished what he was doing and paid little attention to Yellow Wolf. This angered Yellow Wolf even more. If it were anyone else besides Two Crows, he might consider killing them, but Two Crows was his lifelong friend, so he didn't think he could kill him for such a trivial thing, at least not today. He needed him to show the way to the Mexicans. He would speak to Two Crows when they were alone. It was important that all the warriors of the Kutsutɯɯka camp be respectful of him, even if only because he was the War Chief. Two Crows would understand this. Yellow Wolf would not like to kill him as an example, but kill him he would, if he had to. As they rode past Runs Like a Bear's lodge, Yellow Wolf did not take notice of the big clumsy warrior watching them sourly. *I will kill him someday*, Runs Like a Bear thought, scowling as they rode past. *Maybe both of them.* He turned and went into his lodge. He was not a very good hunter so his lodge was poor, and because of this, he had no wife to care for it. He blamed this on Yellow Wolf and Two Crows. If they showed him more respect, his life would be better. Yes, he would kill them both someday.

Yellow Wolf and Two Crows traveled as fast as they could, but they were going a very long way through some of the other tribes' territory, and Yellow Wolf was not on the best of terms with them so they had to be careful not to be discovered. It took them eight days to cover the one hundred sixty five miles between the Buffalo Eaters camp, situated on the Guadalupe River near San Antonio, and the buffalo swamp in the east, where Logan and the Texas militia were stationed. (In later years, the whole area around this swamp would be known as Houston.)

The two Comanche warriors could hear the White Men's marching long before they got to the buffalo swamp. They were chasing the Mexican Army, but it seemed that Santa Ana did not know they were there. How could he not know? They made so much noise that Yellow Wolf would have been able to find and kill them even on the darkest of nights. He and Two Crows watched and followed alongside the army of the White Diggers. It would not be good to get too close and find themselves caught between the White Diggers and the Mexicans.

The Texians stopped in the morning mist beside the buffalo swamp to rest and cook food. They were stupid. Santa Ana could've swept down and killed them all had he not taken his army and kept marching. He burned a settlement of the White Diggers and killed many who lived there. After another half day of watching the Mexicans, Two Crows stopped his horse for a moment, a look of amazement spreading across his face.

"They are crossing over the river to die," he said matter-of-factly.

"What do you mean? How will these slow, stupid White Diggers kill them? The Mexicans are twice as many," Yellow Wolf demanded, scowling at Two Crows. He was unfamiliar with the area around the buffalo swamp. Still, it did not seem logical. Two Crows drew on the ground with a stick.

"Across the river they are trapped between two rivers, heavy with rain, and a swamp," Two Crows explained. "There are only two ways the White Diggers or the Mexicans can cross with many men at once. If the White Diggers know this, they will destroy the tree path in the west," he said, pointing in the direction of the wooden bridge, "and the great canoe to the north." They looked in the direction of Lynch's Ferry. Yellow Wolf realized the Mexicans had set up their camp on what was effectively an island during a time when the rivers ran high and the swamp to the east flooded. They had no retreat and were unaware of the Texians. Still, he doubted the White Diggers could kill the Mexicans. Either way, he was glad that many would die on both sides.

Two Crows said that they should cross the buffalo swamp and wait beside the Mexicans, after all that is where the White Diggers would go, even if they didn't know it yet. Yellow Wolf looked the area over again, Two Crows was right. He nodded and they made their way across the buffalo swamp very carefully.

The water was very high and they struggled to keep the horses calm so they wouldn't be noticed. They crossed over and found a place where they could watch unseen as the Mexicans arranged men and cannons on a rise overlooking the open field above the river.

They waited all night and into the next day. When the shadows were getting longer, the Whites appeared at the bottom of the open field. They were standing in long straight lines.

"They are very stupid," said Yellow Wolf. "Many will die if they try to attack the Mexicans this way." Two Crows agreed, then pointed at the Mexican camp. Almost no one was visible. There were no scouts watching. It seemed as if they were sleeping and didn't know the Texians were just at the bottom of the hill, ready to attack. Yellow Wolf and Two Crows looked at one another, wondering if it might be a trap by the Mexican army. They watched in amazement as the Texians began to move slowly and quietly up the rise. He and Two Crows would return to their camp once the battle was over and come back with many warriors to kill all who remained, White Digger and Mexican alike. There would be many coup counted and many new scalps hanging from Comanche lodge poles very soon.

When the Texians were well over halfway up the rise, they charged and shouted a war cry that neither Yellow

Wolf nor Two Crows could understand. Then the Mexican thunder started and Yellow Wolf smiled; even a young Comanche warrior could kill many of the White Diggers before they reached the top. The White Diggers began to move faster and faster. Yellow Wolf and Two Crows looked on in amazement. It seemed the White Diggers had some medicine that protected them. The Mexicans were shooting from very close, but the White Diggers were not dying in great numbers like Two Crows and Yellow Wolf thought they would. They just kept going up the hill. The Mexican thunder became so thick that the White Diggers had to stop and turn back. The Mexicans went after them, but not as fast as Yellow Wolf thought they should. They must be afraid of the White Diggers' medicine. Two Crows nudged Yellow Wolf and pointed to a spot near the top of the hill. There was one White Digger fighting alone among all the Mexicans. He was tall, dark, and very muscular. A long wound stretched down his side, but he seemed not to notice it. He killed one Mexican by hitting him with his rifle, and then he began to fight many others with a great knife. Yellow Wolf was sure he would die soon. He seemed like a brave warrior: brave, but stupid. Yellow Wolf and Two Crows watched in wonder as he continued to stand and fight. The Mexicans could not kill him, even though he was completely surrounded. One after another died under his great knife, but still the Mexicans came and still he stood.

Two Crows looked at Yellow Wolf. "His medicine is strong…they cannot kill him."

Yellow Wolf watched him fight on bravely. "He will die soon," he said matter-of-factly. They watched as more Mexicans died under the big warrior's great knife, then there was a shout from below and the White Diggers surged back up the hill, driving Mexicans before them. Many Mexicans died as the White Diggers moved up the hill, but few of the White Diggers went down. Finally the White Diggers were near the big warrior and the thunder stopped. The Mexicans were running from the White Diggers, but still the White Diggers chased them down and killed all they could. The open field was scattered with the bodies of many Mexicans. Some White Diggers met their end, but most were still alive. This battle had taken less time to end than it would to smoke a pipe. Yellow Wolf looked for the big warrior but couldn't see him. Two Crows pointed to a group of the White Diggers moving back down the hill. They were carrying the big warrior, struggling under his weight.

"He must be a great chief," Two Crows said. "Look how they care for his body. He will go to his ancestors with great honor." Yellow Wolf had to agree. It was too bad. Yellow Wolf would like to have met and killed this warrior himself. He imagined the power he could have gained from this man's medicine. It would have made him an even greater war chief than he already was.

They watched a while longer, then skirted around the area, hiding carefully, watching. It was clear that more than half of Santa Ana's army was killed or wounded. The White Diggers took all the weapons, stock, horses, and food. Yellow Wolf just shook his head. This was not what he expected. These White Diggers were not to be taken lightly. They were obviously going to be a great enemy, one all the tribes would have to be careful of.

Yellow Wolf's plans to kill the survivors of the battle changed. For the first time in his life he began to doubt the immortality of the plains tribes, the greatest horse warriors of all.

As he and Two Crows rode back to their camp on the Guadalupe River, he thought much about their future. He could not live peacefully with these White Diggers, but he wondered if even the combined strength of the Comanche and the Kiowa would be enough to rub them out. The White Diggers' medicine was great. They would have to be patient, like when they hunted the Tatsiwoo, the great buffalo that roamed over the vast prairie. They would wait patiently; an opportunity would come.

When they neared the camp of the Buffalo Eaters, Yellow Wolf turned to Two Crows and said, "I don't think we should try to kill the White Diggers' army. We will kill all White Diggers within two days ride of our camp, after all, they are only diggers, but we will not try to kill the warriors, yet." Two Crows understood this and nodded.

When they arrived at their camp, Yellow Wolf told the Medicine Chief, Tu Paruwa (Black Elk), to call a council. He and Two Crows told the council what they had seen at the buffalo swamp. Any intruder into this part of their territory must be considered an enemy. The elders spoke on this matter far into the night trying to decide what they should do about this new and powerful enemy. Yellow Wolf spoke of his thought that they should kill all the White Diggers within two days ride of their camp, but some of the elders thought that might just anger this new enemy and cause more trouble than they could survive. Yellow Wolf called those elders "women" and it caused an uproar around the council fire. Yellow Wolf stepped forward and said it was time for the Comanche, Kiowa, and all the other tribes of the plains to drive these people from their lands. They should prepare for war.

"Are we not, after all, the Lords of the Southern Plains?" he asked. All were stunned into silence for a few moments. Those who opposed the idea remained silent. The remainder agreed with Yellow Wolf and it was decided: All the Whites must be driven from their lands or die. They would send messages to all the other bands and tribes around, telling what Yellow Wolf and Two Crows had seen at the buffalo swamp, and asking the other tribes to also drive the White Diggers out or kill them.

That night Yellow Wolf could hardly sleep, even though he was very tired from the trip back and the long council. He had much to consider and many things to plan. He hoped they could kill many of these white enemies and drive them from their area.

In two days, Yellow Wolf had gotten all his warriors and their horses readied for war. All wore medicine designs of yellow paint that would protect them from their enemy's weapons. All had sharp knives, many new arrows, and strong lances to kill the White Diggers. In the early morning chill of the third day, Yellow Wolf and more than a hundred warriors rode out of their camp on the bank of the Guadalupe and into what would eventually become the end of life as they knew it.

The large group of painted warriors swept out to the west a short distance and then turned north. They only encountered one family trying desperately to get to the Trinity River so they could cross it to safety. Yellow Wolf had them killed with only a glance. As the band turned east, they encountered more small groups coming back into the land. This angered Yellow Wolf and many of the other warriors. None showed mercy for the unfortunate few caught in the path of this fearsome band. They came across seven small groups, mostly single families. All died quickly, none died easily. As they crossed the Navidad River, the scouts brought news of a larger group moving due west toward them. Yellow Wolf spread the warriors out on the side of a hill among the trees and waited. When the wagons came angling down the slope, they were overwhelmed, and in less time than it would take to retell the story around the fires at night, it was over. All the white men, women, and children were dead and everything burned. Yellow Wolf's band was moving fast and traveling light. All that was taken were scalps. They continued to the south, but encountered no more of the White Diggers, or even Mexicans. After nine days, they were back at their camp along the Guadalupe, dancing and celebrating their victories. Even Runs Like a Bear killed two of the white enemies and took a horse. He had gained some respect among the people. He was happier that night, but he still avoided Yellow Wolf and Two Crows.

CHAPTER 3

WAGON TRAIN

As the small troop of soldiers headed west from Harrisburg toward Mina, they were in high spirits. They were free men on the plains, and though they were soldiers bound by the duties and the day-to-day grind of army life, they could all see the brightness of their future, and none more so than Pvt. Logan Vandeveer and Sgt. W.H. "Will" Magill. The two talked and planned almost constantly. They were intent on raising cattle on the lush grass of the Texas hill country. They were involved in just such a discussion when Logan got a faint feeling that something wasn't right. He wasn't sure what had caught his attention first, the faint smell of death, or a glint of something shiny on the hillside to their right, but the small troop stopped and waited while Logan and Will rode carefully up the hill into the trees to see what it was that had caught Logan's eye. They had no idea that what waited for them would change all their dreams and plans for the future. Even if he had known, Logan would not have been able to ignore the small bright sparkle in the corner of his eye.

When they were about seventy yards up into the trees, the smell became much stronger. Being familiar with death, they knew what they were looking for long before they found it. Logan saw the glint again another hundred yards up the small hill as he wound his way through the thick oak trees. He kicked his horse to a faster pace as they made their way upward, with Will falling in behind.

The first thing they came across was a small blanket with a baby's rattle and several beads stitched to the corner. It lay crumpled on a small ledge about four feet across. It appeared to have been dragged through the mud. The beads must have glinted in the sunlight catching Logan's attention. Will was leaning down from his saddle to pick it up when he realized it wasn't mud on the blanket. It was dried blood—lots of it. He sat looking down for a moment and then quickly scanned the area. Nothing seemed amiss, but the smell of death was strong. He looked up the hill and saw Logan sitting stock still on his horse. There was a look of distress on his face. Will rode up, but before he got to Logan he saw a scene that made his stomach sour. The smell of the burned out wagons with charred bodies still inside and the scene of destruction were worse than anything he had seen in the time they had been in the Army. They just sat and looked around trying to piece together what had happened. Finally, without a word, they moved on into the small clearing and began to survey for tracks. As they rode around the edge making wider circles, it didn't take long to figure out what had happened here. They both wore a look of anguish as they headed back down the hill to report to Lieutenant Tucker, the officer leading the small troop. They rode in silence to the file of soldiers waiting at the bottom. Logan was surprised that when they got there Will was choked up, unable to report what they had found, so Logan filled the Lieutenant in on the specifics.

"It looks like maybe seventy-five or a hundred Comanches or Kiowas waited to ambush a small wagon line coming from the east. The wagons were trying to find an easy track to the bottom of this hill. The Indians waited in the trees and then had at 'em. They never had a chance. Don't know for sure, but it's possible it all happened so fast no one in the wagon line even got off a single shot," he said, glancing back up the hill. "Every man, woman, and child was killed, stripped, and scalped. Some of 'em was burned with the wagons. They took nothin' but scalps. Everything else was left or burned." Logan was barely able to cover up the catch in his voice at the end. There was a lump in his throat so big he couldn't say another word. Lieutenant Tucker sat looking up the hill for a moment.

"Sergeant Magill," he finally said. "Scout the other side of the hill and make sure there aren't any more surprises waiting for us." Will nodded and then gestured toward Logan and two privates named Amos Edson and Joshua Mulgrew.

As they started back up the hill, Lieutenant Tucker called out, "Corporal Huggins, take the men to the first clearing." He was pointing to a small clearing about half-way up the hill. "Picket the horses, post guards, and take the rest of the men to the top. Let's bury these poor devils. Gather any personal belongings and report back to me."

"Yes sir!" the corporal snapped, giving two brief hand signals to the rest of the troop. The small troop broke into a flurry of activity. Every man checked his rifle and pistol to make sure they were all charged, just in case, and hurried up the hill. Will, Logan, Edson, and Mulgrew split up and went in different directions, making long arcing sweeps around the hill. When they were sure they knew what had happened and where the Indians had gone, they went back to report to the lieutenant. "Looks like there were about a hundred coming from the east," Will said, pointing off to a line of oaks near the top of the hill. "They must have spotted the wagons from quite a distance away. They had time to pick a spot, hide their horses, and then wait for quite a while till the wagon line was right where it couldn't change direction or run."

"Think anyone might've escaped?" the Lieutenant asked, with little hope in his voice. All four shook their heads.

"The Indians, Comanche from the looks of the arrows and lance wounds, turned south from here," Logan said. "They left a plain track, sir." When the lieutenant looked puzzled, Logan added, "Meanin' they're not hidin' nothin'."

"We could follow 'em if you want, Lieutenant," Will said. "See where they're headed."

The lieutenant shook his head. "No Sergeant, there are too many of them for us." He gazed off to the south as if looking for a dust cloud. "These aren't Santa Ana's lazy Mexicans; these are Comanches, and I doubt we'd catch 'em nappin'," he finished and turned to the corporal, who had just come up with a pouch containing the personal items found among the bodies.

He told the corporal to inventory and list all the items, and then turned to Will, saying, "Sergeant, let's finish up here and put a few miles between us and this place. I don't relish sleepin' so close to this many fresh graves." Once they finished the last of the cleanup and assembled at the bottom of the hill, the lieutenant gave the order and all moved out to the west at a quick pace. They all wanted to be away from this place.

That night, Logan and Will talked little about what they had seen that day. It bothered them both much worse than the slaughter of Mexican soldiers they had participated in just two weeks earlier. As the night drew around them, they hunkered down into their bedrolls. They both slept with their pistols in hand and kept their rifles close. Having grown up in Kentucky, they were familiar with Indian trouble. Both knew better than to think Indians wouldn't attack at night. The two privates that had scouted the hill with them, Edson and Mulgrew, rolled their blankets out close by. They trusted all the men in their small troop, but none so much as William Magill and Logan Vandeveer.

The troop saw nothing unusual for another day and a half. They had just made camp on the second night and were starting to cook some food when one of the night scouts came in with a young boy riding a worn-out old bay horse that looked to be thirty if it was a day. As skinny and lathered as it was, Logan wondered that it hadn't died already. The boy was filthy and looked exhausted and hungry. The lieutenant took the boy away from the other men and had some food brought to him.

"What's your name, son?" he asked, looking at the boy, who had stuffed his mouth so full with beef jerky that he couldn't speak at first. The boy looked up at the lieutenant.

"Ezekiel Morgan, sir," he said through a mouthful of jerky. "Folks call me Zeke."

"Well, Zeke, tell me how you come to be out here all alone. You're a might young," Tucker said.

The boy stopped chewing as if he had forgotten for a moment and just then remembered. A sorrowful look came across his face. "They's all dead, sir; I'm the only one left. Me and ol' Boss," he said, looking at the tired old horse, standing with his nose almost touching the ground. The Lieutenant tensed a little and seemed to know what the boy was going to tell him before he said another word.

"Injuns," Zeke said as tears filled his eyes. "Lots of 'em. They come outta nowhere and kilt ever'body before they could do anything. My Ma and Pa, sisters, even my baby brother Titus." Tears were rolling down his face and he began to sob.

"Take it easy now, son," the Lieutenant said.

"They kilt the Ryersons, too," he said wiping his face on a sleeve. "Four a' them. All dead…'cept me." He began to sob again. "I took ol' Boss out early, huntin'. Thought we might get a deer or maybe a couple a' turkeys. When we come back, we found 'em. They's all dead. Cut up real bad and scalped, even my Ma and sisters." He hung his head unable to speak. Lieutenant Tucker put an arm around the boy and tried to comfort him. Finally after a long while the sobbing subsided.

"If you can show us where they are we'll help you bury 'em proper," Tucker said at last. Zeke looked as though he'd been slapped. "No sir, I can't…I can't go back there…I can't look at 'em again." He began sobbing all over again.

"It's okay, son, you won't have to look at them. Just show us where they are and we'll take care of it," Tucker said as he pulled the boy closer to him. "They deserve a decent burial and we'll say some words over 'em."

Nobody slept well that night, and in the morning, the troop was ready to move out just after first light. Zeke pointed them to the north and they set off. No one looked forward to what they knew they'd find. It wasn't until the next afternoon that they found the tracks of the Comanches. They followed them several miles further north and eventually found what they were looking for. After they buried the Morgans and the Ryersons, they hurried on riding into the night. The moon set about two hours after sunset and they were forced to pull up and camp. At least they'd put a few miles between themselves and this last set of graves. The men seemed restless and walked around the camp, peering out into the darkness, trying not to go night blind from the small fire that was still burning. Will kicked dirt over it, and you could almost hear the sigh of relief from each and every one of them. They were all on edge, all except Zeke. He seemed to have slipped back inside himself during the last two days, and was almost completely unaware of anything happening around him. Several of the men tried to engage him in conversation hoping it would snap him out of it, but it didn't work. He was listless and his eyes were vacant. He was not with them.

In the morning they turned due west at a fast pace toward Mina again, but hadn't gone more than three hours when they ran across the Comanches' tracks again. They were several days old, but this time they were headed back the way they had come from, south toward San Antonio. Lieutenant Tucker had the entire troop scout the area around them for any fresh signs. When nothing was found, he gave the order to ride double time to Mina. They needed to report this to Colonel Burleson, the commanding officer there.

Three days later they were in Mina and had reported all that had happened on the way west. The colonel told them to rest up for two days but to prepare for a long-range patrol. There had been rumors that a Comanche war chief named Yellow Wolf had stirred up his band of horse warriors, and they were thought to have been out raiding. Nobody knew where they might be, or if it was even true, until now. Patrols went out and within four days, all the wagon attacks were located. What was left of the dead was buried, and all the personal items had been brought in to Colonel Burleson's aide.

Will, Logan, and Amos were in the patrol that found the first family killed by Yellow Wolf and his band. It was apparent that the Comanches were more ruthless with this group. The bodies had been hacked apart to the point of being almost unrecognizable. The patrol carefully and dutifully collected the parts the animals had left, and buried them. The patrol lasted seven days. They were one day out from Mina and had camped beside a small stream beneath some old live oaks. Will had just finished eating supper and was sitting back against his saddle to smoke his pipe when Logan dropped his saddle beside him, arranged it to face the small fire, and sat down next to him. They both stared into the fire for a few minutes letting their minds wander.

"I'm gonna muster out when we get back to Mina," Logan finally said matter-of-factly, gazing into the fire. Will took a long puff on his pipe, letting the smoke escape from his mouth and nose as he thought this over.

"I don't know that you can muster out whenever you want," he said, looking over at Logan. "I think Colonel Burleson might have something to say about it."

"I've already talked to the lieutenant about it, and he said that since we came in as militia, we are free to go now that the trouble with Mexico is over," Logan said, picking up a small stick by his feet. He felt uncomfortable springing the news on Will this way because he was certain Will would think he was quitting. Will sat for a long time smoking, not saying a word. His expression never changed.

Finally, he took his pipe from his mouth and said, "You seem to have thought about this for some time." He was looking straight into Logan's eyes. Logan looked straight back and nodded.

"What made you want out of the Army?" Will asked.

Logan snapped the small twig into pieces. "The Comanches have been a problem to white men on the plains for quite a while, and the Army isn't doin' nothin' about it, 'cept buryin' dead folks." Logan tossed one of the little sticks into the fire. "I want to settle down here, build a cattle ranch, maybe get married and raise a family, and I don't want the Comanches tryin' to kill me, my beeves, or my family, and the Army ain't gonna protect us," he said, his voice rising a little at the end.

"So what do ya wanna do, go out and kill all the Comanches by your own self?" Will asked, with the slightest of grins on his face. Logan was looking back into the fire and didn't see it; he took Will's statement more seriously.

"Well, hell no," Logan said, a little exasperated "I know I can't kill 'em all, and I don't know that I'd want to. I just think that if the Comanches and Kiowas know the folks comin' in here to settle have some protection, they might just leave 'em alone."

Will reached out and put his hand on Logan's arm. "Easy brother, I hear what you're sayin', I just don't know what we can do about it," he said soothingly.

Logan looked back at the fire. "There's a fella in Mina name of Boales, Calvin Boales. He's a captain with the Rangers. He's startin' up a new troop there and he's lookin' for volunteers." Logan leaned back against his saddle and tossed another piece of the stick into the fire. "It's likely to be a might dodgy as far as pay goes, but he says the outfit's sole job is to protect folks hereabouts from anything and anybody that might do 'em harm. Mex'cans, thieves, rustlers, killers, even Injuns… anybody that might harm 'em. Says they're here to help civilize this area, and that's what it needs, Will, civilizin'." He was looking straight into Will's eyes now and he was dead serious. "Folks need to know there's somebody on their side so they'll come and build homes and churches and schools. So stores can open and then it'll all grow. Civilization is what it needs." Will's mouth was open just a little; he'd never heard Logan talk with passion like this, except when he first started talking about coming to Texas. "I'm gonna join up with Boales when we get back to Mina," Logan said firmly, a very serious look on his face. Will sat in silence, thinking.

"Well, Brother, if you're so all fired set on it, I reckon I can't hold it against ya'. I know you'll probably be getting' yourself into scrapes ya' won't be able to get out of on your own. Reckon I couldn't never go back to Kentucky and face your Ma if anything was to happen to ya', even now. Speakin' of which, have you wrote your Ma and Pa of late? I imagine they're mighty worried about you, what with all this Mex'can trouble and warrin' and such goin' on, and don't you think they don't know about it, neither." Will took a long drag on his pipe. "Why, I bet they've heard all about how you won that little scrap at the buffalo swamp and captured Santa Ana all by your own self," Will said, as he tapped the ashes out of his pipe on a small rock between his feet. Logan's head snapped around to face Will, and then he saw the twinkle in his eyes. He ducked his head and got red in the face.

"Dang you, Will," he said, and punched Will playfully in the arm. "You had me believin' you was serious."

"Serious! Why, Brother, more serious never came outta my mouth before. I'm as serious as a broke leg in Injun country," Will said with a knitted brow and a sparkle in his eyes. "Why, while I'm roundin' up all these wild beeves out here that's just free for the takin', and getting' rich and fat, I'll sleep better at night knowin' Captain

Calvin Boales is patrolin' the countryside with you and a buncha' underpaid, overworked rawhides a-lookin' out for me." Will decided to indulge himself with another smoke and started packing his pipe again. "Yessiree, I'll sleep like a newborn baby. I bet my whole herd could stampede right through my house and I'd never even know it, I'd be asleepin' so sound."

Logan shook his head. "William Harrison Magill, you're so fulla' crap your eyes are turnin' brown," he shot back. They bantered back and forth a couple of times until Logan got a serious look on his face. "Will, I don't want you to think I'm a quitter, I just think I can do more for civilizing this country as a Ranger than as a soldier," he said, looking straight at Will. There was silence between them, and Logan knew it was at this point that Will would probably tell him they would have to part company, something he wasn't sure if he was prepared for. Will lit his pipe with a small twig he picked out of the dying fire, took a long drag, and as the smoke rolled up his face said, "Well, Brother, I personally don't think Captain Calvin Boales can do it." He tossed the burning twig back into the fire. Logan looked sidelong at him.

"Don't think he can do what?" Logan asked, a little more defensively than he meant to.

Will pulled his pipe from his mouth and pointed at Logan with the stem. "I don't think he can make me sleep sound at night with just you and a bunch of wet rawhides, and Brother, you can bet that's what they'll be. All runnin' around out there, probably lost half the time, botherin' folks with all your protectin' and civilizin'." Will took another drag on his pipe and let the smoke roll out his mouth. "Likely folks'll be shootin' at y'all rather than the Comanches or the Mex'cans. Reckon I best come along too. At least I can keep you on the straight and narrow even if I can't none of them other knotheads you'll be ridin' with." He reached down to spread out his bedroll and took something from his vest pocket. "Besides, I'm guessin' you'll need help fillin' out this." He handed Logan a folded piece of paper. Logan unfolded it and leaned toward the fading light of the fire to read what it said. It was a Request for Discharge form. He looked up at Will with shock on his face. Will stopped what he was doing and said, "You best get that filled out so you can turn it in as soon as we get to Mina. Calvin Boales is leavin' day after tomorrow, and you gotta get signed up with him." He pulled another folded piece of paper out of a different pocket of his vest. "Already got mine filled out. Reckon they'll want to make me a Sergeant, again, being the far thinker I am and all," he said as he unfolded his own discharge request.

"Damn you Will Magill, I worried about you bein' mad at me for a week now, and here you already got your request filled out. You was probably planning this all along. That's just plain mean," Logan said as he sat down and folded the paper and put it in his own vest pocket. They would be in Mina by noon the next day. He'd have time to get it filled out and submitted. Then he'd go find Captain Boales.

They arrived in Mina at about a quarter past noon and were dismissed as soon as their mounts and gear were taken care of. It was one thirty when Logan sat down to fill out the discharge form, and two o'clock when he, Will, and Amos Edson knocked on Lieutenant Tucker's door. Tucker let them in and was noticeably disappointed that all three wanted to muster out right away, but when they explained about Captain Boales, his whole demeanor changed.

"Boales is definitely the man for the job. He fought Indians in Kentucky and Tennessee and was a Town Marshall in Fort Smith for a while. He knows the law and he knows how to fight Indians," Tucker said, and then he sat down and looked over the forms. "I'll have to take these to the Colonel. The final say is his, but I don't think he'll have a problem with it. I know he'll hate to see you three go, but he knows Calvin Boales. They fought Indians together about ten years back. He says there ain't none better than Boales for such an impossible task." Tucker took the papers to Colonel Burleson straight away. The three sat and waited. Burleson's office was close by and they could hear raised voices. Shortly Colonel Burleson came striding into Tucker's quarters where Logan, Will, and Amos were waiting.

He looked from man to man, "Lieutenant Tucker informs me y'all want to muster out," he said. It wasn't a question. All three snapped to attention and saluted, something they had seldom done in the past. They all looked at one another and nodded, still saluting.

"Yes sir," Logan said a little nervously. "We want to sign up with Captain Boales and he's leavin' tomorrow." They all stood and continued to salute. Burleson paced the room several times as he looked over the request forms. He stopped once and looked at Amos as if he was going to say something to him, but closed his mouth and paced on. Finally he stopped and turned to face them. "Y'all sure this is what you want to do?" he asked, looking from one to the other. All three nodded again, and since he hadn't returned their salute, they still had their hands to their foreheads. He shook his head with a look of disappointment on his face, and then just stood looking at them. "Well, hell boys, I guess I can't stop ya, but if I was y'all I don't think I'd be salutin' Calvin Boales like ya'll are doin' now. He don't like it at all, and since you ain't in this Army anymore I can't imagine what you're doin' still standin' there saluting me." He laid the forms out on a small table and signed all three. He turned to the three bewildered ex-soldiers and said, "Boys, I hate to see you go, but if you're planning on joining up with Calvin Boales, you best get a move on, 'cause he won't wait for no man." He strode from the room and stopped at the door, turning to say, "Y'all stop in by and by. I got word two days ago they plan to give away land tracts to certain… ahem…heroes of the recent conflict. Nothing definite yet, but I expect to hear more sometime this month." He looked again at the three, turned, and stepped out the door. Logan, Will, and Amos stood in silence looking back and forth at each other.

"Is that it?" Logan asked. "Just like that we're outta the Army?"

"Reckon so," said Amos, looking confused.

"Boys, if we're fixin' to be Texas Rangers we better get over to find Captain Boales," Will said, clapping Logan and Amos both on the shoulder as he stepped between them and out the door. They followed him out, and the three of them headed up the street to become Texas Rangers.

CHAPTER 4

LAME BADGER

The first months of their time in the Rangers were trying beyond belief. The endless patrols, the heat, the lack of food, supplies, and equipment. On top of this, they had to supply their own mounts and weapons. Their only pay came in the form of vouchers, but there were few places to use them.

Will said they must be the "poorest citizens in this here new Republic." Several times, in those first months, Will, Logan, and Amos felt they were at the end of their ropes and were about to quit Rangerin' when Captain Boales would say or do something that would renew their faith. Then they would feel ashamed that they had considered giving up in the first place.

Finally, the last time they ever lost their morale was when they were out looking for a group of what seemed to be some of the worst renegade Comanches, Apaches, and Mexican bandits in Texas. This group had raided the settlers and small towns to the north, killing more than two dozen people. The worst part was they were stealing children and teenagers from their families. Several times the Rangers had come across the bodies of captives that couldn't keep up. The victims usually had their throats slit and were left for the coyotes.

Captain Boales was sure these Mexican bandits were taking the stolen children into Mexico to sell, but the Rangers could never quite catch up to them. This little band of renegades seemed to be able to slip past the Rangers and get away clean every time. Boales' Rangers were frustrated beyond reason, and several of the men had given up and gone home.

On this last particular occasion, the Rangers had followed the group up a streambed, out to the west, near a place the Comanches called the Dripping Spring. Boales had decided they would wait until late into the night when the renegades were sure to be asleep, and then they would go in quietly and take them. As the Rangers waited, the bandits slipped right past their camp and were heading south before the Rangers made their move. A smoldering fire was all that was left in the camp when Boales and his men got there. The renegades had spent part of the night dirtying up their tracks and then wiping them clean when they were a little ways off. The only thing the Rangers knew was that the renegades had slipped within five hundred feet of them with six young captives, and then had vanished. The Rangers were fit to be tied. They had spent five days tracking and following them, being careful not to give themselves away. To lose them at the last minute made the Rangers feel cheated, but none more so than Captain Boales. He sent small patrols out for several miles in an effort to pick up their track, but it was as though the small band and their captives had flown out of the country. Finally, he ordered the men to water their horses and fill their canteens. He knew where this mixed band of cutthroats and killers was going and decided they were going to race them for the border. They left the Dripping Spring long before noon and headed south fast. Logan and Will feared the horses might not last at the pace the Captain set, but they kept on, and by nightfall they were skirting San Antonio. The horses were done in, so Boales ordered a stop at a small ranch just east of town. It belonged to a family named McMasters, Hardy and Delfina McMasters. They were young and had not been married long, but Hardy had worked hard to build up a nice little ranch. They were living as comfortably as possible out in this part of Texas. They gave the Rangers hot food and some grain for their horses. The McMasters were obliging and patient with this rough bunch of recruits. Delfina bustled around the kitchen making food and taking it outside to the Rangers while Hardy and Captain Boales sat at the kitchen table and talked about the renegades.

"Where do you think they're goin', Cap'n?" Hardy asked, pouring them both a second cup of coffee. Boales held up his hand when his cup was half-full. Coffee kept him from sleeping well at night.

"I know they're headed for Mexico, so I figure we'll race 'em to the Rio Grande and then start tryin' to pick up their tracks on the Mexico side. I figure they'll ease up a might once they're across."

McMasters leaned forward on the table. "You mean to take 'em in *Mexico*?" he asked, obviously surprised. "Won't arrestin' 'em down there cause big trouble, especially now?"

Boales raised his coffee cup to his lips, stopping midway to peer back at McMasters through narrowed eyes. "Mister, they've killed more'n two dozen settlers in their own homes and taken at least that many children to sell in Mexico. I don't intend to arrest 'em. I intend to catch these damn killers at all cost and send 'em straight to hell, by bullet or by rope. I don't care if they start the trip from Mexico or Texas, but by God they're goin' to hell." He finished the last of his coffee and sat his cup on the table. "I'll find the most likely spot for 'em to cross from Marshall Willard when we get to Laredo. I figure he might have some ideas about that." He started to stand up and excuse himself for the night, but McMasters reached out and took his arm.

"I don't want to try and tell you how to do your job, Cap'n, but they're not gonna cross at Laredo." His face was serious. "Willard ain't the Marshall there no more. He got sick about six months back and a fella by the name of Murdoch took over. Walt Murdoch." Boales sat back down. "He's been givin' em holy hell down there. Got so's the Mex'can bandits and renegades won't go near Laredo. That man Murdoch hunts and kills 'em with a vengeance they ain't used to."

Boales slumped. If they weren't crossing over at Laredo, then where? There were a thousand places to go across unseen.

"Well hell, I'd like to shake the man's hand, but he sure made this more complicated," Boales said, pondering what he would do next. Seemed they weren't going to get any good breaks chasing down these devils.

"Quemado!" McMasters said simply, looking into Boales' eyes intently. Boales looked puzzled. "They're likely headed for Quemado," McMasters continued. "Instead of headin' south, they've headed west fer sure and fer certain." He went to a small table next to a straight-backed chair in the corner. From the drawer he pulled out a roll of parchment. He moved the coffee cups and spread it on the table. It was a map, and a pretty darned good one at that. Boales looked it over carefully as McMasters traced a line with his finger to the west.

"There. Quemado. That's where they'll cross. No law there. It's a real hellhole. Good or bad, nobody goes there without lots of guns behind 'em. Not if they want to live," he said, peering at the map. They studied the map intently for a long while, the captain tracing out parts with his finger and peering closely.

"This is a fine map." Boales said appreciatively "I don't believe I've seen better, especially of this border area."

McMasters smiled, "Made it myself, so I do have a little bit of experience with Quemado." He continued to look at the map, but it was obvious he was remembering something unpleasant. Finally, he looked at Captain Boales and said, "My granddaddy was a map maker with a young upstart surveyor back in the east by the name of George Washington, years ago. My daddy and me used to make 'em for the railroads back there. Reckon it'll be awhile before the railroads need any for this area," he said with a grin. "You can have this one." Captain Boales started to protest, but McMasters wouldn't have any of it. "A good map could make all the difference," he said, as he rolled it back up and handed it to Boales. They shook hands and both retired for the night. The Rangers rested until first light, and then were gone again. They were heading west for Quemado. There was justice to be served there in more ways than they knew.

Yellow Wolf sat beside the small stream in the shade of a big oak tree. He stared at the fresh deer tracks in the soft mud at his feet. The deer had been there just minutes before. He could track and kill him easily, but he wasn't hunting deer. He was hunting solitude. He needed to think. He had recently become very popular among some of the other camps nearby. Since the raids on the White

Diggers, warriors had come from all around wanting to stay at his camp and make war on these "diggers in the dirt." His camp had swollen until he could hardly think; he had to leave camp and go somewhere quiet, like this. He had to put a stop to it, and warn all the other camps that no one would be allowed to come to his camp and stay except for elders coming to council. That was something else that had begun since the raids. Other camps wanted to hold council with him and the elders of his camp. He didn't like that either. He had enough trouble keeping his own council; now he had to think about the problems of other camps. No, he didn't like it at all. He would have to find a way to make it stop, without breaking relations, of course. Good relations with the other camps was crucial, especially now. But he had another problem to think about, one that seemed more important at the moment. It was Wihnaitʉ Huuna (Lame Badger), the son of his mother's brother from the Hanataibo (Corn People) camp. His mother's brother, Tsuhni Kwasu, (Bone Shirt), had captured and kept an Apache woman, something most Comanches would never do. Bone Shirt was considered a vain man, and he thought she was pleasing to look at, for an Apache. It was thought that his vanity had kept her, not his wisdom. Apaches were not well liked by the Comanches, and Apache captives were usually killed because they were too much trouble. With this woman, he had fathered a son with a bent leg, Lame Badger. Deformed children were thought to be cursed and therefore were unwanted, so his mother had tried to kill him, but Bone Shirt would not let her. No one in camp understood why Bone Shirt would not let her take the cursed child to the river. He was, after all, just a crippled half Apache child of no consequence, but Bone Shirt would not allow it. The woman was determined that the boy should be killed. She had tried several times, but Bone Shirt watched her closely and had stopped her each time. The Apache woman eventually became so troublesome that Bone Shirt traded her to a Piute trader. She screamed like a demon when the Piute dragged her from the camp, spitting at Bone Shirt, cursing him in Apache. He heard later that the woman had killed the trader in his sleep and was skinned alive to pay for it. Lame Badger was still only a baby at the time, but he grew up hearing the stories of Tuhkwasipia, his 'Demon Mother', in the taunts of the other boys in camp. He quickly grew to hate these boys, but he also learned young that it did not hurt when he fought them, and since his bent leg was shorter than the other leg he was able to drop to the ground and get in below another boy's guard very quickly and easily. Sometimes the other boys would try to fight him two at a time, but he was too wily for even that. Eventually they steered clear of him altogether and never spoke to him. He was just a crippled half-breed and they hated him for it. Lame Badger didn't let them off so easily. Even with his peculiar gait, he learned to sneak around and go unseen. He would often lie in wait for one of the other boys to be foolish enough to go somewhere alone. He took particular delight in beating any he caught this way until they were bloody and senseless. This disturbed many of the other people in the camp, and Bone Shirt had to beat Lame Badger many times for this, but Lame Badger didn't care. It was as if he felt no pain. Finally, at the end of his thirteenth summer, he turned his attention to a young girl. She was called Tomo'atua (Sky Child). She was younger than he and small for her age, but to her father, who was old and childless, except for her, she was like warm sunshine on his face in the cold winter. Many times Lame badger lay waiting for Sky Child, and when he finally caught her, alone and farther from camp than she should have been, he grabbed her and threw her to the ground. He wasn't sure what to do next, so he sat on Sky Child's chest, making it hard for her to breathe. She was afraid of him and tried to get away, but he held her down on the ground and just laughed at her. Sky Child tried to scream, but he slapped her in the face, very hard, to shut her up. Her whole life, she had been a good and dutiful daughter and so had never been beaten. It was more than she could take. He began to taunt her as he hit her harder and harder. The terror in Sky Child's eyes seemed to be just what he was looking for. He kept her there for a long time and continued to brutalize her until she fainted. He slapped her face until she came around, then started over again, laughing almost hysterically. Finally, she fainted again and he couldn't make her wake up, so he simply hit her on the head with a rock and killed her. Without a second thought, he covered her body with leaves and sticks and washed himself in a small stream nearby. When he finished and was dry, he waddled calmly back to camp.

Everyone in camp helped to search for Sky Child, or some sign of her, and when her body was finally found, everybody knew what had happened to her. The camp's medicine man was furious, as was the girl's father and the chief. This was something that had never happened before in their camp. Men did not do this to women, at least the women of their own tribe. Slave or captive women maybe, but not a Comanche woman. There was a discussion in council about what to do. The medicine man wanted Lame Badger skinned alive and then burned to pay for it, but some in the council wanted him killed more quickly and quietly. Bone Shirt knew that whatever was decided would stop his son's breath. This type of public death would reflect badly on him, and it was his vanity that made him take Lame Badger out into the hills while the elders of the Hanataibo discussed his fate. Bone Shirt told the boy they would go out to hunt and talk to their spirits. He was intending to kill Lame Badger quickly rather than have him tortured to death while the whole camp watched. When they stopped to make camp for the first night, Bone Shirt turned his back on the small waddling boy. It was his last mistake. Lame Badger plunged the knife into Bone Shirt's back to the hilt and began twisting and rotating it so it would cause more pain and damage.

As Bone Shirt slumped to the ground, Lame Badger smirked. "I think you will not kill this little cripple today, father." He leaned over Bone Shirt, who lay on the ground prostrate and writhing in agony. "It is true what people have always said," Lame Badger stated calmly as he looked down at his dying father with disgust. "You are vain and it will cause your death." He gave an evil laugh as he mounted Bone Shirt's horse, gathered his own horse's reins, and rode directly over top of Bone Shirt, allowing both horses to shy and dance around, pummeling Bone Shirt with their hooves. Bone Shirt lay on his side, unable to sit up, and watched as his only son rode away laughing, almost hysterically, and then he died.

Lame Badger rode north to the Llano Estacado, the Staked Plains, and stayed gone for many years. Yellow Wolf was now troubled because Lame Badger had gathered a group of renegades of all types, even Apaches, and was raiding the White Diggers and Mexicans. This didn't bother Yellow Wolf so much as what else Lame Badger was doing: He was causing trouble among some of the Comanche camps as well as several Kiowa camps. He knew that peace among the Comanches and Kiowas was necessary to fight the White Diggers. Yellow Wolf feared what might happen to the Comanche if that peace was broken and all were left to fight the White Diggers alone. Lame Badger needed to be rubbed out, and Yellow Wolf felt it was his responsibility. After all, he and Lame Badger shared blood. Tomorrow he would take a group of warriors, track Lame Badger and his renegades, and rub them all out.

◠◡

As the Rangers were getting ready to leave the McMasters' ranch, they were surprised to find out that Captain Boales was turning west instead of continuing on south. This news came at a time when morale was particularly low. Some of the Rangers were grumbling, and Will took it upon himself to set them straight on Captain Boales. His task was made easier by his close association to Logan. Every Ranger there had heard the story of Logan Vandeveer fighting the whole of Santa Ana's army. Besides the stories, Logan stood a full head taller than any of them, and the sight of his massive muscles often made people stop and stare. No one wanted to end up on his bad side. Logan would have been somewhat abashed had he known how they felt. Will, on the other hand, did know, because several of them had asked him about Logan on the sly, and he never missed an opportunity to talk Logan up, even to the point of slight exaggeration.

That first day out of San Antonio was every bit as brutal as the day before, except there were more rivers and streams to cross. At each one, small patrols would scout up and down the river for any sign of those child-stealing devils. None was found, but Captain Boales held firm to his plan, even during his own spate of doubt and frustration. Three hours after dark, the moon set, and they were forced to stop and camp beside Sabinal Creek, about halfway between San Antonio and Quemado. The grain given them by the McMasters helped the horses greatly, but they had just traveled close to fifty miles and the horses were completely done in. Several had balked right about sundown, and it was feared they would go no further. With a short rest, their riders got them to go a little further, and eventually they caught up to the rest of the troop at Sabinal Creek. Although Will trusted the captain, he was worried nonetheless. If they lost their horses out here, they were dead for sure. He decided to find out what the captain had planned. He cautiously approached Captain Boales and asked if he might speak with him. Boales motioned for him to sit.

"Don't mean to pry, Cap'n, and surely don't want you to think none of us boys'd be second guessin' you, but I want to talk straight with you, sir," he said, squatting on his haunches. Boales was afraid the men were losing confidence in him and he wasn't sure how to handle it. Even he was unsure about the change in course he had made. After all, he had taken the advice of a man he'd just met, something very unlike him. Now he regretted it and was worried they might be on a goose chase. He looked into Will's face, but said nothing. Will began, "We all respect you, sir, and we figure you must have a good reason to head west instead of south to Laredo, but we're all afraid of what might happen if we lose even one of our mounts.

This breakneck pace is startin' to show on 'em. We got two that'll be lame by noon tomorrow if we keep this up...sir." Will felt very self-conscious about whether he was stepping out of line here.

Captain Boales rubbed his chin and gazed into the fire. "I appreciate your honesty, Magill, and I share your worry, but I feel what we did was very necessary. I think this band of renegades slipped past us and deliberately set us to thinkin' they went toward Laredo, when in fact they only went a short distance south to fool us and then turned west to cross at a place called Quemado. Since we rode south to San Antonio, they had a big lead on us and we needed to get some of it back." He looked over at Will and took a sip of coffee. Will sat waiting. Captain Boales continued. "I intend to catch these devils and get those children back, and I'm going to hang or shoot every last renegade in the bunch." His look was as stern as any Will had ever seen. "And, I will gladly go into Mexico to do it if I have to. So, any that choose to come with me need to set their minds right about the task at hand, because there won't be any falterin' later. When we ride into Quemado we will be in Satan's lair for sure, and some of us may not ride out." He tossed the gritty dregs of his coffee into the fire and turned to face Will. "Magill, you were a Sergeant in the Army, and you have the ears and respect of the men. It would make my task easier, no, I should say possible, if they knew you and I thought alike. I know I haven't been generous with information, but I have my reasons. Just know that I fully believe these murderin' bastards are going to Quemado, and we need to be there first."

Will gazed into the fire for a moment longer. "Cap'n, if you say it's so and you believe it, then by God, every last man here will ride his horse into the ground to back you up." Will stood up and the two men locked eyes, then he turned and strode back to the circle of Rangers sitting around a small fire.

The next morning Captain Boales was awakened before first light by the sound of a quietly bustling camp. The Rangers were not only ready to move west, they were almost eager to do so. The ones with questionable horses had split their gear up among some of the others, and all were dropping anything that they wouldn't absolutely need. Amos had marked a large pecan tree with three slashes of his knife, then went to the third pecan due east and dug a hole to cache any completely unnecessary gear, and even some food. These men had determination and grit, and Boales was indeed glad they were on the same side of the law. The troop rode out into the receding darkness toward whatever fate awaited them. Had the Rangers known that Lame Badger and his band were but a few miles north and heading for the same place, they surely would have ridden screaming into the renegades' still sleeping camp and slaughtered every last one of them.

Quemado awaited.

Lame Badger was not up before dawn as he probably should have been, but he was up before any of the rest of his band was even awake.

Lazy dogs, he thought to himself as he surveyed the jumble of dirty renegades he had drawn together. If they weren't so ruthless and so good at killing he probably wouldn't have let them live, but ruthless they were, and kill they did.

He limped around the camp with his familiar seesaw gait, kicking and rousting these dregs of humanity, these near devil dogs into semi-wakefulness, cursing them until they were all up and breaking camp. They moved out without any idea of the tangle of briars that fate was about to throw them into, but the Mexican Rancheros waited, just past Quemado.

❦

Yellow Wolf called a meeting, but not just with the elders. He summoned ten of his most trusted and bravest warriors to explain what he was intent on doing and why, but Two Crows, his lifelong friend and companion, was not among those summoned. After Yellow Wolf finished speaking, several of the elders tried to warn him against taking the best and bravest warriors from the camp. He held up his hand and silenced them all.

"I have found my own wisdom in a dream. I stand here now to speak to the Kutsutᵾᵾka." (Buffalo Eaters). He held out his hand toward the warriors sitting on one side of the lodge as he faced the elders and spoke directly to them. "It is for them to say whether they will go with me to kill Lame Badger and his band. I am not asking for a blessing for myself. I ask only that the brave ones who go with me be blessed so that they may return to their families. Whether I have brought shame or honor to the spirits of my ancestors will decide if I live or die, but the brave warriors that go with me shall be honored." He was not seeking their wisdom or approval; he was simply telling them what would come to pass. The elders looked at each other and whispered quietly among themselves very briefly. Then the medicine man, Black Elk, stood and stepped forward to face Yellow Wolf directly.

"You have spoken with the spirits and they have set a path for you to follow. We cannot say otherwise. Your warriors will have our blessing, and we will dance for the strongest medicine we can. Yellow Wolf shall also have the blessing of all in the Kutsutᵾᵾka camp." There was silence as Yellow Wolf and all the warriors left the lodge to prepare for the battle to come. They all knew this would be a dangerous battle and felt they must purify themselves with herbs and smoke. They spent the rest of the day preparing weapons to seek out their enemies' hearts, and then they prayed. That night the entire camp gathered for the blessings given by Black Elk, and the dancing lasted far into the night.

At first light Yellow Wolf stepped out of his lodge to find that all ten of the warriors chosen were there waiting for him. There was one other waiting as well: Two Crows. Without exchanging a word, these two lifelong companions looked at one another and it was settled. Yellow Wolf smiled slightly. It was good that Two Crows had decided to come. Though a better horse stealer than a fighter, he was still a very valuable warrior to Yellow Wolf and all the Buffalo Eaters. They mounted their horses as the entire camp came out to see them off and wish them well. As the small band of warriors rode off in the early morning light, they all knew that whatever waited over the horizon was meant to be.

CHAPTER 5

QUEMADO

At times, Lame Badger longed for the familiarity of his father's lodge and the easy life he had known while living there. He had learned young that his father felt guilt and shame because Lame Badger was crippled. Bone Shirt felt he was being punished by one of the gods for his vanity. He knew that bringing an Apache woman into the camp and keeping her was not a good idea and that he should expect trouble, but he could not put his vanity in its place. It ruled over him, making him do things he shouldn't just to prove that he could. As a result, Bone Shirt had been too easy on Lame Badger, more so than any of the other fathers in the camp were on their sons, more so than was good for anyone living in that part of Texas at the time. Lame Badger became resentful and lazy because of it. These two traits became a way of life for him. He resented everyone and everything because deep down he felt everyone and everything was better than he was. His laziness would have faded in time, but he grew to enjoy it. He preferred stealing over work, and so he became a great thief around camp. He was very adept at taking food or belongings right out of other people's lodges without being seen. Even more than stealing, he liked making people feel guilty for no reason, but when they felt sorry for him and gave him food and other things, he hated them for it. Sometimes he would snatch whatever it was they offered and waddle away without showing any gratitude. Sometimes he would look over their gift and then throw it to the ground right in front of them. He had been known to throw things on the ground and stomp on them until they were broken and useless. He was like that with this band of killers and thieves he had drawn to himself, but still their numbers grew whenever they came near a town or settlement. It was as if Lame Badger called to the evil, soulless men of that region, but as evil as they were, Lame Badger was worse than all the rest. All in his band feared him but one, a Mexican they simply called Asesino: Killer. His name was Alberto Negron, but his lust for killing earned him the name Asesino. He was the worst of these killers and his heart was as black as night. There was no question about his lust for killing. It bothered Lame Badger that this lowly Mexican killer seemed not to fear him. He was sure he would have to kill Asesino someday, probably sooner rather than later. Oh well, no matter. There were plenty more killers out there that would ride with Lame Badger to kill, rape, and steal. He would find another when he needed to.

As the band of killers drew near Quemado, Lame Badger stopped them and sent a scout ahead to see what might await them. It did not pay to be unwary in this area of back shooters and bandits. Those who were so foolish never lasted long. After several hours the scout came back and reported that the little village was quiet. There were two gringos partially skinned and hanging just outside the town, but there was no real activity. He also told Lame Badger that there were six Rancheros with at least five Vaqueros each, just on the other side of the river in Mexico, waiting. Even though it was almost sundown, Lame Badger decided to go the remaining two miles; however, they would stop and wait just outside of town. Several of the children were very tired and nearly unable to stay on their horses. One young girl of about five years old was whimpering. Asesino slapped the ones that were swaying on their horses and beat the young one to make her quit whimpering, but it only made her scream and cry louder. Lame Badger finally stepped between them, his war club in hand, ready to finish it with Asesino right then. He knew the girl would bring more silver if she had no marks and did not cry when the Rancheros looked at her. Asesino backed off with a scowl on his face, grumbling. Yes, Lame Badger would have to kill this one; perhaps when their business with the Rancheros was finished. Lame Badger gazed toward the west for a few moments and then signaled the band to move out. He told four of the Apaches to skirt around to the south of Quemado. He wanted them to take up positions near the Rancheros so they could watch and cover his band of renegades, just in case. Four very mean looking Apaches veered off to the south and disappeared into a line of trees that followed a stream to the west. They would skirt the stream and travel unseen through the trees.

Yellow Wolf took his small band of warriors out to the west where Lame Badger had been raiding. He knew Lame Badger was lazy and held himself in high regard as a very bad man. Yellow Wolf thought Lame Badger wouldn't try to hide his tracks. Yellow Wolf was a very careful man and rarely mistaken, but this time he was. They had to make many sweeping arcs across a very large area before they picked up the tracks, but in doing so, they also picked up the tracks the Rangers had left as they headed south. At first Yellow Wolf was surprised that these White Diggers hadn't followed Lame Badger, but then he thought it would be surprising if they actually did. The White Diggers were stupid and usually unaware of what was going on right around them. He didn't know how they would ever be able to hold this land, even if they stayed. He was sure his people could just come back later and kill them off a few at a time until they were all dead. That would be good. Yellow Wolf had already been making such plans, and had heard that Kuhtsuna Kwapipu (Buffalo Hump), the Chief of the Penatɨka (Honey Eaters) camp and Parua Sɨɨmarɨ (Ten Bears) of the Napɨ Watɨ (Don't Wear Shoes) band thought the same as he. When he was finished with Lame Badger and his band of renegades, he would go meet with Buffalo Hump and Ten Bears to discuss these plans in council, but now he must rub out Lame Badger and his renegades.

He pushed the small group of warriors hard for the first two days, covering a great distance. Always, there was a fresh scout out front, just in case. If Lame Badger was as lazy as Yellow Wolf expected, they could easily happen upon him at any time. It was best to be ready, so they pushed on until Two Crows, who had been scouting, came back and reported to Yellow Wolf that Lame Badger was only a half-day ahead.

He looked long at Yellow Wolf and said, "The White Diggers have turned west and are catching up to Lame Badger." Yellow Wolf was very surprised. How would they know Lame Badger was headed for the 'crossing of the tall grass'? He had always gone south to Laredo or back north, onto the Llano Estacado. Finally Two Crows spoke again. "The big warrior is with them; the one from the buffalo swamp." Yellow Wolf was visibly startled. He looked long at Two Crows; his eyes were wide with wonder. He was sure the big man had been rubbed out by

Santa Ana's soldiers. This warrior's medicine must be very strong, to be able to bring him away from his ancestors. Yellow Wolf stepped up the pace. If this warrior was going to try and kill Lame Badger, Yellow Wolf would like to see it. If the big warrior failed, then Yellow Wolf wanted to be in a position to move his warriors in and kill Lame Badger himself. Either way, Yellow Wolf needed to get his warriors to the crossing of the tall grass.

Captain Boales pulled his horse up just before the troop of Rangers topped the low ridge overlooking the stream just north of them. He dismounted and moved low and slow to the edge of the ridge. He scanned the area around the stream below. There was plenty of cover in the trees and some good grass for the horses. It was almost dark, so he decided they would camp beside this stream, just outside Quemado. He would send Magill and Vandeveer in to scout out the town. If it were as bad a place as he was lead to believe, they would have to be very careful.

After surveying the area for quite a while, he got back on his horse and led the line of Rangers quietly down to the stream. Will and Logan moved slowly along the south bank toward the town while the rest of the Rangers set up a 'cold' camp. Boales warned them all to picket the horses separately where they couldn't be seen, and then settle in quick and be quiet. He didn't want anyone spotting them and sending word of their presence to the band of renegades they were after, if the killers were even here. The Rangers picketed their horses and vanished among the trees. There was no guard posted. Captain Boales didn't want anyone moving around. The Rangers all settled in under the trees in pairs, watching out for each other while eating jerked beef with water for their meal. All were quiet and sat with their pistols in hand.

Logan and Will had moved down the stream about a mile before it opened out into a break of tall grass where it flowed into the Rio Grande. They stayed under the trees for a long time making sure no one was around before moving closer. They were finally able to gain a low hill just to the south of the little village that gave them a good look at the area. From there they could see the town, the Rio Grande, and a group of Mexican Vaqueros camped across from it on the Mexico side. They lay on their stomachs and got a good look at Quemado. Logan cupped his hands above his eyes and pressed his thumbs against his cheeks. It was a trick he'd learned in Kentucky when he was younger. His father had taught him to do this to help him see farther and more clearly. He could see something hanging in a tree just to the north of town, but at first couldn't quite make it out. After a moment, it seemed to move slightly and he could see it more clearly. It was two men hanging from the tree. The filthy, poor little town seemed remarkably quiet for all the bad they'd heard of it. Not a soul was seen on the one disorganized, dusty track running through the middle of town. There were two saloons in town, and sounds could be heard coming from them, but not much else. Logan peered into the impending gloom for as long as he could, but saw no movement, so he and Will got comfortable. They were going to spend a good part of the night here.

It was well into the afternoon and Yellow Wolf knew they would be coming to the crossing after nightfall, so he decided to swing a little further to the north. This way he was sure they wouldn't run into any surprises with Lame Badger or the white men. When they were close to the little town, they slowed and waited for the scout he'd sent ahead. The scout came to Yellow Wolf and told him that the white men were waiting in the trees on the south side of the stream. He also told him that Lame Badger and his band were following the stream on the other side. He was sure that Lame Badger didn't know the white men were waiting for him. Yellow Wolf thought about this. He felt it was his responsibility to kill Lame Badger, but if the White Diggers did it quickly, that might be good. Why risk the lives of his best warriors for such a one as Lame Badger. This would not be a fight that would be sung of in later times; the whole affair was an embarrassment. As long as it was done quickly, he would not interfere with the White Diggers. Then he and his small band could just go home without losing anyone and it would be finished.

They found a ridge on the north side of the crossing that was thick with trees and settled in, to wait and watch. They could see where the White Diggers were, but the Rangers were being very smart. They were well hidden and not moving. Yellow Wolf spotted the Apaches moving down the stream. He did not like Apaches and would like to kill these, but that could wait. Then something made him wonder if he were seeing things. Two of the White Diggers were hiding in the tall grass, waiting for the Apaches. It was apparent that the Apaches would move right to them. He closed his eyes a moment and then opened them to give himself better night vision. One of the White Diggers in the tall grass was the big warrior. Yellow Wolf watched very closely, then signaled Two Crows and several of his warriors to move down and intercept the Apaches. If anyone were to kill the big man, it was not to be an Apache! They moved silently down the slope and soon were close to the men moving through the tall grass. All three groups of men were trying to be silent. None could afford to have anyone in the town know they were there.

Logan and Will had just decided to head back to camp and report to Captain Boales when Logan caught a very faint sound back in the tree line by the stream. It sounded like a horse stamping, but it was so faint that he couldn't tell for sure. He signaled Will and they began a slow crawl down the low ridge into the tall grass. They were moving so slowly that it had taken almost an hour to make it back to the tree line. The moon was just starting to rise by the time they got to the tall grass. They lay still at the edge of the grass and waited. As they lay there, they saw a slight movement ahead and could just make out what sounded like whispering. They watched, and eventually counted four men coming slowly toward them. Apparently the men didn't know Logan and Will were there because they were approaching low in the grass, but were not crawling. Logan and Will were well covered by the grass at the edge of the stream. The four men were Indians for sure; there was no mistaking the way they moved through the night. Will rolled over onto his shoulder so he could see Logan more clearly.

He mouthed the words, "Four Injuns…prob'ly Renegades." Logan nodded. They both slid their knives out silently and slipped them into the mud of the tall grass to dirty them up. They didn't want to give themselves away with the flash of a shiny blade. They lay in wait, hoping the four men would go past them and they wouldn't be seen. The last thing they wanted was a knife fight with Indians in the dark, especially being outnumbered as they were. But, as the men crept closer, it became obvious to Logan and Will that they were right in their line of movement. All they could do was wait and be ready.

One of the men was so close to Logan that he was almost on top of him. Logan could see he was Apache. He didn't understand how the Apache could not see him, but it seemed he couldn't. Logan waited until the man was about to step on his leg, then he reached up and grabbed the short man by the throat and pulled him down quietly into the tall grass. He immediately rolled over on top of the smaller man. Still grasping the man's throat with his crushing grip, Logan sent the big knife home, straight into the man's heart. The Apache didn't make a sound or a movement. He died, quickly and silently. Logan snaked a little further to his left near where Will was lying, waiting. Just as Will was getting ready to reach up and pull the second Apache down, he saw the unmistakable flash of a knife blade off to his left. He couldn't tell what was about to happen, but he simply pointed with his own knife, and Logan immediately dragged the second Apache down. The scene was much the same as the first, except that this time his knife hit a lung, and there was a faint gurgling sound. The other two Apaches heard the sound and stopped to listen. Logan hung on and continued to crush the man's throat. Pretty soon the faint gurgling stopped and that one was dead, too. The remaining two Apaches stood frozen, waiting and listening. While Logan was taking care of the second Apache, Will slipped over to where he thought he'd seen the flash of a blade. He peered through the tall grass, and as he moved forward, he wasn't sure he believed what he was seeing. There was one of the other two Apaches lying face up in the grass. The cut was made with a very sharp knife and went from ear to ear. Will slowly edged further back into the grass and began scanning all around. He didn't want to be next. He was just about to move back toward Logan when off to his left he saw another Indian with two black feathers tied into his hair moving silently through the grass. This one was not Apache. He was Comanche. Will tensed for the kill then noticed the blood on the Comanche's hands. Had he killed this Apache? As he waited, Will noticed yet another Indian moving very slowly through the grass, just behind the oncoming Comanche. The second man was definitely Apache, and it was obvious he meant to kill the Comanche with the black feathers in his hair. Will didn't know why, but he somehow knew that he had to try to save the life of this Comanche. He seemed to know this one could not die. He very carefully and silently rolled to his left and began to snake his way in behind the Apache. He didn't know if he could get into position in time, but he was going to give it everything he had. He had to stop this Apache, and maybe find out why a Comanche would be trying to help him and Logan. The entire scene began to unfold in slow motion. Everyone crept slowly and silently. The only thing that had happened quickly was the deaths of the three Apaches. Will was almost there, just a little farther. He saw the Apache tense for the strike. He wasn't quite close enough, but he knew he had to make a move now or he would be too late. The thought of looking around to see if there was more danger went through his head like a bullet, but he knew there was no time. He was on his feet, running the few remaining steps to the Apache without regard for his own life. There was a blur of movement behind him and to his right. It was another man coming at him. He knew he would likely die in the next instant, but he had to stop the Apache. Will was on the Apache in the blink of an eye. He was quiet but not silent, so the Apache had some warning of Will's presence. It did him little good. Will was on top of him pinning him with all his weight before the Apache could react. The Apache writhed and struggled, slashing blindly behind himself, trying to score a hit with his own knife. He did score and the blade cut Will on the upper thigh just below his butt. It was deep and long, but Will didn't let up. He held the Apache and slipped his own blade beneath the soft skin of the neck and violently jerked upwards, then he rolled away quickly into the grass. He felt the wind on the back of his neck as a knife blade whipped by him so close it cut the kerchief he wore. As he rolled onto his back, knife at the ready, he saw two men drop into the grass. He knew he was about to die, but by god, he was resolved to take some along for the ride. He lay there, knife at the ready, staring into the confused face of the Comanche who was looking, first at him and then at the dying Apache, writhing and bloody in the grass. The Comanche looked back and forth several times, the black feathers in his hair waving as he turned his head from one to the other, and then realized that Will had saved his life. He cautiously stood and slowly sheathed his own knife. He put the edge of his hand to his lips, a warning for Will to be quiet. He dropped beside Will and looked at the deep gash on Will's leg. He took the kerchief that had been cut from Will's neck and packed it with grass, then bound the wound very tightly. The bleeding slowed and would likely stop altogether soon. He and Will sat looking at one another.

There was movement to their left and another Comanche crawled into the circle of trampled grass. He surveyed the scene with a questioning look and made a sign with his hand that unmistakably asked, "What happened?" Two Crows made several hand gestures toward the dying Apache, then toward Will followed by a sign that resembled shooting an arrow, and then he pointed back to the Apache. Will couldn't say for sure that they were friends, but he figured that if these two were going to kill him, they would have already gotten around to it.

Suddenly, he saw something in the grass that made his blood freeze. He jerked his hand up, palm out. It was Logan, moving silently up behind the second Comanche, his knife poised to plunge into the man's heart from behind. Logan, startled by Will's quick movement, stopped the thrust midway, but he did not pull back. He would keep this Comanche very close to death, at least for the time being. He waited to see what Will would do next. Both Comanches knew they should make no movement whatsoever and froze where they stood.

Very quietly, Will whispered, "Easy Brother, I don't think they mean us no harm. This one kilt one of the Apaches," he said, pointing to Two Crows. Logan eased back just slightly and sheathed his big knife. Two Crows turned to face Logan, looked him up and down, and lay a lingering eye on the big knife. He was beginning to think this knife might be the source of the big man's medicine.

He pointed toward Logan with his chin and said, "Big warrior," then he pointed at the knife and said, "Piapuha Nahuu" (Big Medicine Knife). He said this with unmistakable respect. "See you kill many Mexicans at the buffalo swamp. See you die." The other Comanche stood staring at Logan with a look of awe. He had never seen such a big man or such a big knife. Two Crows quickly told him in Comanche who Logan was. He blanched and staggered back a step. He fully understood now how close to seeing his ancestors he had been this day.

Two Crows indicated that they should follow him and all four moved slowly and silently back into the trees along the stream. Two Crows led them up the small slope to Yellow Wolf. When they came into the clearing, every Comanche there, including Yellow Wolf, was startled by Logan's size. Yellow Wolf hadn't seen him up close before. When Yellow Wolf stepped forward, Logan and Will knew without question who and what he was. He bore himself as a natural born leader and it was obvious that every Comanche there respected him. Two Crows spoke briefly, telling him what had happened. Although Yellow Wolf had watched everything from a distance, Two Crows, out of respect, could do no less. Yellow Wolf turned to Logan and eyed him closely. He looked at the big knife and there was a sparkle in his eye.

He held his hand straight up, shoulder high, palm out, and said, "Big Warrior, strong medicine." He then placed his fist in the middle of his own chest, and said, "Oha Isa."

Logan stepped forward and repeated the action, "Logan." He then pointed with his chin toward Will. Yellow Wolf turned to face Will and raised his hand again. "Will," Logan said.

Yellow Wolf pointed to Two Crows, his lifelong companion. "Waha Tuwikaa," he said, completing the introductions. Yellow Wolf desired to speak with Logan and Will to find out what their intentions were for being there, but he did not wish to give himself away. He motioned for them to follow him and Two Crows into the trees a short distance. They sat in the deep shadow of a big oak. Logan and Will were both surprised that Two Crows and Yellow Wolf could both speak passable English, but they made no mention of it.

Yellow Wolf led the conversation. "See White Diggers hide in trees," he said pointing to where Captain Boales and the Rangers were in hiding. "Why here?" He gave Logan an open but very stern look.

Logan tensed slightly. He hadn't planned on sitting in the dark talking to a Comanche.

"Hunting," he said simply. Yellow Wolf looked puzzled and inclined his head slightly toward Two Crows who replied in Comanche. Yellow Wolf understood.

"What game?" he asked. Logan was uncomfortable, but knew he couldn't lie to this man.

"Renegades," Logan said flatly. Again, Yellow Wolf turned to Two Crows who responded. Yellow Wolf did not look pleased. Logan began to think maybe Yellow Wolf was leading the renegades and perhaps they had killed the wrong Indians. He was about to say so under his breath to Will when Yellow Wolf spoke to Two Crows, while indicating Logan and Will with his left hand.

Two Crows turned to face Logan directly. "Wihnaituu Huuna, bad spirit. We come to kill. You come to kill?" he asked, pointing toward the spot on the stream where Lame Badger was waiting. Logan looked in the direction Two Crows was pointing, and in the moonlight he could just see the faintest shadow of movement. Could it really be? Was it possible that after all this way, the renegades were unknowingly camped less than a quarter of a mile from where Captain Boales and the rest of the Rangers waited? Logan peered into the moonlight. Suddenly a figure appeared at the edge of the trees. It was short, stocky, and walked with an exaggerated waddle. The waddling figure stopped, turned, and seemed to look directly at them. Logan caught his breath, but realized they were still squatted in the deep shadow of the big oak. There was no way the waddling figure could see them.

Two Crows pointed with his chin, stating, "Lame Badger," with a slight smirk on his face. "Bad one. Many bad ones there." Logan turned and looked into Two Crows' and Yellow Wolf's eyes. There was determination there and Logan knew they meant to kill this figure waddling in the moonlight. Their cold expressions made him shiver. He would not like to face either of these two men in a fight.

"We've come to kill him too. Me, Will, the Cap'n, and ten other Rangers," Logan said, holding up all ten fingers and looking at the two fearsome Comanches.

Yellow Wolf stepped toward Logan, and Will tensed. "You are the great warrior from the buffalo swamp," he said, staring deep into Logan's face. "See you die. Now here." He paused, as if in thought, and then spoke slowly. "We will watch you try to kill Lame Badger. If you do not, we will kill him, then we will kill you." His words had a finality about them that left no doubt about his intentions. Logan and Will were escorted to the far edge of the heavily treed rise; from there they made their way slowly down into the tall grass, crossed the stream, and disappeared into the tree line on the other side. It took them so long to make the tree line that there was a faint lightening in the eastern sky.

Lame Badger awoke with a start. He had been dreaming. It was a dream he had many times in the past. He was trying to run from a black shadow, but he could not make his legs move. He did not run well anyway, but in his dream his legs kept getting tangled and he would fall as the black shadow loomed over him, menacingly, then there would be a bright flash and a crushing weight on his chest. He would thrash in his sleep, feeling unable to breathe as the flash moved closer, and then he would wake. The dark shadow was much closer this time, and he could almost make out a face swirling in the blackness, before the bright flash and the crushing weight woke him. He was covered in sweat, and felt genuine fear. He lay looking up at the early morning stars through the trees. Something was wrong. The Apaches had not sent word back about the town. Lame Badger didn't hesitate; he scrambled to his feet and began waddling as quickly as he could through the camp, quietly waking the band of renegades and killers. They all began moving quickly and quietly. Everyone knew the consequences of Lame Badger's anger. Soon they were all mounted, and the captive children were gagged with wads of leather in their mouths so they couldn't make noise even if they screamed. They were riding down the stream, and had just moved out of the tree line into the tall grass, when Asesino caught a glimpse of something in the trees to their left. It was the briefest of glimpses, but he was sure of what he'd seen. He kicked up his horse and caught Lame Badger. Leaning over in his saddle, he whispered to him what he'd seen. Lame Badger told him to take two men and go take care of it. He immediately signaled the two brothers from Sonora, Philippe and Pancho Madrigal, two of the worst among them. Lame Badger rode back down the line, whipping the horses into a gallop.

It was fairly light when Logan and Will finally crept back into the Rangers camp. Captain Boales listened carefully to what they told him about the events of the night. He was startled by the news that the renegades were so close to them. When they got to the part about Yellow Wolf and his small band, Boales grew stern.

He was quiet for a short while, pondering, then he motioned all the Rangers to gather around him.

He spoke in a whisper. "Okay boys, this is what we came here for, and we need to move now or I fear we may lose 'em yet again". He scanned the faces gathered around him. There was grit in every man there, no question, but this damned band of renegades had slipped by them more than once, and he meant to stop 'em for sure this time. He whispered orders to each pair of men. Will and Logan were given the job of scouting the renegade camp. The Rangers moved silently to their already saddled horses and began to move out quietly in different directions. The Captain had laid out plans for an ambush as the renegades moved from the tree line to the tall grass. He wanted to catch the renegades in the open, where the tall grass would hinder them.

Logan and Will moved more quickly than they liked toward the renegade camp. They were quiet, but not silent.

When they got close to the spot where the stocky waddling figure had been they dismounted and crept toward the camp. Something was wrong! There was no one there. The devils had slipped past the Rangers again! Logan began to trill out the call of a thrush, the signal to the Captain that something had gone wrong. They ran back to their horses and began to trot quickly through the trees to the spot where Captain Boales was waiting for them.

Yellow Wolf watched the big warrior and the other white Ranger move slowly down the heavily treed ridge and into the tall grass. By the time they made their way to the tree line, it was beginning to get light. He lost sight of them in the trees and began scanning the area where Lame Badger's camp was. He and all eleven of the other Comanche warriors watched for movement among the Rangers and Lame Badger's band. Finally, Two Crows pointed to where Lame Badger was camped. It was barely light, but there was movement. A line of riders was coming out of the trees, but there was no movement among the Rangers yet. Yellow Wolf signaled his group to go into the tall grass. They would have to kill Lame Badger themselves.

Captain Boales had sent the Rangers into the trees in pairs, with orders to wait until the renegades were committed to the tall grass before making their move. Then he would signal them with a single shot and the Rangers would ambush the renegades. With twenty-five or thirty of the worst killers that part of Texas had ever known, Lame Badger's band was more than twice as big as the Rangers were, and Boales knew their only chance was an ambush. He also knew that total surprise was the only way they could hope to take the renegades, but it was their only chance at survival. The stakes were very high, but Boales was intent on stopping these killers and baby stealers once and for all, no matter the cost.

He watched Vandeveer and Magill disappear into the trees toward the renegade camp. Then he checked the other Rangers. They were all well hidden and prepared. It looked like this plan could possibly work, but he didn't try to fool himself; the price would be high. It was something he would have to live with, so that they and the rest of the people in this area could finally be rid of this band of evil men, for good.

Just as he was about to settle into the spot he'd picked to shoot from, he saw the line of renegades coming out of the trees into the tall grass. This was what they had waited for. Every muscle tensed, but he made himself comfortable and remained quiet. Boales was an expert shot with his Morgan-James Rifle. He had recently obtained an experimental telescopic sight, and after some practice, found he could put ten shots in a row into a group that could be covered by a two-inch circle of paper at over 100 rods (550 yards). He would wait until they were close enough that, even if they ran from him, he could still shoot them out of their saddles.

He was trying to count them when suddenly, a thin Mexican rode forward to the short stocky Indian in the lead. They whispered quickly and then split up; the short one rode back along the line whipping up the horses. The thin Mexican doubled back and took two other Mexicans with him. They headed directly for the trees where two of the Rangers were hiding. Just as they entered the trees there was a shot. Suddenly the whole line of riders began galloping into the grass. Several were obviously children; their hands were bound and they were gagged. Then there were three more shots and he saw Vandeveer and Magill break out of the trees and make a rush for the running line of horses. There were several shots from the line of renegades, but Vandeveer and Magill seemed not to be hit. They answered the challenge of the renegades and two fell from their horses. The two Rangers kept the pace and at this rate, would soon over-take the line. They fired again, and two more fell from their saddles. Boales could only wait, as did the other Rangers. As they watched, Boales saw two more Rangers emerge from the trees from where the first shots came. They must have been seen and had apparently killed the three men sent back to check it out. These two Rangers were also giving chase and firing at the renegades. Boales could only hope they realized how careful they needed to be in order to keep from hitting any of the captive children. As the line approached Boales and the eight remaining Rangers, another group of riders came out of the trees across the break of grass near the bottom of a heavily wooded ridge. They were riding hard for the renegades. Were they here to reinforce or fight them? He couldn't tell at first until one of the riders, a Comanche, shot a renegade from his horse with an arrow and all hell broke loose. Boales fired the signal shot and a renegade leading one of the children's horses fell from the saddle. The Comanches were pressing the renegades hard, and it began to show. Pandemonium ruled the tall grass. Horses scattered in all directions. Some of the renegades, realizing they were trapped between the Rangers behind them and the Comanches in front, dove from their horses into the tall grass and tried to get away. Boales signaled the two pairs of Rangers that he'd instructed to get the captives; now was the time to move. The four Rangers were out of the trees, and their horses were running at full speed through the grass to head off the line when shots began to erupt from the town. Two of the Indians coming out of the trees fell, as did two of the renegades. A Ranger's horse went down and the scene took on a nightmarish quality. Boales knew this could be a blessing or a curse. In the confusion, it was difficult to tell who was friend and who was foe. The rest of the Rangers fired at will as the line of renegades broke and began scattering. They were still quite a ways off, but most of them were running toward Boales' position. Boales was methodically firing; he was taking the renegades without a miss. The pressure from the combined force of the Rangers and the Comanches was so heavy that the renegades scattered and dove for the grass. Boales watched as his Rangers dashed into the grass and began shooting at the killers that were trying to crawl away to safety. He looked up and saw two of the Indians that had come from the other side of the break riding hell bent for the spot where the stocky renegade leader had disappeared into the grass. He was fairly close to that spot himself and briefly considered running into the grass, but Calvin Boales was an excellent shot with a rifle so he kept his head and began watching the scene, offering cover and support wherever he saw a captive or Ranger in trouble. It was then that he realized one of the biggest threats to all concerned was coming from Quemado itself. Whoever was there shooting, was doing so indiscriminately. He watched closely and saw the smoke from the rifles. It was a very long distance, but Boales trusted his Morgan-James. He sighted the first puff of smoke and guessed the distance at around 75 rods. He adjusted the elevation in his sight, took careful aim, and a Mexican wearing a wide brimmed sombrero fell forward out of the closest puff of smoke. He scanned the edge of the town and saw three more men, further off, shooting into the melee. He adjusted again and killed the second. He missed the kill on the third gunman, but saw him run behind a building holding his bleeding hand. Boales didn't hesitate, and killed the fourth gunman. He was so intent on the gunmen in the town he didn't notice the squat, waddling Indian coming at him from the grass to his left, until it was too late. When he did notice, Lame Badger was on him, war club already in motion. Boales tried to duck the blow, but didn't have a chance. The blow was glancing, but it still took him on the side of the head practically lifting his feet off the ground.

The four Rangers that rode out into the melee in the grass were J.D., Cherokee Jim, Shorty Hayes, and John Liddel, who everybody called Little John. Shorty was the first to go down, his horse shot from under him. He was stunned at first, but recovered himself just in time to see two of the renegades galloping toward him leading four horses carrying captive white children. He laid himself down in the grass quickly and waited. When they were almost on top of him, he jumped up between the two lead horses. He shot the Mexican riding the horse on his right and turned his attention to the Apache on the other lead horse. He should have shot the Apache first. As the war club clipped the top of his head, stars began jumping around in front of his eyes. He kept his feet, but the Apache was on him, trying to connect with the war club a second time. Shorty wrestled him to the ground and was on top of him when the Apache bucked Shorty up over his head and laid him out flat on his back. The Apache was up and almost on top of Shorty, war club raised high for the deathblow, when Shorty pulled his knife and ran it clean and quick up into the Apache's left arm pit. The Apache froze for a brief second, which was just long enough for Shorty to put it straight into the Apache's throat. Blood spurted out into Shorty's face and he quickly rolled to the side, dropping the Apache to the ground and giving him one more between the shoulder blades. The Apache went limp immediately, but before Shorty could get to the frightened children and horses, another Texian renegade was on him, pistol in hand. Shorty took the shot in his chest. It was high up on the right side, but he knew it was bad for him. He only reflected on it for a split second and then jumped at the renegade as he rode past, trying to club Shorty with his rifle butt. Shorty dragged him from his horse, cutting him several times on the way down. As they hit the ground, Shorty buried his blade to the hilt with an upward stroke just below the Texian's breastbone. The Texian died quickly, but so did Shorty. Little John was there as Shorty gasped his last breath with a weak smile on his face. He knew the children would be all right.

As Little John began to gather up the horses, Will, J.D., and Cherokee Jim rode onto the scene. J.D. looked down at Shorty in anguish. He and Shorty had been friends since childhood.

"SHORTY!!" He screamed, jumping from his horse.

Little John stepped in front of J.D. and shook his head. "He went with a smile on his face, 'cause he knew the kids was gonna be okay." J.D. picked up the fallen man and they put him across a saddle as several bullets whizzed into the grass around them. Then they all turned back to the kids who were by this time panicked beyond reason. They had no idea who was friend and who was foe. They all screamed and tried to whip their horses into a run every time anyone even looked at them, especially Cherokee Jim. The horses were spooked and confused from the noise, the smoke, and the smell of death around them. The children were unable to do more than add to their panic. Considering what had happened to them, and what was happening now, it was admirable how well the children held up. Cherokee Jim had just caught the last horse as it spun backward circles in the grass and was heading back to the others when two Apaches galloped up swinging their clubs. One tried to jerk the reins out of Cherokee Jim's hand, but Jim held firm while J.D. put a ball into the Indian's head and he dropped like stone. The other Apache jumped from his horse onto J.D., but Little John was close at hand, slipping his knife under the Apache's chin and sending him to meet his ancestors. The children were frantic by the arrival of these new killers.

Little John grabbed a handful of reins and held up his bloodied hand. "Hold on there. We're Texas Rangers." Only one of the children knew what that meant, a girl of sixteen named Rebecca Pensana, and she wasn't sure she believed him. Will rode up at that moment and could see what was happening.

He caught her eye. "Honest, little lady, we mean you no harm. We're here to help you. We've come to take you home," Will said in the most soothing voice he could muster. Rebecca felt doubtful, but then looked at one of the Apaches. He had a long scar along his chin down onto his neck. He had beaten and abused her terribly from the beginning. She would never forget him. She sat, unsure whether to kick her horse over the top of Little John, this tough looking man with the bloody hands, or not. However, she had seen him kill the evil Apache with the scar. Finally, she just slumped in the saddle and began to sob uncontrollably. She was all in. She had tried to take care of the other children as best she could, though there was little she could do. She was just plain worn out. Will rushed forward and steadied her in the saddle.

"It's okay, honey," he said in the most soothing voice she'd ever heard. "We'll get you home, but right now I need you to help me get these other children into the trees so's they'll be safe. Can you help do that?"

He was looking into her eyes, which said, "No, I can't take anymore," but she sat up straight, took the reins from him, wiped away her tears, and nodded, a very determined look etched onto her face.

J.D., Little John, and Cherokee Jim were already mounted and ready to go. Will's horse had shied and run off a short distance. He told them to go on, that he'd be right behind 'em. He started after his horse, and was about half way to it when a big Mexican renegade rose up out of the grass holding a machete, the preferred blade in many parts of Mexico. Will just looked down at the pitifully small knife in his own bloody hand. Now he wished he'd gotten himself one as big as the one Logan carried. His knife had done plenty of work, especially today, but he wasn't going to kid himself; it was suicide to try to take down this big man wielding an even bigger blade. The Renegade saw the thought through Will's eyes and smiled an evil smile, showing big yellow rotten teeth. Will knew he had no choice. He had to kill this big man or he would die trying. He wiped the blood from his right palm, gripping the knife firmly, and just as he was about to scream his war cry and charge the man, a horse shot past him out of the grass from his left, straight at the big bandito. The big man was caught off guard, unable to get out of the way. There was a look of complete surprise on his face as the horse hit him full on, stumbling over top of him and stepping squarely on his head and torso. Rebecca reined the horse up and spun him around for a second pass. It was unnecessary, but she was going to make sure. She reined up again next to Will, offered her hand, and he swung aboard.

She took him to his own horse, and as he slid down, she said, "How would we get home if I let you get hacked up by that big ugly devil?" Will looked into her eyes and saw nothing of the frightened girl that had been there just minutes ago. He swung into the saddle and off they went at a dead run to catch up to the others headed for the tree line.

Lame Badger was recoiling for his second and final swing when Logan veered his horse to the left and jumped headlong from it. He hit the ground running and screaming. His big knife leapt into his hand as he ran. Lame Badger heard the man's war cry, and seeing the biggest man he'd ever seen in his life running toward him with knife in hand, he dropped to the ground and crawled to his right as fast as he could. When Logan got to Boales, he found him sprawled on the ground, blood pouring from the gash in the side of his head. He pulled off his own neckerchief and held it against Boales' head to staunch the flow. Boales' eyes were rolled back in his head and he was as limp as a rag. Logan carefully cradled the captain's head and tried to stop the bleeding. After a minute or so, the bleeding began to slow and finally it appeared it would stop. Logan felt for Boales' heart. It was slow and faint. He bound the captain's head and laid it down carefully into the grass. That waddling little devil would pay for this. He picked up his knife, set his jaw, and went into the grass. It was hard to see where the crippled Indian had gone, but Logan did not get down and crawl as Lame Badger did. He stood upright and waded deliberately through the grass. The trail seemed to turn and twist many times as Lame Badger tried to confuse the trail, but Logan wasn't fooled and kept his head. He followed steadily until he heard movement in the grass ahead. Without thinking, he began shrieking like a banshee. He had never done this before this day, but it was his own war cry, and it unnerved Lame Badger until he stood upright and tried to run. Logan spotted him instantly and turned after him. Lame Badger was more frightened now than he had ever been in his life. He tried to run faster, he willed his bent leg to move quickly and surely, but he kept tripping. The grass kept tangling his feet and he fell time and again. Logan saw him fall down several times and knew he had this devil. He didn't hurry. He just kept up his war cry and kept coming after Lame Badger who was struggling frantically with the grass. He was whining now, as he tried to untangle himself and get away from this giant of a man with the big knife. Finally, Lame Badger could go no further, and rolled onto his back, trying to scoot backwards into the grass. Logan stepped forward, his shadow falling across Lame Badger. As he loomed over him, Logan could see the stark terror in Lame Badger's eyes. It was as if Lame Badger were looking at some demon on earth. He swung his war club, trying to break one of Logan's legs, but Logan stepped back, easily avoiding the blow, and pinned the war club to the ground. Lame Badger struggled, trying to pull it free, giving Logan the chance to put his other foot in the middle of Lame Badger's chest. The big man rocked forward and sent all his weight crushing the wind from Lame Badger's lungs. Lame Badger let out a shriek of terror that made Logan's skin crawl. He looked down at this helpless, disgusting insect under his heel and felt his conscience stir. He stood pondering what he should do when a look of defiance passed over Lame Badger's face and he spat up at Logan, screaming with the last breath of air in his lungs, hatred seething inside of him. Lame Badger remembered his dream as he lay dying, looking up at Logan. He knew this was the dark shadow that had loomed over him in his sleep. A new level of fear came over him, and for the first time in his life, Lame Badger knew he was going to a hell reserved for only the most evil men. Logan looked down at Lame Badger with disgust.

Logan lifted his big knife, and as the morning sun hit the blade, he could see the glint of steel flash into Lame Badger's eyes. He leaned forward and shifted his weight, which caused several of the evil man's ribs to crack and break. Without remorse, Logan plunged his knife into Lame Badger's throat, pinning him to the muddy ground with it. Lame Badger's eyes opened wide and he began tearing at the powerful leg crushing down on him with one hand, and clawing at the knife with his other. He writhed and hit Logan's leg with his fists; tears were streaming down his face. His mouth gaped open in a silent scream, but there was no air left in his lungs to cry out with. Death seized his muscles, and he flopped on the ground for a moment until the strength began to go out of him. His writhing grew less, but his tears increased. He twitched a few times and went still.

He died poorly, just as he had lived. Logan withdrew his knife, wiped the blood from it on Lame Badger's chest. As he turned to leave, he started. Yellow Wolf was standing directly behind him, knife in hand. Logan tensed, but Yellow Wolf didn't move. He had watched Logan kill this evil little man and had not made a sound. He and Logan stood looking at one another for a moment; tension filled the air. With a somber, satisfied look on his face, Yellow

Wolf sheathed his knife and nodded at Logan. Without a word, Yellow Wolf turned on his heel and walked back to his horse, which stood waiting nearby.

Logan could still hear shooting and the occasional scream of someone dying as he hurried back to his own horse. He gathered the reins and surveyed the situation. All that could be seen were Comanches riding through the grass, shooting arrows into the last of the renegades. Three Rangers were coming out of the grass leading horses with captive children aboard. Amos and another Ranger named Smithwick were riding up from behind the scattered line shooting into the grass as they passed renegades trying to escape. No quarter was given these killers. Shooting still rang from the town, but at that distance, it seemed ineffectual. Logan hurried back to the Captain's side. The Rangers with the six captive children rode in and gathered around. All of the children were crying except one, Rebecca Pensana. The Rangers were helping the children from their horses and trying to comfort them. Bullets continued to ricochet off the ground and whiz around them. The children screamed every time one did. Simon Whitley, one of the Rangers that had stayed in the trees to give rifle cover, was with Boales putting on a proper bandage made from a piece of clean shirt that he had found in the Captain's saddlebag. Logan dismounted and knelt beside Captain Boales. He had a troubled look on his face.

"He come around once," Whitley said, tying the bandage snugly around Boales' head. "Asked if we got 'em all or not, then slipped away again." Several bullets ricocheted out of the dirt around the group as the Rangers got the last of the children behind the trees. Cherokee Jim was having trouble getting close to them. Whenever he tried to get near one they would scream, and try to shrink away from him. Boales' eyes fluttered open. "Be gentle with 'em Jim, they're just children, not rough old cobs like us," he said, almost in a whisper.

Logan took his hand. "Sure am glad to see you back with us. I thought we'd lost you for sure."

Boales grinned weakly. "Tell me we got 'em all." He winced at a sharp pain in his head, then added, "...and I'll live to be a hundred." Will rode up at that moment with Rebecca.

"We're cleaning the last of 'em outta this damn grass," he said. "I'm afraid we lost Shorty Myers. His horse was shot from under him and a whole passel of 'em got him in the grass, but they paid high for it. He kilt three of them." The little group around the captain was silent for a moment as more bullets ricocheted past them.

Boales looked up at Logan. "Corporal Vandeveer, would you please take our boys over there and teach those bastards in that hellhole of a town how unwise it is to shoot at Texas Rangers?" he asked with a slight grin on his face. Logan was visibly surprised because he'd been called Corporal. He wasn't even sure there were Corporals in the Rangers. At least, he hadn't heard of any in Boales' rangers.

"Right away, Cap'n," Logan said, as he turned and pointed at Will, Amos, Noah Smithwick, J.D., and Little

John. Will and Amos snapped to attention and saluted, hardly able to keep straight faces. Logan hesitated in mid-stride and then, looking down at the ground in embarrassment, he stepped astride his horse.

"Corporal," Boales called out weakly. Logan stopped and turned in his saddle, "I'll have Simms, (meaning Skylar Simms) cover you with my target rifle. He's a fine shot."

Logan nodded "Thank you Cap'n." Not having seen Boales kill the gunmen who'd been shooting from the town from more than a quarter of a mile, Logan didn't have much confidence that it would be of any help, but he said nothing.

The Rangers that stayed with Boales and the children began getting everyone and everything back into better cover, lest a lucky shot hit home, while the seven mounted Rangers rode up the tree line to come at the town from the road.

As Will started to mount up, Rebecca reached out and took his arm. He stopped, and as he looked into her face, he realized how pretty she was; young, but very pretty.

"I don't even know your name," she said, stepping closer to him. He'd never felt such a thrill as the feel of her touch on his arm.

"William Harrison Magill, ma'am, but everybody calls me Will," he said, feeling a tingling sensation inside his chest.

She looked directly into his eyes. "My name's Rebecca. Rebecca Pensana." They stood looking into one another's eyes a moment, then Will swung into his saddle and rode after the others.

"You be careful, William Magill!" she called out to him as he rode away. Rebecca stood and watched him ride off through the tall grass, knowing in her heart that she would be seeing Texas Ranger Magill again. When they got back to Mina, she would make sure of it. She became aware of the other children crying, and turned to tend them. She helped several of the smaller ones from their horses and led them further into the trees until they were well out of sight and range of the bullets ricocheting around Captain Boales. She told them to hush and wait there, and that she would be right back. As she was headed back with three more, she saw a man dart through the trees. She recognized him as one of the renegades and screamed. Cherokee Jim came running, pistol in hand. She pointed in the direction she had seen the man.

He pulled a second pistol from his belt and handed it to her. "You know how to use this?" he asked, looking into her frightened eyes. Rebecca nodded and he moved quickly into the trees. She ran to the other children and gathered them to her, backing them against a huge oak tree and standing between them and the spot where she had seen the Mexican bandit. She held the pistol ready. They all waited for the worst; because that's all the past days had offered any of them. Rebecca heard quiet rustling in the brush and wanted to call out, but knew better. She just waited and watched. There was a shot close by, and soon afterward more rustling in the brush near the tree. She was sure Cherokee Jim would emerge from the brush and waited anxiously, the big pistol trembling in her hand. Suddenly her heart stopped as Asesino staggered into the little clearing. There was blood on his shirt and malice in his eyes.

Rebecca went white. "Jim!" she called out. "Jim, he's here. Jim, help!" she practically screamed the last.

There was an evil grin on Asesino's face, "He won't be coming, senorita," he said with a sadistic laugh. As he began to move toward her, she raised the pistol, pointing it directly at his face. He stopped, but continued his evil grin. "Please be careful, senorita," he said, slowly reaching for the pistol in his belt. "Someone might get hurt, perhaps one of these children." He jerked the pistol from his belt, cocked it, and pointed it at the group of scared, huddling children, laughing aloud as he did so. Without so much as conscious thought, Rebecca jerked the trigger and saw a piece of Asesino's cheek explode and fly away. He was spun to the side, knocked off his feet from the force, his own pistol going off harmlessly. He grabbed his face and began cursing her in Spanish. There were footsteps behind Rebecca, but she never took her eyes from him as he writhed in agony on the ground.

"Does it hurt?" she asked with as much of her own malice as she could muster. "I hope so. I hope it hurts like hell for a long time, you bastard." She cocked the gun again. Hearing the gun cock, Asesino scrambled around the big oak, jumped to his feet, and was gone before she could pull the trigger, though it wouldn't have done any good. She was holding a flintlock pistol and had already fired her one shot.

Logan led the Rangers up the stream a safe distance, and then along a trail that went into the dirty little town.

He stopped them, and as they gathered around he looked each one in the eye. "Well boys, I guess this is what Rangerin' is all about. We're in a tight spot and I don't see any easy way out of it. We came here to kill those baby-stealing bastards and I reckon we can't go and leave these killers here either. Anybody think they can't do this?" He looked around, as did all the other men.

Will spoke up, "We'll back ya, whatever move you make, Brother." The other Rangers all nodded.

They checked their guns. "We don't know what's down there," Logan said as they turned toward town. "But then they don't know what's up here about to come down on their heads. Let's make 'em wish they was all church goin' folk." He kicked his horse into an easy lope and the other six Rangers fell in behind their new leader, two abreast.

As they rounded a small bend in the trail, they passed a tree with two skinned men hanging. The sight enraged them all. The seven kicked up their horses to a run and gave their best war cries as they thundered toward the settlement. Shots rang out and Will felt one sting his left leg. He didn't even look down; he just took aim at the puff of smoke up ahead and held it until he was in range, and then killed the Mexican that had shot him. Shots boomed all around them, but they ran on, yelling and shooting. Will saw four others drop. Suddenly they were at the end of town and the edge of the Rio Grande. They stopped, turned around, and faced the town. They could see movement in a few shadows.

Logan stepped his horse several paces forward and called out in a voice everyone was sure to hear,

"My name is Corporal Logan Vandeveer and we're Texas Rangers. We've come here for any bandits, renegades, or killers we can find. Any who want no part of this can throw your guns in the street and come out now, holdin' your arms up in the air." There was silence, and then some muffled chuckling started. Soon there was outright laughter and from one of the buildings on the right side of the street someone called out,

"What if we don't feel like getting' arrested." Laughter erupted from several buildings. Will held up six fingers, indicating his estimate of known voices.

Logan sat calmly until the laughter subsided a little. "What you want doesn't matter to us at all," he said icily. "'Cause, we didn't come to arrest you, we come to kill you, and kill you we will, to the last man." There was silence. "Unless you throw your guns in the street and put your arms up in the air, now." There was some scuffling around inside the first building as one lone Mexican in a battered old hat and ragged clothes came out, hands in the air. As he opened his mouth to say something, a shot rang out from the saloon across the street. The front of his shirt puffed out and a red blossom began to grow on it. He glanced down with a confused look on his face then fell forward into the street. At once all seven

Rangers kicked their horses in different directions. Two went behind the buildings on either side of the street shooting in from the backside. Logan and Will each took a side of the street and began to calmly ride down, alert for any movement. Amos rode straight down the center. A bullet whizzed through a window and hit Logan's saddle horn, shattering it. He kicked his horse through the door and into the building. The two men inside were caught unprepared. He shot one with his rifle and one with his pistol. He heard Will keeping pace across the street. They both exited, and the three of them resumed their slow assault down the street. Amos shot a skinny man from the roof of one of the saloons. They were fired on two more times. The first shot rang out from a saloon, and Little John killed the gunman through an open back door just as Logan entered. Will got the second, and as they reached the other end of the street, they heard a thump, a grunt, and the distant boom of Boales' rifle, then another Mexican bandito fell from the roof of the last building. While they watched the Mexican writhe in the dirt, there was a crash on the other side of the street and the distant boom of Boales' rifle again, and another gunman fell through a porch roof and rolled into the street, dead.

"Damn!" Logan exclaimed in wonder. "That rifle of the Captain's does shoot long don't it." The other Rangers chuckled. Then they gritted their teeth and started back down the street. This time they all rode slowly and deliberately, scanning every building. There was movement in the shadows of two of them. J.D. and Amos found and killed the last three banditos in the town.

As they neared the end of the street for the second time and approached the Rio Grande, they heard shouting and whooping from the Rancheros and their hired men. Logan stopped his horse and watched them. It was as if he were pondering a decision.

Across the grassy break among the trees, Boales had regained consciousness for the third time, but this time he remained awake. When the shooting started in the town he had Whitley help him sit up so he could see what was going on. It was hard to catch all that was happening in the dirty little town, but he was able to see the Rangers ride up and down the street three times, and Whitley counted all seven in the end. He coached Simms on making adjustments to the barrel length telescopic sight on his Morgan-James Rifle, and when he killed the first bandito trying to ambush the Rangers Boales clapped him on the shoulder and shouted, "Damn fine shot, son!" then staggered slightly. Whitley tried to get him sit back down, but Boales brushed him off and stood over Simms as he killed another one just seconds later. "Skylar," he said proudly, "I place that second shot to be well over a quarter mile."

Simms just looked at the Captain and smiled. "This is a mighty fine rifle Captain," He said, holding it easily in his hands. When Logan and his group reached the west end of the street for the second time, they were too far for even Boales' fine rifle. All Boales and Simms could do was watch. The Rangers seemed to be just sitting, watching the Rancheros taunt them.

"Come on boys," Boales said under his breath as he watched, "go get the bastards. Don't let 'em live to buy another child into slavery." Simms looked at the Captain and grinned. He'd always suspected Boales was an abolitionist at heart, though politics was something Boales had a hard and fast rule against in his command: No ifs, ands, or buts, just no politics!

When Logan and the Rangers stopped at the edge of the Rio Grande, Boales caught his breath.

"Go ahead boy. They're cowards. Go get 'em. Kill 'em all!" he said out loud. He knew how dangerous it was for them to cross over, but he knew it was up to Logan and the other Rangers. They would have to choose to turn back or go on, and possibly die in Mexico. He feared what might happen to the Rangers against so many Vaqueros. He knew it was the right thing for them to do, but he feared for them. They had come through so much. He didn't want them to die over there.

❧

"Boys, we ain't finished with this business yet," Logan said, while watching the group ride along the bank of the river shouting insults at them. "These Rancheros came here to buy stolen children. In my mind that makes them every bit as evil as any we've kilt here today. I say we show 'em the real cost of stealin' children in Texas." Without hesitation, every man nodded and rode up beside him. At once they all began running for the river and yelling their war cries as they crossed over into Mexico and drove straight at the Rancheros. Boales, Whitley, and Simms cheered as the Rangers drove for the river.

The Rancheros and the hired Vaqueros were startled, to say the least. Their horses danced in confusion as they pulled them up and attempted to turn from the charging Rangers. The Mexicans had all been certain the Rangers would never cross the Rio Grande and were stunned to see them come running and screaming through the shallow river to the Mexico side. Several pulled their pistols and fired, but the shots were ineffective. The rushing Rangers were more than they could take and they began to run. Will expected Logan would only chase them for a little ways, but he was wrong, and glad of it. Logan kicked his horse into a dead run and shot a Ranchero out of his saddle. The rest of the Rangers were right behind him, taking their fair share of the toll. Apparently, they were getting better at shooting while on the run, what with all the practice they were getting. Logan holstered his pistol, pulled out his knife, and closed in on the last Vaquero in line. The Vaquero heard him coming up from behind and swerved his horse at the last minute. Logan continued on, catching two more that weren't quick enough. They chased the Rancheros and their men for more than two miles, shooting, clubbing, and stabbing them. Before the Rangers pulled their horses up, fourteen Vaqueros and four Rancheros lay on the dry, dusty ground, dead or dying from gunshot or knife wounds. Logan's horse wanted to continue the chase and danced in circles, but Logan pulled him back and the Rangers turned to survey their day's work. Bodies littered the trail and empty Mexican horses were beginning to stop and breathe. Logan sent J.D. and Amos to gather up all they could catch. He figured they might need them later. Noah Smithwick came up leading one of the Rancheros on a very fine, lathered black horse. Logan stepped his horse up next to the Ranchero, pistol in hand. He put the muzzle against the Ranchero's eye and cocked the pistol. Everybody held their breath. This wasn't what they expected, and no one was sure it was the right thing to do, but they sat and watched. The Ranchero was shaking with fear as he waited for his death.

"¿Habla inglés?" Logan asked, looking into the terrified Ranchero's eye.

The Ranchero nodded "S-Si, I s-speak a little," He said.

"Good," Logan said as he pulled the trigger...click. The Ranchero and all the Rangers jumped as if he had actually shot the terrified Ranchero.

"It's just that easy," Logan said, leaning toward the Ranchero. "You tell everybody you know what happened here today. You tell 'em how the Texas Rangers mete out justice and vengeance, and you be sure and tell 'em we're not afraid to come across the Rio Grande to do it.

We might even come right into your own houses." The Ranchero was so terrified of this crazy gringo from across the river he was sweating and crying. Logan pulled the big pistol away from the Ranchero's eye then laid it up side his head, knocking the blubbering Mexican to the ground. He reached over and took the horse's reins. "You walk back to your Rancho, you baby-stealin' cabron". Logan kicked his horse at the Ranchero, who scrambled to his feet and began running south, looking over his shoulder to see if these 'loco Tejanos' would shoot him in the back. When Logan turned his horse to face the rest of the Rangers, they were all just sitting and staring at him. He sat on his horse and looked back at them. There was no embarrassment or apology in his eyes.

"Didn't know you spoke Mex'can so well, brother," Will said with a look of pride and more than a little mischief in his eyes.

In the fight, Boales had lost only two Rangers: Shorty Myers and Cherokee Jim. Yellow Wolf was not so fortunate; three of his bravest and best warriors had been lost. Clearly, the Rancheros across the river had fared far worse, but none as bad as Lame Badger, his renegades, and the gunmen in Quemado. Between the Rangers and Yellow Wolf's Comanches, every known bad man in the immediate area was dead or had disappeared. Since no one knew how many there were to start with, it was impossible to know if any had escaped or who they might have been. Had they known, the Rangers would have spared no amount of searching to find one for sure. He was closer than they knew...and he was waiting.

CHAPTER 6

LUCINDA

When the Rangers got back to Mina, they were surprised to find it had been renamed. It was now called Bastrop once again, and was the new county seat of Bastrop County. Life for Logan and Will became routine, at least by their standards. It seemed all they ever really did was patrol, chase down Mexican and Texian bandits, and fight Indians, mostly Comanches from Buffalo Hump's camp, but sometimes Kiowa or Apaches. They never crossed paths with any from Yellow Wolf's camp, at least not then. After one such patrol to the east, while chasing several Kiowa horse thieves that happened to get away clean, they rode back into Bastrop and were greeted by a very long wagon line camped just outside of town. It stretched well over half a mile from lead wagon to drag. There was even a traveling Medicine

Wagon. These Medicine Wagon wanderers were usually unique travelers that would offer up anything they had, or could lay their hands on, for sale. Some offered goods like copper pots, knives, lightning rods, and other various and sundry items, while others offered services like health or dental care, knife sharpening, or tinkering (repairing pots). However, the Medicine Wagon that accompanied this wagon line had something completely different; something that would change Logan's life forever.

It wasn't quite sunrise yet and Logan had already washed and shaved. He had just walked to the stove and poured himself a cup of freshly boiled coffee when Will tapped on the door and came in. Logan offered a cup and Will nodded.

"There's a medicine wagon camped just outta' town," Will said eagerly. "Wanna' go see what they got?" Logan poured the cup of coffee and handed it to Will, shaking his head.

"Naw, I need to take my saddle apart and fix the tree," he said, blowing into the steaming cup and taking a sip. "Ever since that Mex'can shot my saddle horn off in Quemado I been tryin' to fix it and it ain't worked. I'm just gonna have to rebuild the tree. Found a nice fork from a big oak limb, over behind the barracks, that fell during the wind we had last week that'll work fine. Figured I'd get started on it today. If I hurry, I can get it done before we go back out. I surely don't want to have to ride that old spare 'packin saddle' the cap'n keeps for the rawhides." 'Rawhides' was the term used for new recruits. He rolled his eyes at the thought of a week in the seat of that torturous old thing. Any one of the Rangers would have been embarrassed and butt sore to ride the old open seated saddle. It had originally been built to ride or pack and was unpleasant for both. Having an open seat was excruciatingly uncomfortable, even after just a short time in the saddle. Even the pack-horses and mules hated it. As a matter of course there were teeth marks in it where two of the more surly mules had grabbed it while being saddled, drug it from their backs, shook it soundly and then kicked at whoever tried to put it on them. Logan shivered at the thought.

"Come on, Brother, it won't take long, and I'll help you fix that big old Mex'can saddle of yours when we get back," Will said anxiously. Logan was rarely able to deny Will a request, but he tried to stay firm. Logan had complained about a sore tooth about two weeks earlier and Will latched onto the possibility like a bulldog. After several minutes of bantering back and forth, Will won out, although not with the argument that maybe there was a dentist.

Logan grinned at Will. "You just want to go to look for some pretty do-dad for Rebecca," he said, sipping the steaming cup. "You think if you buy her fancy things, she'll like you."

Will grinned. "Shoot boy, there'll be a day real soon when Miss Rebecca Pensana will be changin' her name to Rebecca Magill."

"Hah!" Logan laughed. "Not if she's half as smart as I think she is." Will just grinned and sipped his coffee. Logan relented, and after they finished their coffee, they rode out to find the wagon. They found it quickly enough because the owner, a Dr. Thomas Mayes, deliberately set up his camp close to town. Logan and Will rode up to find a slightly balding man of medium height and weight sitting on a stool being shaved by a small, thin, well-shaped woman. He saw the two Rangers ride up and dismount, but sat very still.

"Good day, gentlemen," he said pleasantly, still not moving from the stool. "How can I be of service to you?" Logan and Will loosened the cinch straps on their saddles and turned to face the man. What hair he had left was dark and straight and his eyes were blue and clear. He met their gazes, but held very still. The woman had her back to them so all they could see of her were her small strong hands. "Pardon me if I don't stand and shake hands, but Lucinda gets a might bossy when she shaves me." There was a mischievous sparkle in his eye. "She knows the only time I mind her is when she has that razor to hand."

Will chuckled. "She wouldn't be the first wife to bend a man to her will with a sharp blade," he said with a grin. The woman turned quickly and gave him an icy look, which caused him to shrink back, and then she turned to Logan. When Logan looked back into those big violet eyes, he felt as if he'd been kicked in the gut by a mule. His breath came hard, like he was drowning, his ears began to ring, his skin tingled, and to his complete surprise, he began to sweat, but for the life of him he couldn't take his eyes from her. She stood looking at him for a long time, then blushed brightly as she turned back to her task at hand.

"You're mistaken, sir," she said to Will, turning for one more furtive glance at Logan. "I am no man's wife. This is my father, Dr. Thomas Mayes, and I am Lucinda."

Her father rolled his eyes at her. "Lucinda!" he snapped. "Haven't I taught you better than to be so forward with strangers? Why, your mother would take you to hand if she were alive." He was frowning, but Will and Logan both knew he wasn't angry.

Lucinda stopped scraping and stepped back. With narrowed eyes she replied, "I'm sure she would, Father, and if yours was alive she would do the same, for not remembering your manners and making the introductions properly in the first place." Then she resumed scraping the whiskers from his face. Logan had let out an audible sigh of relief to hear she wasn't married, but he still found it difficult to breathe and couldn't stop sweating to save himself. Will grinned, seeing that Logan appeared to be smitten by this dark haired slip of a girl with violet eyes.

"Well sir, my name is William Magill, and this big sweaty lout is Logan Vandeveer," he said grinning at Dr. Mayes. "We're Texas Rangers, and we're pleased to meet you, and also you ma'am." He and Logan both stood and tipped their hats to Lucinda. She glanced over her shoulder and nodded slightly making a slight dip with her knees.

Dr. Mayes jumped and grabbed the towel from around his neck. "Damn girl!" he gasped, holding the towel up to staunch the trickle of blood running down his neck. "Please be careful, a man only has so much blood to give for any cause, and I fear I've near reached my limit."

Lucinda snatched the towel from him and began wiping the little trickle of blood from his neck. "Oh, Papa! Don't be such a baby, it's just a scratch, and besides if you'd hold still I wouldn't keep cutting you." Logan and Will grinned at each other.

Will continued, "I've not slept as well as I'm used to of late, and my love-struck friend here needs some dentistry performed on him." He held out his hand as if to present Logan. Logan was flabbergasted, first by Will's reference to him as a 'big sweaty lout' and then as being 'love struck'. Why, he was no such thing. He was just about to tell Mr. William Harrison Magill that very thing when Lucinda turned around and faced him again. When he looked into those big beautiful eyes, he forgot about everything and just stood there with his mouth open. After a moment, Will began to feel embarrassed by these two blatantly staring at one another. He reached out and smacked Logan on the arm and Logan jumped. Dr. Mayes looked at his daughter, then grinned and wiped the rest of the shaving soap from his face. He handed Lucinda the towel and held out his hand toward the wagon.

"Well, Ranger Magill, if you'll step this way we'll see what we can do for your sleepless nights and your friend's dental needs." Then with a chuckle, he added, "I fear it's Lucinda that will have to address his love struck nature, though." Will snorted. Logan felt his ears get warm and punched Will in the back. They all stepped to the back of the wagon. Dr. Mayes lowered a shelf built onto the side of the wagon and exposed all manner of sundry bottles. He searched the middle shelf and took one from the right end. He pulled the cork stopper as he lifted a small folded envelope from a slot and blew into it to open it up. He poured a small amount of a white powder into the envelope and then folded it closed. He corked and replaced the bottle and handed the envelope to Will. "Take a pinch of this in some water or tea before retiring at night. It should help." He started to turn to Logan then added, "And abstain from coffee after sunset." Will's face fell. There were few things in life Will found more enjoyable than sitting with Logan passing the time over a cup of coffee, day or night. "Now let's take a look at that tooth, big fella." He motioned for Logan to sit on the stool. Logan was caught off guard.

"Oh, I don't know… I just came along with Will…I…I don't really need a…a…" he stammered.

"Nonsense," said Dr. Mayes, "I get that all the time. Most folks just don't like the idea of someone pokin' around their mouth, but once I get started you'll feel differently." He pushed Logan against the stool so that he had no choice but to sit. "Now open up and let's have a look." He was grasping Logan's jaw with one hand, and his forehead with the other, trying to pry his mouth open. Logan felt panicky and began to struggle, clamping his jaw shut.

"Come now son, I can't help you if you don't at least let me look, now….open…up!" Dr. Mayes said as he put all his strength into trying to pry Logan's jaws apart. Logan struggled on the stool. He was beginning to feel very foolish as he thrashed about unable to shake this strange man holding onto his face.

"Lucinda!" Dr. Mayes called out through gritted teeth, "Come here and hold his head still." He nodded to Will, "You hold his hands. Maybe sit right down on top of him so's he can't flop around. It'll be impossible to pull any of his teeth with him thrashin' about so."

Lucinda came over and just stood, arms crossed, looking down at Logan sweetly with those big violet eyes, and he began to melt. Will rushed in and climbed up into Logan's lap, grabbing his wrists to restrain him. The spell was broken. Logan roared and stood up, throwing Will and Dr. Mayes to the ground. Lucinda jumped back just in the nick of time.

"Dammit, Will!" Logan roared. "What are ya' doin'?" He looked menacingly at both of them. "I ain't havin' no teeth pulled today, maybe never." Will and Dr. Mayes sat in the dirt looking up at him. Will knew the fight was over. If Logan set his mind to a thing, well, that was it. He was just too damn big and strong to bend against his will.

Then with a devilish look in his eye he jumped to his feet and ran at Logan "Come on, Dr. Mayes, we got him now. I'll hold him down, Lucinda you sit on his chest, Dr. Mayes, his head's all yours." He grabbed Logan around the waist and pretended to be struggling to lift him off the ground. Logan just stood there, looking down at him with an exasperated look on his face. "Be careful now, when he sets his jaw to a thing, why that's it. There ain't no amount of good sense'll change his mind." Will grunted loudly. "Stubborn as a dang mule he is. If he goes fer that big knife, scatter. Why, he plumb near wiped out the whole a' Mexico with it at San Jacinto." He continued to throw himself about as if he were really struggling with an immovable object. Logan was getting more than a little peeved when he noticed Will's shoulders were shaking and he could hear him chuckling. Logan felt his ears warming up as he looked around at a crowd of about ten people that had stopped midstride, watching the spectacle. Lucinda and Dr. Mayes were trying unsuccessfully not to laugh at the sight. More chuckling broke out around them. Logan panicked and grabbed Will by the upper arms and lifted him cleanly from the ground, he spun around and sat him forcibly onto the stool. The force was more than the stool could take. It collapsed and they began to fall to the ground. Logan tried to catch his balance, but stumbled over Will and went down too, smacking his head on another small shelf attached to the side of the wagon. It had the pan of shaving water on it. The shelf bowed as if it would collapse and the pan of soapy water sitting on it flew up into the air and came down, right onto Logan's head. Logan jumped up banging his head on the shelf again on the way up. This time the shelf let go and collapsed to the ground. The shaving soap ran into his eyes, burning like fire. Logan howled and staggered backwards, wiping at it, then stumbled over Will and fell into a heap beside the wagon. Laughter erupted from everyone. Logan jumped to his feet, spun around, and glared at everyone present. The soap continued to burn his eyes. The laughter continued as if no one noticed his menacing glare. Lucinda stepped forward, and as she cleaned the soap from his face, everything else seemed to disappear. When his face was dry, she stepped back, smiling sweetly at him. He was lost in her eyes again, but the stinging soap snapped him back to reality.

"Damn you Will," he said as he reached down to help Will to his feet. "You ought to be ashamed, carryin' on so." Will was limp with laughter, and so was everybody else. Lucinda was the only one trying to contain herself. She couldn't, but at least she was trying. Will held up a limp arm. Logan grabbed it with an angry look on his face and lifted him to his feet as if he were a child. Will staggered and doubled over, laughing harder. "People are gonna' think you're simple. Cut it out," Logan said, looking around at all the people laughing. Will went limp again and Logan had to drag him to his feet.

Will pointed at him, laughing so hard no sound came out, tears streaming down his face. "Me!" he finally sputtered, "I ain't the one stumblin' around like a bull in a china closet tearin' up these good folk's wagon," he gasped, as another fit of laughter swept over him. His knees grew weak and he sagged. Logan glared again, but this time only at Will. He reached out and placed his hand in the middle of Will's forehead, shoving gently. Will toppled over backwards and just lay there laughing, gasping for breath.

Logan turned, tipped his soaking wet hat at Lucinda and said simply, "Ma'am," then with soap still burning his eyes and streaming down his neck, he strode from the camp to where they had tied their horses. He turned Will's horse loose, slapped its rump to send it on down the road, mounted his own, and rode away to the sound of laughter fading into the distance.

Logan had recently bought a small, two-room house on the next street over from the Rangers' barracks. Will had decided to stay in the barracks with the other Rangers, thinking he and Logan would enjoy their time together even more if they didn't live together. Besides, they saw each other every day. Logan was disappointed at first, but soon realized they did enjoy their time together more.

When Will got to Logan's house, he banged on the door, yelling out, "Open up Brother! I need help gatherin' up my old caballo, providin' you've finished your bath." Fresh laughter sounded outside the door. Logan had indeed washed up again, toweled himself dry, and was putting on a fresh shirt.

"Go away. I don't need no crazy folks hangin' around me," he said, almost laughing himself. He had taken the time to reflect on what had happened and found it to be more than a little funny.

"Come on Brother, don't leave me afoot. If Injuns get their hands on that worthless ol' nag o' mine they'll probably eat it just to put it out of its misery," Will pleaded.

Logan jerked the door open, then turned and walked back across the room as he tied up the lacing on his shirt. Will came in grinning. He was still having trouble keeping the laughter back. "Don't be mad, Brother. Why, I probably did you a favor. I hear gals like a good humored fella. Shoot, you probably got a leg up, now," he said with a snort.

Logan turned his head and looked solemnly at Will. "They might like good humored fellas, but I doubt they like humorous fellas, like jesters or clowns," he said, with a look of mock seriousness. "They don't see 'em as the marryin' type."

Will froze, his eyes got big, and he strode across the floor to Logan, "Marryin'! Why Brother, are you thinkin' that skinny little slip of a gal might marry you?" he asked.

Logan looked serious. "From the moment I saw her. Will, I plan to court and win her heart, and no amount of funnin' me will change it." Will stood up straight and gazed at his lifelong friend. He could tell from Logan's look that he'd never been more serious.

"I can see it won't. Not that I'd want to." He reached out and put his hand on Logan's shoulder, saying, "I wish you all the good luck I can," then with a mischievous look added, "With what little we two know about women, you're surely gonna' need it."

Logan and Will worked on the saddle together for the rest of the day, unstitching the leather cover and pulling the tree with the shattered saddle horn out. They even found the bullet buried deep in the wood. After removing the broken pieces, Will set his hand to shaping a new tree and horn while Logan oiled the leather to make it more pliable so that it would stretch back into place around the new wood. Every now and again Logan would glance over at Will and catch him chuckling, obviously thinking of the events of the morning. They finished around sunset and stepped back to survey their work. It looked as good as new. Will beamed. Logan nodded his satisfaction, "Mighty fine woodwork there, Brother," he said, clapping Will on the shoulder. Will put his arm around Logan's shoulder and they stood gazing into the sunset.

Then, from behind them, they heard "Ahem!" They spun around to see Lucinda watching them with a slight smile on her face. "I'm sorry to disturb you gentlemen in the midst of your reverie, but I'd like to take a walk and was wondering if you could tell me if it is safe for a woman to walk out here alone?" She stared straight into Logan's eyes. His mind had started to go blank when Will spoke up.

"Well, I'll tell you ma'am…" he started, but before he could get any further Logan reached out, put his hand on Will's shoulder and shoved as hard as he could. Will flew sideways into the dirt as Logan stepped forward and held out his arm for Lucinda.

"Just about anywhere here is safe for you to walk," he said, as they turned, "so long as you're with me." Neither seemed to notice Will lying in the dirt grinning.

The next day, when Will knocked on Logan's door expecting to find Logan there with a ready pot of freshly boiled coffee, he was surprised. There was no Logan. Will reckoned he knew where to find him, so off he went to the Mayes' wagon. What he didn't reckon on was finding Logan sitting on a freshly repaired stool letting Dr. Mayes work on his teeth. Will just sat on his horse dumbfounded, staring. After the ruckus Logan had raised the previous day, Will figured Dr. Mayes had no chance of ever getting even a finger in Logan's mouth, but here he sat as docile as could be, with Dr. Mayes working away. Lucinda noticed Will sitting with his mouth hanging open and quietly walked over to him. She reached out and touched his leg. He just looked down with wonder on his face.

She smiled knowingly at him and said, "You just have to know how to let him make the right choice." Will smiled back at her.

"I see now that Mr. Logan Vandeveer has met his match," Will said, shaking his head and adding, "and then some." She smiled and patted his leg. Logan got a sheepish look on his face when he looked up and saw Will. The lump Logan had gotten from hitting the shelf on the side of the wagon with his forehead was still big and was now black and blue. Will just kept shaking his head and smiling.

"I'll go make a pot of coffee and meet you back at your house," he said, turning his horse. Logan mumbled something incoherent and Will rode away.

Dr. Mayes and Lucinda didn't leave with the rest of the wagon train as they had planned. In fact, people came from miles around Bastrop to call on Dr. Mayes for dental and health care. He felt a strong need to help these honest, hard working people. It took him no time at all to make the decision to stay. But even as quickly as he had made that decision, he was far behind Lucinda. She had decided within five minutes of meeting Logan Vandeveer that she wasn't going anywhere...without him!

Logan had been given a 1470-acre tract of land west of Bastrop by the newly formed Republic of Texas for his heroic service during the War for Independence from Mexico. It was at this time, in 1838, that he and Will decided they would try to get on with their original plan and build ranches. However, it seemed that every time they made such plans, something would come up and they would have to keep on with their duties as Rangers. In early 1838, a Mexican bandit was taking a heavy toll on the hill country of Texas. He was one of the worst anyone had ever heard of. It seemed he killed just for the pleasure of it. Several times Captain Boales' Rangers would find settlers heinously killed, with nothing taken but their lives. This one seemed to hate without prejudice and kill without mercy. Twice they found Kiowas killed and cut to pieces. Logan and Will suspected the killer was Mexican because the wounds often times resembled those made with a sword, or more likely a machete. Their first lead came from Ellis Parser, who was able to give them a description. He had originally come from Virginia, and was the only known survivor of an attack. He was interested in buying a small ranch from Pop Van Der Groot. Pop and his brother Max owned small spreads next to each other over on the Clear Fork of Plum Creek just west of Lockhart. They'd worked their small places for three years. One day, as Pop was in town picking up some supplies, Max started to dig out an irrigation ditch on the river. It had rained the night before and he thought it would be a good time to dig since the ground would be soft. Max had only dug for about two hours when he opened up a nest of Copperheads without realizing it. Pop found him face down in the river with eighteen snakebites on his legs. Two were high up on the inside of his thigh. They had hit the main artery; Max didn't even have time to get his feet out of the mud. When he died, Pop inherited his ranch. But, because he had a working ranch of his own and didn't need or want another one, Pop agreed to sell Max's ranch to Mr. Parser. After the two had come to an agreement on price and terms, Pop asked Mr. Parser to stay for supper. As they sat eating beef and beans at the kitchen table, someone shot through an open window and hit Mr. Parser just to the left of the center of his chest.

The impact knocked him backwards out of his chair. He looked up in time to see Pop's forehead disappear. He tried to stand, but couldn't get his legs under himself, and finally he just lay back on the dirt floor. In strode a man wearing trousers with wide legs at the bottom and silver conchos down the outside seam. He wore spurs with big spiked rowels. When Parser looked up into his face, he caught his breath. The man was Mexican for sure, but what set him apart was his face. Most of his left nostril and part of his left cheek were missing. The wound had not healed well, leaving ragged scar tissue. Even more startling than his face was the hatred in the man's eyes. He kicked Pop out of the way as if he were a piece of garbage, then calmly walked over to Parser, spat down into his face, and shot him again in the chest. Everything started going black for Parser. In his last moments of consciousness, he watched the scarred man calmly sit down at the table and begin to eat the food on Pop's plate.

In the morning, Parser tried to get up, but a searing pain in his chest kept him on his back. He opened his long coat and undid the lacings of his shirt. Blood was dried and caked down his front, but not as much as he would have thought. Then he noticed his Bible. He always carried a small Bible in the inside pocket of his coat to read during the long days and nights on the trail out to Texas. There were two holes through it. It hadn't stopped the bullets, but it had slowed them considerably. Both bullets had hit the same rib and shattered it, but had not gone deep enough to hit anything vital. Pop wasn't so lucky.

Varmints had gotten after Pop in the night, but had left Parser alone. He finally steeled his nerves against the pain and dragged himself to the table and into a chair. Whoever the scarred man was, he wasn't interested in stealing. Everything seemed the same except him, Pop, and the empty plate. He made it to his horse, which was still saddled from the night before, and then rode to the small settlement of Lockhart. Parser was very lucky. Not only did his Bible take the brunt of the impact, but there also happened to be a man in Lockhart named Wilkes that had been a medic during the War with Mexico for Independence. Wilkes removed both bullets, bandaged his ribs and gave him laudanum to sleep, then sent word to Captain Boales.

Boales and his Rangers had been searching for this killer for almost a year without knowing who or what they were looking for. Parser gave them a description and everything became clear: It was the same killer that Rebecca Pensana had shot in the face outside Quemado.

Will wanted out of the Rangers, but Logan was adamant about helping civilize the territory. They never really argued about it, but Will rarely missed an opportunity to try to get Logan to settle down and start raising cows. Will had been spending less time with Logan and more time with a certain Miss Pensana. She was at the age for marriage, according to her father, and Will had seriously entertained the idea. However, it seemed that whenever he'd just about talked himself out of the

Rangers and into Rebecca's open arms, they would have to go out after another bad man or group of bad men, which would take him away from her for a time. This scar-faced one bothered Will more than the others because it was Rebecca who had shot him, and Will could see where the varmint might have cause to come looking for her. Rebecca was anxious and impatient, telling Will in clear language that he'd best make up his mind 'cause she wouldn't wait long for him. She knew it was a lie, but Will didn't, and it fretted him something awful.

Where Rebecca was impatient, Lucinda was extremely tolerant. She seemed almost content to live in the small house Logan had provided for her and her father as long as she was able to see Logan often, and spend as much time with him as his Rangerin' allowed. Every now and again she would test the waters with a pointed question about when they might get married. Logan always seemed ready, but he hesitated, unwilling to commit her to the kind of life Rangerin' imposed on women.

She decided that she would just have to learn to live that kind of life. She went to Barclay's, the little General Store in town, and ordered some white taffeta: yards and yards of it. It took a month to come in. Logan knocked on her door two days after it arrived and was greeted very warmly by her father. When he ducked through the short door, he found Lucinda almost swallowed up by white taffeta, happily sewing.

He stood and watched silently for a long moment. Lucinda never looked up or slowed down. Her strong, nimble hands were gathering folds and stitching them together as surely as could be. Dr. Mayes watched them both for a moment, and paced around the room a time or two before snorting and striding to the door.

"If you need help pickin' him up after, Lucinda, I'll be right outside," he said with a grin as he stepped through the door and patted Logan on the shoulder. Logan gave him a puzzled look, then turned back to face Lucinda, who never looked up.

"Your Pa sure seems in good spirits today," he said, still a little puzzled. "I don't believe I've seen him so anxious though. I wonder what's got him so up on edge." A small smile crossed Lucinda's pretty, full lips, but she just kept stitching. This perplexed Logan even more.

Lucinda broke her silence by saying, "Oh I reckon he's just tickled." She had a sparkle in her eye. Logan stood quietly for a moment waiting for her to elaborate, but she didn't.

"What's got him tickled?" Logan asked, starting to feel the old tightness in his chest. He had a hard time speaking to her for long periods at a time. He would be caught up in her beauty, finding it more and more difficult to breathe, until Lucinda did one of a dozen different things to put him at ease, like touch his arm or caress his forehead. This time he was having trouble with his breath and she wasn't doing anything except sewing. She just kept sewing...and smiling. Suddenly she stopped, bit the thread off, and stood up, holding the dress against herself. It looked awfully puffy around the bottom and might have fit her fair, but for the length. She was a very good seamstress and had made numerous dresses for the ladies around the county, but of late she had not been too occupied with it. He wondered whom she was sewing for now. He just stood there looking at her. The white dress set off her dark hair and violet eyes and she looked so beautiful at that moment Logan thought he might just choke to death.

Lucinda realized he didn't get it. She rolled her eyes and her lips puckered into the cutest pout he'd ever seen. That helped his breathing a little, but he felt as if something was up and he didn't have a clue what it might be.

Lucinda spun, making the puffy bottom of the dress swirl out, then she stopped and stared into his eyes.

"He's tickled to be giving away his daughter in marriage," she said, peering deeply into Logan's eyes. It hit him like a ton of bricks and suddenly the tightness in his chest disappeared.

"So am I to take it you have a sister that I don't know about?" he asked, looking dumb. Lucinda spun around with fire in her eyes.

"You know very well I don't have a sister, Logan Vandeveer," she said, taking a step toward him. He stood as if still clueless, and shrugged. Then his brow knitted and he looked as if he was getting angry.

"Don't tell me that no account John Liddell's been hangin' 'round while the rest of us was out on patrol. I knew he was just pretendin' to be sick. Why I'll run him clear through. Imagine, goin' behind a man's back after his gal!" he said with disdain on his face. Lucinda looked up at him with a look of despair. Surely, he wasn't this dense. Then she saw the twinkle in his eye.

She gathered the dress in one arm and took another step forward, smacking him on the shoulder playfully.

"Darn you, Logan Vandeveer, don't you play dumb with me at a time like this," she said, shaking her finger in his face. "I've been sewing my fingers to the bone to have this pretty dress ready, and here you are acting like...like...oh, I don't know what. Why, I ought to..." she was truly exasperated. Logan stepped forward, grinning, then took her in his arms and kissed her cute little pouty lips. She started to struggle, but soon melted in his arms. When he pulled away, she had a dreamy look on her face. She turned back to the chair to finish the dress.

"You go on now, I've got work to do," she said, waving him toward the door. "Go catch a killer or something."

Logan ducked out the door smiling from ear to ear.

Dr. Mayes was standing just out by the corral smoking. He looked up as Logan approached.

"Congratulations, son," he said with a smile. Logan pulled out a thin cheroot of his own, but found it difficult to light because of the smile on his face.

He got it lit, and as he exhaled the thick grey smoke he said, "That's the first time I've spent more'n five minutes with her that I didn't feel like I was bein' smothered'." He turned to gaze into the sunset, adding, "Well I did at first, but it just seemed to go away.

Dr. Mayes chuckled, "Her mama used to make me feel the same way." They stood side by side and watched the Texas sun go down. It was one of the happiest days of Logan's life.

When he got to his house, Logan found Will sitting on the porch sipping a cup of coffee; it was strong from the smell of it. Logan unsaddled his horse, and with a light heart went to the porch to visit with his friend. He rolled his eyes at the cup of coffee in Will's hand, but never said anything. He was waiting for the right time to tell Will that he and Lucinda were going to marry, soon. Will watched him out of the corner of his eye as Logan poured himself a cup and sat down next to him. The sun had set and it was almost dark.

"Sure was warm today," Logan said matter-of-factly. "Probably gonna be extra hot this summer. Ain't had the rain we oughta'." Will said nothing. "I expect we'll have to go back out after that damned Mex'can tomorrow or the next day."

"I expect so," Will said agreeably. Then they sat in silence. This was one of the things they liked most about one another; they could spend hours, even days, together and remain quiet, just enjoying each other's company.

Finally, Will turned to Logan and just stared. Logan was caught a little off guard, but still said nothing. Will continued to stare.

"What?" Logan asked, feeling self-conscious.

Will just shook his head.

"What?!" Logan asked again. He was starting to think that maybe Will was mad at him, something they had never experienced before. Will stared for a while more.

"Well," he said, looking Logan in the eye expectantly.

"Well what?" Logan was getting exasperated.

"You really fixed it for me this time, Logan Vandeveer." Will said with a stern look on his face. Logan was truly baffled by this conversation. He didn't have any idea what was eating Will.

"What are you talking about?" Logan said, getting more nervous and trying to think what he might've done to Will. He couldn't think of a thing. His mind was blank, a great big goose egg. He just looked at Will and shrugged.

Will shook his head and looked down at his boots. He didn't want Logan to see him grinning.

"Well Rebecca says that if you're gonna marry Lucinda, then it's high time her and I tied the knot too." He kept looking down. "Said if Lucinda can tolerate life as a Ranger's wife, so can she. Don't see as I've got a choice." Will tried to look serious, but he was having a hard time. Logan was dumbfounded. It seemed everybody knew he and Lucinda were going to get married; everybody, except him. He jumped from the chair and paced across the porch.

"Well I'll be!" he said louder than he meant to. "Is there anybody in this whole part of Texas that don't know we're getting' married?" He was a little irritated, mainly because he wanted to see Will's face when he told him they were getting married. But here Will had done it again. It was as if he knew what Logan was going to do or think before he did it or thought it.

Will just looked up, all serious like, and shook his head. "Ol' Ely Duncan over to Lockhart might not know, but, I figured to swing over that way tomorrow and fill 'im in."

Logan guessed he must've been about to catch a fly, because Will reached up and closed his mouth, then broke out laughing. Logan just shook his head and stared down at his feet.

CHAPTER 7

THE HUNT FOR SCARFACE

Logan was right about one thing, the next day they were told to prepare for a long patrol. Captain Boales was determined to catch up to this scar-faced killer. They would stay out and track him for the next two months if they had to. Lucinda, being anxious as only a soon to be bride can be, wanted to know when they would be back.

Logan just shook his head. "No tellin'." He stooped slightly and slipped his arms around her waist. "I reckon we'll stay out till we get the murderin' devil." Lucinda looked troubled, and Logan figured she was worried about him now that they were getting married, for sure. "I know it's hard for you. It's hard for me too, but as much as I don't want to go, I do want to go. This is the very kind of thing we can't stand by and allow. We've got to stop him, for everybody's sake, for the sake of Texas."

He peered into her eyes, making sure she understood what he was saying. "What with the way this one moves around, I want to go get him before he finds out that Rebecca lives here and comes for her. She's been real lucky so far, but I don't know how long her luck will last." He looked into her eyes. "I want to ask something of you," he said, holding his hat in his hands. "It would be good if you was to check in on them, Rebecca and her Pa, to see that they're okay." He reached into his belt and pulled a double-barreled pistol from it, then took her small hand and laid the big pistol into it. It looked huge in her hand. She knew he was worried, so she slipped it into her apron pocket, then raised up on her tiptoes and kissed him as if he were leaving for months, and perhaps he was. He turned and walked out into the cool predawn darkness, mounted his horse, and rode off to meet the other Rangers. Since Lockhart was the last place this killer had been seen, Captain Boales headed them south.

Time passed slowly for Lucinda and Rebecca as they waited for Logan and Will to return. They had become fast friends, and were spending more time together lately. They were about the same age and came from similar backgrounds. Lucinda's family had moved from Kentucky, as had Rebecca's family. They both loved life in Texas, even as dangerous as it was, and they were both in love with and planned to marry Rangers. They had talked at great length about the possibility of Logan and Will being Rangers from now on, but neither wanted that. They wanted their men to settle down, raise a family, and make homes and better lives for their families. No more chasing around the country, hunting bad men, or fighting Indians. They both trusted their future husbands and understood Logan and Will's need to see the territory civilized for the sake of their families and everyone else, but still, it was difficult.

The Rangers had been gone for more than two weeks when Lucinda, Rebecca, and both their fathers decided to take a small wagon and drive over to the Colorado, just west of Bastrop, and pick blackberries. It had gotten warm early that year and there were plenty to be had for pies and jams. They loaded up several baskets and boxes, packed some food and water, and were ready to leave when Dr. Mayes got called away. The Marcus' youngest son fell from a skittish horse and broke his leg. The others were going to cancel the trip, but Dr. Mayes insisted they go without him. Mr. Pensana drove the wagon and the two young women sat in the back and talked of anything and everything, giggling like schoolgirls at times. Mr. Pensana smiled; it had been a long time since he had heard Rebecca laugh out loud like that. They had started out early, and since it didn't take long to get to the Colorado, it was still cool when they began picking berries. There was an abundance of blackberries that year. It seemed they had found a spot no one else had picked over. They were able to fill their baskets and boxes quickly, giving them time to relax under the big oak and pecan trees before spreading out the picnic lunch the women had packed. Mr. Pensana took his cane pole from the wagon and hiked downstream to get in a little fishing, something he rarely got a chance to do. He was a blacksmith, and though there was already a blacksmith's shop in town when he first arrived, there always seemed to be plenty of work for both. As a matter of fact, he and the other blacksmith became friends and would help one another out whenever either needed it. He had only gone a short distance when he found a very likely looking catfish hole and settled in, baiting his line, and planting it just where he thought it might do some good. He didn't plan to stay long. He had smelled the fried chicken and biscuits Rebecca made that morning before sunup and he didn't want to miss out on them. Rebecca was a fine cook, and he especially loved her fried chicken and biscuits. He lay back in the grass, pulled his hat down over his eyes, and began to doze. When he awoke, he thought he was dreaming. He wasn't sure what it was that woke him. He must've been dreaming that Rebecca was in trouble because he thought she must have screamed in his dream, startling him awake. He started to breathe a sigh of relief, but then he heard both women scream again. He was on his feet running back down the river before the blood-curdling scream finished.

Lucinda and Rebecca had spread a quilt in the grass and laid out the picnic lunch they had prepared. They laughed that there was too much food, especially since they had cooked for four and had naturally gone a little overboard. As they lay on the quilt in the cool shade of a giant pecan tree, talking and laughing, they began to feel like long lost sisters. They were both amazed at how much alike they were. They felt the same about many things and discovered they had been raised much the same way, with similar values and ideals. They were destined to be friends and sisters for life. The sun was straight overhead when Rebecca stood to call for her father. She knew how much he liked her chicken, a recipe her mother had taught her. Just as she stepped to the edge of the quilt, a man with his kerchief pulled up to cover his nose and mouth stepped from behind a tree, machete in hand. Both women were startled, and Lucinda cursed herself for not bringing the pistol Logan had given her. They stood for a moment in terror before the man lunged at them. Rebecca screamed and dodged his first attack. Lucinda threw a plate of chicken at him, but he just let it bounce off him and drop onto the quilt. Rebecca had stumbled and was trying to crawl across the quilt when he grabbed her ankle and jerked upward. He held her ankle so high he was almost lifting her off the ground by the leg. She and Lucinda both screamed and Rebecca kicked out several times blindly. She was lucky, or perhaps unlucky, that one of her blind kicks connected with the man's nose. He yelped as his nose broke and blood spurted from it. He threw Rebecca violently to the ground and cupped both hands over his bloody nose, eyes tearing heavily. Lucinda grabbed Rebecca and they ran for the trees. They had a good head start, but as soon as he could see again he was after them with a vengeance.

"Come here, puta!" he shrieked, as he dashed after them. "I will show you how breaking bones feel." Lucinda grabbed an oak limb and turned to face him. Both women knew they couldn't outrun him; all they could do was turn and face whatever was about to happen, together. Suddenly the man's eyes widened and he stopped dead in his tracks.

"Puta que apesta!" (stinking whore) he spat out hatefully. "I know you. You are the puta that shot me in the face." He pulled the kerchief down around his neck. Rebecca gasped, and Lucinda screamed. The ragged scar shone white in the bright light of day. Lucinda had never seen anyone so disfigured before; she felt nauseous and threw up. He stepped forward and hit her with the back of his fist, knocking her unconscious.

Then he turned to Rebecca and said with an evil sneer, "Now I will show you what a scarred face is like." Rebecca had not seen Asesino since she had shot him in the face, but she knew who he was. Asesino had seen her many times in his thoughts and dreams. He had prayed for this day, and now he would make her pay with the skin off her own face. He would peel and rip it from her, drinking in her screams of agony. Yes, this would be a day he would relish forever. He stepped forward with a most evil look on his face, laughing sadistically at Rebecca's horror. He grabbed her by the hair and dragged her back onto the quilt. He threw her to the ground and kicked her viciously several times, and then straddled her, dropping to his knees to pin her wrists under them. Rebecca screamed again as he laid the machete down, and pulled a thin blade from his waist. He grinned maniacally as he leaned forward and placed the point of the knife against her cheek. He was going to take his time and enjoy this. He would probably have to finish tomorrow. After he had skinned her face, he would start skinning the rest of her. He was so excited by the prospect he drooled onto her face. She was so terrified now she couldn't move or make a sound.

"What puta, you can't scream no more?" he hissed, leering at her. "I bet you scream plenty before I finish with you." He thought scalping her was a good place to start so he grabbed her by the hair and jerked her head up off the blanket. He laughed gleefully as he brought the knife down to scalp her, slowly, but before the edge touched her skin, he seemed to lift up into the air and fly backward off her. He rolled over in the dirt and lay stunned for a split second, not realizing what had happened. Then, the boom of a rifle sounded in the distance. Asesino slithered behind the trunk of the pecan tree and looked down at his chest. There was a large red blossom spreading across the right side. He felt a dull ache in his shoulder, but no real pain, at least not yet. He looked around frantically. Both women were lying where he had left them. He wanted to run, but the need to kill this 'chorra puta' (stupid bitch) was strong. He gripped the thin knife and darted from the tree zigzagging toward Rebecca, still lying on her back gasping hysterically. The front of his vest flew up and he spun almost a full circle before hitting the ground again. A split second later, there was another boom from the rifle. The bark from a nearby tree exploded, sending splinters into his neck. He cursed as the rifle boomed again, and headed for the river. Neither of the last two shots had hit him, but both were close,: very close.

Rebecca lay gasping and crying, helpless from hysteria. Lucinda rolled over groggily, taking in the scene with dazed eyes. She jumped up, still holding the oak limb, and ran to Rebecca. As she was comforting her, Rebecca's father ran into the little clearing and grabbed Rebecca up in his arms.

"It's okay, honey, it's okay. You're all right now. We're here. You're okay," he said, holding her to him. Lucinda petted her head saying much the same. Just then, they heard the sound of hoof beats almost upon them. Lucinda spun, club in hand, and there were Logan and Will dismounting on the run. Will grabbed Rebecca and held her tight, then pulled away and caressed her hair. She was hysterical and tried to pull away, but he held her tight, whispering into her ear.

"It's alright," he said, trying to soothe her and reassure himself. "He's gone. He won't hurt you. I'm here sweetheart. It's okay." She looked up, finally focusing on his face, then burst into tears of relief mixed with fear and grief. He held her tight for a long time.

Logan ran to Lucinda and swept her off her feet. "Are you alright? Did he hurt you?" he asked, looking her over. The side of her face was swelling and beginning to discolor. He kissed her face all over and held her tight. She began to wriggle so he put her down. He hadn't realized that he was holding her more than a foot off the ground.

She stepped back with a serious look on her face and said, "Logan, go get him. You can't let him get away." She backed up a step. "It's the one you were after, the one Rebecca shot in the face." Logan and Will looked at each other. Rebecca held onto Will tight, she wasn't letting him go anywhere.

Logan nodded at Will, saying, "Keep 'em safe, I'll take care of this." He let go of Lucinda's hand and turned for his horse. He pulled the big pistol he had given Lucinda from his saddlebag and handed it to her, again. "This time keep it close…and use it if you feel the need." Then he grabbed his rifle and ran for the river.

He picked up Asesino's tracks quickly, but this killer was an expert at confusing his trail. He had years of practice while he was with Lame Badger. It wasn't long before Logan had to slow down to read the trail carefully. He was very aware that this was the worst killer he'd ever encountered. Death was so close he could almost smell it. Several times, as he slipped along the river, quietly following one small sign after another, he came across signs of blood. Then he found where Asesino had gathered some bunch grass and clay to pack into his wound.

Logan smiled tersely. *He must be hit pretty good,* he thought to himself. He noticed the trail becoming more visible. Either Asesino was becoming careless, or he thought he was in the clear. Logan figured he was losing blood and not thinking clearly, and he knew there was a good chance Asesino was hit so hard, that left alone he would possibly bleed out in an hour or less. But he wouldn't take the chance. This one could go no further. He noticed that the track was veering off the river, which meant he would be leaving the trees soon. However, Logan didn't think Asesino meant to expose himself like that and was becoming more confused. He only thought about it for an instant and then left the trail for the river. Logan was sure he would try to get back to the cover of the trees once he realized what he'd done. Since Logan was no longer following Asesino's trail, he picked up his pace. If Asesino lived long enough to double back, Logan wanted to be there waiting for him. He hadn't gone more than a hundred yards when he heard a very quiet rustling just over a small sand bank beside the river. He smiled in satisfaction. He had been right; Asesino was coming back to the river. He crawled slowly and silently, foot by foot, until he caught the tiniest of movements out of the corner of his eye. Slowly he turned his head, ever so slightly. There he was. Through the low brush, Logan saw the hideously scarred face just a few feet from his own. He lay very still and waited.

Asesino thought he caught movement out of the corner of his eye as he moved along the base of the sand bank. He froze and waited a very long time. He must have been mistaken. He felt very confused. He couldn't recall why he was crawling on the ground like an insect in the first place. He just felt that he should. He was so tired now, he really needed to rest, maybe even sleep. He would rest by the river, and then go back to skinning the 'puta' that had shot him in the face. He moved further down the bank, and just as he was about to lie down and rest, he was seized from behind. At first, it felt as if his jaw was being crushed, but then he went numb. He saw something that shone in the sun flash by his face. The blade slipped past his ear and into his throat so quickly that he didn't even know it had happened until he felt the warm wetness on his chest. He was puzzled. What had happened? The ringing in his ears drowned out everything around him. He was thrown onto his back. Asesino looked up into the face of the biggest man he had ever seen. He wondered if the man was injured. He had blood on his hands and arms. His vision went very bright for a moment, and then he felt himself falling into a very deep, very black hole. He tried to call out, but no sound came from his mouth. When the blackness seized him, he realized he was very tired. He couldn't hold his eyes open any longer, and simply went to sleep.

Logan washed Asesino's blood off in the river. When he got back to where Lucinda and the others were waiting, Lucinda ran to meet him. She threw her arms around him and held him tight, then stepped back to look for any injuries. Satisfied that there were none, she held him again. On the way back to Bastrop, Lucinda asked how they came to be there just then. Logan told her that they had been unsuccessful in finding any sign of this killer, and Captain Boales had finally turned them back to rest and re-outfit. When they got to town, they ran into Dr. Mayes, who told them where to find the picnickers. Logan and Will had decided to ride out to surprise the women, but were surprised themselves. Obviously no one was more surprised than Asesino.

CHAPTER 8

MATILDA LOCKHART

In 1838, the fate of many Texans and Comanches was changed forever. Common sense, honor, and decency were not in evidence in much of central Texas that year. Several events occurred that would change the lives of Logan, Will, Yellow Wolf, Two Crows, and their families and friends.

It all started with one man, Mirabeau Lamar. Lamar was elected the second President of the new Republic of Texas in December 1838, replacing Sam Houston. Houston's policy toward the Indians had always been one of peace and trade, and it was always held firm. Lamar, on the other hand, stayed true to a policy of war, especially when it concerned Comanches. He wasn't just determined to drive the Indians from Texas; he wanted to eliminate them, their culture, and their memory, from America, starting with the Cherokees and then Comanches. He was relentless in his campaign. Lamar helped pave the way for the Buffalo Hunters to come to Texas and slaughter the mainstay of the Plains Tribes. His plans began with the total eradication of all the buffalo, the Plains Tribes' main food source. Millions of buffalo were slaughtered on the plains by the Buffalo Hunters by any means. Buffalo hides had become a valuable commercial product, but often times the buffalo were killed for no reason at all, their carcasses left to rot in the sun. To Mirabeau Lamar starvation was the perfect solution.

To the Plains Indians, the slaughter of the buffalo, their Great Spirit of the Plains, and their most valuable resource, was the worst travesty of all. They could not understand what would drive the white man to do something so offensive to nature itself. They sang, danced, and prayed, but to no avail. The slaughter continued, so they did the only thing they knew, war. They fought to drive these 'White Diggers in the dirt' out of their territory, just as they had done for 200 years against Mexico and the rival tribes that tried to take and settle the land. Comanche war chiefs had reigned supreme over the southern plains, keeping all intruders at bay, including Santa Ana, who attempted to negotiate the final treaty between Mexico and the Comanches. Being so desirous of horses, the Comanche terms were simple; they would live in peace and allow Mexico to settle certain parts of the southern plains, "for all the horses in Mexico." Santa Ana knew they had reached an impasse.

Lamar had developed a dislike for the Indians after having fought in several skirmishes with the Cherokees in his home state of Georgia. Therefore, after taking office, he set about organizing a company of Rangers whose sole mission was to fight the Indians. To him, and many other white men of the area at the time, all Indians were the same, and should be run out of the territory, or better yet: killed. Lamar would use the newly formed company as his tool for eradication.

1838 was an important year for Logan, Lucinda, Will, and Rebecca. Logan and Lucinda were married first, in the early spring, with Will and Rebecca exchanging vows just three weeks later. Logan and Lucinda's first baby, a daughter named Eliza, was born in March 1839. Will and Rebecca's first child was also a girl, whom they named Mary. She was born in August of the same year. These two couples' first six children were all born between 1839 and 1848. Logan and Lucinda had four daughters and two sons, while Will and Rebecca had four sons and two daughters. Logan named his first son William Harrison Vandeveer, after Will. Logan insisted that he and Lucinda name their last child, a girl born in 1849, after her mother. Life would have been very idyllic for both families if Logan and Will had been ranchers instead of Rangers, and Mirabeau Lamar had not implemented his policy on Indian eradication.

In the fall of 1838, Runs Like a Bear decided to start making forays out on his own into the settlers' territory northwest of Bastrop. He began by stealing a single horse from a family named Martin. Within the next couple of months, Runs Like a Bear had raided four different white settlers, stealing five horses in total. He had never owned so much or felt so wealthy. He was even able to bargain four of the horses, a pitiful amount by Comanche standards, for a woman named Yepa (Snow Woman), who came from a different camp. She was homely and not young, but Runs Like a Bear felt he had made a good bargain. Then his luck changed; whether for the better or worse was hard to say. He caught a young boy unaware, leading a mule down a well-traveled road, and took him and the mule. The boy was a slave belonging to a family named Morgenstern. Runs Like a Bear traded the mule to a group of Lipan Indians, but kept the boy as a slave of his own. Snow Woman, being homely and considered lowly in her own camp, liked the idea of having a slave, even a small black one. She began to feel important, and soon suggested to her husband that he should steal more horses and take more slaves. Runs Like a Bear, sensing the prospect of more respect from many of the other people in camp, was easily swayed by her desires. He decided that he would steal many more horses and slaves. He would be wealthy by Comanche standards and all would respect him. There were, however, two that didn't respect him, Yellow Wolf and Two Crows. They saw through what he was doing. They understood his feeling of being outcast among the people of camp, but they also lived by the natural law of 'survival of the fittest'. They could in all good conscience only help him so much, then they would be forced by their natural instinct to let him make his own way in life. To them, the fact that they had not already killed him was the only help they could offer, and perhaps they were only delaying the inevitable. In any case they both began to watch him carefully. They knew kidnapping children of the White Diggers was dangerous and could get out of hand quickly. They had no idea how quickly it would do just that.

In the winter of that same year, Runs Like a Bear happened upon a small group of white children gathering pecans along the bank of the Guadalupe River. They were young and on foot, so he and two other Comanches were able to capture them easily.

The oldest was a seventeen-year-old girl named Rhoda Putman. Along with her were three of her siblings, a ten year old boy named James, and two smaller girls named Elizabeth, who was six, and Juda, who was two. The fifth captive was a thirteen-year-old girl named Matilda Lockhart. None of the Comanches knew how important this young girl was, or how much she would affect their very existence. They could not have predicted that this one small white girl was to become the spark to set off a powder keg that would mark the beginning-of-the-end for all the tribes of the southern plains.

Runs Like a Bear was sure that taking these slaves would make Snow Woman happy. Now she would have more slaves than anyone else in camp. Perhaps he could even trade one or two for a better horse. The Comanches coveted a special type of horse found on the southern plains; the painted mustang with a particular color pattern on its face, chest and legs. They came in many combinations of colors, but two specific variations, the War Bonnet and the Medicine Hat were most favored. Snow Woman's brother had many fine Medicine Hat horses, but no slaves, and Runs Like a Bear wanted a good Medicine Hat horse.

When Runs Like a Bear and the other two Comanches arrived in camp with the five children, Yellow Wolf and several of the elders were very concerned. They held a hasty council and were in agreement quickly. These children could not stay, at least not all of them. Yellow Wolf, Two Crows, and the camp's medicine man, Black Elk, approached the three. A lump of nervousness and hatred formed in Runs Like a Bear's stomach. Yellow Wolf raised his right palm up in the general open greeting.

"You have brought White Diggers to camp," he said. This was not a question. "Children." He stood looking Runs Like a Bear in the eye.

Runs Like a Bear nodded, saying, "I will make slaves of them." He tried to sound self-assured. Black Elk clucked at this skeptically. "You have no experience with slaves," he said, looking at the frightened, sobbing children. He knew the amount of care they would require, and was sure Runs Like a Bear and the other two Comanches involved were not up to the task. Two Crows stepped forward and took the leather thong binding the wrists of Matilda Lockhart. He tugged it slightly and it came free of her wrists. She immediately shrieked and tried to break for the edge of camp. Two Crows took several quick steps and grabbed her by the hair, jerking back and downward at once. Matilda's feet flew out from under her and down she went, flat on her back. Two Crows put one knee in the middle of her chest to hold her down and rebound her wrists tightly with the thong. He pulled her up and handed the other end to Runs Like a Bear, "You should know which one will run away and make sure she can't," he said, while stepping around Runs Like a Bear to stand next to Yellow Wolf again, adding, "If you want to keep them." Runs Like a Bear felt the old rage welling up inside. Whenever a Comanche spoke without expression, it was because they did not respect you, or were hiding their true feelings about you. Either way, Runs Like a Bear hated it, and he hated Two Crows. Not just for making him look foolish, but also for the lack of respect he showed. Runs Like a Bear took the thong and jerked it, pulling Matilda off balance. She fell in front of him and he slapped her on the head several times, then began kicking her savagely.

Black Elk stood quietly by, watching until the rage seemed to subside in Runs Like a Bear. "You should trade these slaves," he said, pointing at them. "It would not be good to have so many children of the White Diggers in one camp. It would be too easy to find them, and then other White Diggers might come here looking for them." His face was stern. He was suggesting something very plainly, and Runs Like a Bear was getting angrier. It was hard for him to hold his tongue. He wanted to tell them all to leave him and his slaves alone, and that it was not their place to tell him what to do with his own property. He had captured these slaves, not Black Elk or Two Crows. Were they becoming women who feared the White Diggers? He stood and glared at the three elders, but said nothing.

Yellow Wolf placed his right fist against his left palm and gave it one-quarter turn, indicating Runs Like a Bear should heed what he had to say. "You may keep one slave here. The others must be traded to other camps or tribes." He stared straight into Runs Like a Bear's eyes unblinking, then added, "This must be done before the sun sets a second time." He continued to stare directly at Runs Like a Bear, who opened his mouth to speak, but then closed it and glared back at Yellow Wolf. The three elders were satisfied that they had made their point clearly, so they turned and walked back to Black Elk's lodge. The two Comanches that had helped Runs Like a Bear felt they were each entitled to one of these new slaves and began looking the children over more closely. They understood very well what Yellow Wolf had implied, and were content to trade their slaves to other camps. One of the Comanches picked up the youngest of the five, Juda Putman and rode out of camp directly. He took her to another camp about twenty miles to the north and traded her for several good hides and a new pipe. The second Comanche took the oldest Putman child, Rhoda, and headed north to a different camp, where he traded her along with two horses stolen on this raid for a young War Bonnet horse.

Runs Like a Bear tied the remaining three children together, then grabbed Matilda by the hair and dragged her toward his lodge. Snow Woman stepped out of the lodge as he drug her up, the other two children following. Runs Like a Bear told her to pick one, and that he had to get rid of the others. This pleased her; she didn't want the bother two small children would be. The older girl would suffice as a slave, so she pointed at Matilda. Runs Like a Bear grudgingly cut the thong between her and the two smaller children, then he put them both on one of the three horses he had stolen on this raid and left to visit Snow Woman's brother. He was sure he would get a good horse in trade, perhaps even a War Bonnet, but at least a Medicine Hat. He found out later that, as with many other things, he was not very good at trading. He got a War Bonnet, but it cost him both of his slaves, all three stolen horses, the horse he was riding, and the next foal out of the War Bonnet. He was not as happy as he thought he would be, but at least he had a War Bonnet horse. Now everyone would have to show him more respect.

When he got back from trading the children, he found Snow Woman angry and the new slave girl unable to walk. She had tried to run away again and Snow Woman had burned the bottoms of her feet. Runs Like a Bear was furious and beat Matilda with a stick forcing her to her feet. Then beat her while she got water for Snow Woman. Matilda howled in pain, but finally got some of the water back to the lodge. Runs Like a Bear decided she would not eat if she didn't work and make Snow Woman happy. He also told Snow Woman that it was not his duty as a man to beat her slaves. She must teach this slave herself. Finally, Runs Like a Bear went into his lodge to get away from the sound of Matilda's whimpering over her badly burned feet and tried to relax. Taking children of the White Diggers for slaves didn't seem to be such a good idea after all. He was glad to be rid of all the others. Now he wouldn't have to deal with these troublesome children again. As usual he was wrong.

It was November 1839, Logan and Will were at McCutcheon's General Store picking up some supplies, coffee, bacon, and ammunition, when word came about a large group of Comanches that had been spotted camped up on the Llano River. It was believed, or at least speculated, that the Putman and Lockhart children were with them. The children had been gone for almost a year by then, and neither Logan nor Will believed they were still together in one camp. They were certain that if the children were still alive, they would have been split up by now.

Logan heard several older men talking in the store. They were saying that the Army and the Rangers should go get the children back, and maybe kill the whole damn lot of Indians on the plains while they were about it. The more they talked the louder they got. Finally Mr. McCutcheon went over and told them to pipe down; they were upsetting some women that were in the store. The old geezers started to protest, but Logan stepped over behind Mr. McCutcheon to back him up. They all knew Logan to be slow to anger and none wanted to get on his bad side. Grumbling, they all got up and went outside where they continued their ranting, gathering a crowd of sympathizers.

Logan stared out the window getting angrier as more people gathered. Will got their order together and stepped up beside Logan.

"This will go bad, fast," Logan said, looking grim. "Those old coots have lit the match, now let's see who throws the coal oil to it." They stood watching for a few more minutes, not speaking. Just as they were getting ready to leave, they saw a man rush through the crowd, shouting to the gathered people.

Will sighed loudly. "Any idea who that is?" he asked. looking over at Logan.

Logan nodded, watching the crowd getting angrier outside. "That there is Colonel Alton Maybry," he said, looking back at Will. "Wouldn't have of expected him to be the one." Will raised his eyebrows in question. "He was with us at San Jacinto, used to be a good Mex'can fighter, and a steady man. Don't understand the way of 'im now. He oughtn't to be rilin' folks up against the Comanches this way. He'll get people killed for sure." Will just shook his head as they stepped outside.

"Damned red hide Injuns," Maybry shouted. "They's taken these beautiful white children, innocents, they are. They'll use and abuse 'em, and likely kill 'em if we don't do somethin' about it," he shouted. "and if not, they'll ruin 'em so's a man won't want the girls and the boy'll become a gut eater, just like them." The crowd moaned in unison. "We can't count on the Army or the Rangers." He was waving his fist. "Why, we need to form up and go get them babies back our own selves... before it's too late!" The crowd was restless and started to mill around. There was some pushing and shoving, but it seemed to die down quickly. Logan just shook his head and looked disgusted. He and Will headed for the wagon, but before they got more than a couple of steps, Maybry spotted them. "There! There's two Rangers right there!" he shouted, pointing at Logan and Will. "They're getting' coffee when they should be out huntin' down those red hide devils and getting' these children back!" he shrieked. Logan put his hand on his knife, and as he turned to confront Colonel Maybry, Will took his arm and stopped him. Logan glared at Maybry.

"You should be real careful who you try to sully, Colonel, someday you might be outta' town and find yourself in need of a friendly face." The crowd murmured and moved back as he took a step toward Maybry. "Mine might be the only one you see; then again it might not be so friendly." Maybry was visibly nervous, but turned to the crowd again.

"This is exactly the reason we can't count on the Army or the Rangers!" he shouted to the crowd, glancing nervously in Logan's direction. The crowd rumbled louder, finally someone yelled something about getting their guns, and men dashed in all directions. Logan and Will got in the wagon and went to the Ranger barracks to see when they would leave.

Captain Boales walked into the barracks as Logan and Will were distributing the ammunition. They had just gotten new breach loading rifles and had waited two weeks for the paper bullets from McCutcheon's. All were anxious to try out the new weapons: No more powder and balls.

Boales looked at the men and said, "Good. Get outfitted for three days. We're gonna go see if we can head this mess off before it gets outta' hand." He looked at Logan and Will, saying, "I see Colonel Maybry's stirrin' things up over at the General Store. What's he about?" he asked.

"No good," Logan said somberly. "He's getting' people riled up against the Indians and he's gonna' get somebody killed, maybe lots of folks."

Boales looked troubled and shook his head in disgust. "Well then, there's not a minute to lose boys. Let's get on their trail before he does."

The Rangers were outfitted and on their horses within an hour. Colonel Maybry and sixty men, ready to ride, beat them by twenty minutes. Boales was upset, but tried not to let it get to him. He knew Maybry had no real trackers and would be riding in circles for hours, trying to pick up the trail, while every one of his Rangers could follow a skinny jackrabbit over hard rock if they had to. He knew they would probably get to the camp that was suspected of having the stolen children first. The question in his mind was, would the children have already been traded, sold, or killed when they got to them? None had a sure answer.

Logan and Will had hired four Tonkawas to help round up some cattle in the past and had used them to get information about the different camps and tribes. The two Rangers had sought out the Tonkawas when the children were first taken, and had set them to gathering information about them. As they headed northwest, toward the spot where the Indian camp had been seen on the Llano River, Logan and Will began to run the scene through their heads based on the information they'd gotten from the Tonkawas. Which direction did the Comanches come from, what were they trying to accomplish by stealing five white children in broad daylight, and where would they likely go? What they were trying to accomplish was the easy part; it was obvious they were taking the children to raise or trade as slaves. Although neither Logan nor Will had ever held slaves of their own, they had known people their whole lives that kept black slaves. They didn't like it, but in that area of the country, it was accepted. The tough question was, where had they come from and where were they going? Logan and Will discussed it quietly and at length as they rode toward the Guadalupe, until they felt sure that they knew where the children probably were, and that it wasn't where they were going now. Logan rode to the font of the ragged column and moved in beside Captain Boales. The fact that Logan had become the planner of many of their day-to-day dealings, as well as most of their more daring adventures, didn't bother Will at all. Even though the two had lived most of their lives with these roles reversed, Will never hesitated to accept Logan's judgment, and never questioned a plan laid out by him. Logan had proven himself to Will many times; proven he had matured into a very levelheaded partner, with the fortitude to think things through to the end. Besides, he and Will thought alike on most things. Yes sir, Will had no problem deferring to this tall, dark, young man he lovingly referred to as his little brother. Logan would blush and get embarrassed whenever Will used the phrase in public, but the truth was, Logan was tickled that Will considered him a brother.

As Logan rode up beside Boales, the Captain looked over at him and raised his eyebrows, giving Logan the 'go ahead'.

"Me and Will was talkin' to a couple of Tonkawas we know yesterday, and been thinkin' about what they told us, Cap'n," Logan said, seriously. "It's likely there's only one place the children would've been taken to."

Boales continued to stare straight ahead. "Do tell, Corporal."

"Yes sir, and it ain't where we're headed now. It's Yellow Wolf's camp, sir," Logan said matter of factly. Boales looked over at Logan, skeptically at first, but then thought better of it. Vandeveer and Magill's uncanny insight had proven time and again to be correct, even in some of the most unlikely situations, and the Captain respected whatever input these two offered. "With the tension around here so high of late, none of the other tribes or camps have been crossin' territories too much. Good way to get dead, and not necessarily quick or easy." Logan dropped back a half step to dodge around a mesquite. "None of the other camps seem to be taking whites for slaves. They're content just killin' 'em, as many of us as they can, and especially old Buffalo Hump and his bunch, but not Yellow Wolf. He seems to be trying to keep the peace, at least a little." Logan hesitated to let the Captain chew on this thought a minute.

Boales nodded. "Go on."

"Up until pretty recent, Yellow Wolf's camp had near five hundred men ready to make war on any that crowded 'em, but close to a hundred have gone to live at The Honey Eaters camp." Logan used the translated name of Buffalo Hump's Penaṯka group of Comanches. "This didn't make Yellow Wolf none too unhappy, as he was getting' tired of havin' so many trouble makers hangin' 'round. He welcomed the peace of mind it brought when they all left, and Buffalo Hump liked having more warriors." Boales looked out of the corner of his eye at Logan and shook his head slightly. Logan went on. "As near as Will and me can figure, there's probably only a couple of Yellow Wolf's band stupid enough to do something like this. About six months ago Blue Duck, Buffalo Hump's son, got mad at his father for taking a horse he stole from a Kiowa medicine man and giving it to another fella in camp. Blue Duck and Buffalo Hump had words, and Blue Duck left and went to Yellow Wolf's camp. Yellow Wolf felt obliged to Buffalo Hump so he never run Blue Duck off. Blue Duck is a bad one, caused a lot of trouble in Yellow Wolf's camp. It got so bad that Yellow Wolf took Blue Duck down and notched his ear with Blue Duck's own knife, then sent him packin'. He wandered around for about a month, but wasn't welcomed in any of the other camps, so he went back to The Honey Eaters." Boales stopped and pulled out his makins and began to roll himself a smoke. This was getting interesting.

He held his pouch in one hand and dropped the reins across his horse's neck. "You said there were only a couple of stupid fellas out there. Who are the others?" he asked, as he sprinkled the coarse cut tobacco into the thick paper.

Logan went on. "Really there's only one other, we think. Big dumb one name of Runs Like a Bear. Never was much good at horse stealin', but he's getting better. Been out practicing lately. He picked up a few horses lately and it probably made him feel rich. We think he's starting to get greedy. Since he doesn't have a lot of ability for higher thought we think he probably just happened onto these kids, and took 'em without thinkin' it through." Logan was watching Boales for his reaction. There didn't seem to be any. Boales took a deep drag on his crooked little cigarette.

"So you think this Runs Like a Bear took the children to Yellow Wolf's camp?" he asked, smoke puffing out with each word.

Logan nodded. "Yes sir, we do. We think this big knothead don't realize how unhappy this will make Yellow Wolf. I expect Yellow Wolf is probably thinkin' how he might kill Runs Like a Bear, right now, without losing face with the rest of the camp."

Boales had a look of amazement on his face and just shook his head, saying, "Unbelievable."

Logan was puzzled. Maybe he hadn't explained it clearly enough. Usually Captain Boales grabbed the gist of his ideas real quick. "Well, no sir. Not if you think about it…"

Boales chuckled and cut him off. "Not what you just told me. I believe every word. It makes perfect sense," Logan looked even more puzzled. "But the fact that you and Magill seem to know more about the doings of the Comanches, Kiowas, and Lipans than any white man ought to. You two probably know more about what's happening in their own camps than most of them do."

Logan looked a little sheepish. "We got us a couple of Tonkawa spies," he said with a grin. "We hire 'em to help out every now and again and they keep an eye on what's doin' in some of the camps around." Boales chuckled, took the last drag on his smoke, and ground it out on his saddle horn, then turned to Logan.

"Well Corporal what do you and Magill advise?" he asked with a grin on his face.

This was unexpected of Boales, and Logan was a little abashed, but he offered up their plan. "Sir we think it might not be a bad idea to get a few men on over to the Llano to look and see which camp it is that's there'. Maybe they can sneak up and watch for a bit to see if they do spot any of the children. Even if it ain't the ones we're after, there might be others. If it was Blue Duck took the children you can bet they're in Mexico already, or dead." He said the last part quietly. "We're bettin' it was Runs Like a Bear, and think we should take the rest of the men to Yellow Wolf's camp to wait and watch a bit. We probably have some time before Colonel Maybry figures out whether the camp up on the Llano is the right one or not. Most of those fellas he's got with him couldn't find water if they was in a sinkin' boat," he said with a sly grin. Boales nodded in agreement.

As they passed through the area where the Comanche camp had been spotted, Boales sent Amos, Little John, and a new ranger named Micah Hale to find the camp and watch to see if they might spot any of the children. The rest of the troop picked up the pace and continued on toward Yellow Wolf's camp. They rode hard for the rest of the day, not stopping until dark. Boales

pulled them up into a grove of trees where they all hob-
bled their horses and settled down to rest for the night.
They ate a little jerky and drank a few sips of water. No
one built a fire and no one smoked. They just settled
in and tried to sleep for a few hours. They were up and
moving with the rising moon and covered twenty miles
before Boales stopped for coffee. They had a commanding view of the valley and felt a brief stop and a
hot fire would be OK. Besides, the horses needed the
break and the grain. They rested for two hours before
getting back in the saddle. Yellow Wolf's camp was 130
miles from Bastrop, but they would make it by nightfall. Boales was unrelenting, so they made it just before
sundown. The horses were done in, and so were the
men. After graining and watering their horses, they all
fell to the ground exhausted. Boales let them rest and
scouted around to look the area over for any immediate danger. He snuck up to within a hundred yards of
Yellow Wolf's camp and got the layout just before it got
too dark. He sat peering into the fading light trying to
see if he could tell where the children might be kept.
Oddly, he didn't see or hear any dogs in the camp, and
he could see the horses in a small valley over the ridge.
He memorized the camp as best he could, and then
hurried back to the troop. The Ranger's horses were
tired and listless, while the men were starting to mill
around. Boales rounded them up and gave them the
layout, explaining what he wanted to do. They were
going to wait until well after dark, and then sneak up

to the edge of the camp and watch for any sign of the children.

Just after dark Amos, Tyler and Micah rode into the thicket of trees and reported to Boales. They had picked up the other Indian camp's trail very quickly. The new man Micah had ridden into the area, surveyed it briefly, stepped off his horse to look at some sign a little more closely, then mounted up and led Amos and Tyler down along the riverbank to a spot where the Indians had not covered their tracks well. From there they were able to tell which direction the Indians had gone. He pointed out that the tracks clearly headed north and they were all men riding light, pulling no travois'. There were no women or children in this group. Before they left to follow the trail, Amos finished the job the Indians had started. He wiped out the Indians' trail in the immediate area, but made sure it could be found within a mile and then wiped out their own tracks. No sense helping Colonel Maybry do more damage than he had already done. Every Ranger in the troop had fought Comanches, Kiowas, and Apaches, and every one respected them for their cunning and courage, and the fact that the Indians were settlers of the plains long before the white men had ever set foot on the continent. It was truly their land, and the Rangers respected that. No one desired peace with the Indians more than these prairie hardened men who fought for their lives and the lives of friends and family.

An hour after dark, the entire troop, except for Micah, who was left on horse watch, slipped up to the edge of Yellow Wolf's camp and began to watch, hoping to catch a glimpse of one of the children. They had no such luck that night and didn't feel any hope until the next morning when Will spotted Snow Woman dragging a hobbling Matilda Lockhart toward a small stream on the opposite side of the camp. Captain Boales told Logan and Amos to skirt wide around the south end and try to get close enough to steal the girl back. He put all the others on alert and sent two back down the trail to watch their backs. All they had to do now was wait for Logan and Amos to get into position and steal the girl back. She could help them find where the rest of the children were being kept, and with any luck, they could get the other children back without anyone even knowing they were there. Then they could cover each other as they snuck out of the area and rode hard back to Bastrop.

Logan and Amos were less than half way around the clearing when Snow Woman came running back into the camp dragging Matilda Lockhart by the hair and shrieking like a banshee. Logan stopped and waited. There didn't seem to be anything out of the ordinary, but something had set the homely old cow off, so he and Amos hunkered down and watched as the camp began to stir. Amos pointed to a spot directly across from them. Logan shaded his eyes and peered into the dawn light. At first he didn't see anything, but then he caught the slightest of movements, then another, and another. It wasn't long before Logan and Amos could see at least twenty men bunching up under the trees on the lower side of the camp. It was Maybry and his group. How had they found them, in the dark no less?

"Damn him!" Logan whispered under his breath. Amos nodded in agreement. Logan started to turn back toward Captain Boales when two of the men on the far side stepped forward into the open. He looked around quickly to see what effect Snow Woman's shrieking was having. There was movement starting around some of the lower lodges.

Logan couldn't believe his eyes. Yellow Wolf's camp was four hundred strong, and Logan was sure not one of them would care to be challenged first thing in the morning. Logan recognized both of the men standing in the open on the other side of the camp. The first one was Mitchell Putman, the best rifle shot he had ever seen. Logan had once watched as Putman shot and killed four deer running through a field at well over three hundred yards with four shots. The other man was his neighbor, Andrew Lockhart. They were the fathers of the stolen children! There was considerable activity starting in the camp; men ran into lodges for weapons while others ran for the horses.

"Surely they don't think they can stand out in the open and live to see their children home again," Logan whispered to Amos. Amos shook his head in disbelief. Just then, another forty or fifty mounted men broke from the trees all around Putman, Lockhart, and the other twenty or so on foot gathered under the trees. As the shooting began, Logan and Amos began running back to where the other Rangers were. They heard Lockhart call out,

"Matilda! Honey it's me! It's your father! Matilda, run to me!" Logan saw Matilda being dragged down the hill toward the field full of horses. From where Lockhart and Putman stood, a sharp break in the hill shielded Snow Woman and Matilda from their view. At first, there was confusion everywhere, and then Logan saw Yellow Wolf step from a lodge with several others and begin shouting orders at everyone he saw. The Comanches almost instantly melded into an organized group and began fighting their way down the hill toward the attackers. Saddles were being emptied one after another, and there didn't seem to be a Comanche casualty in sight. Logan stopped and began to wait and see if he might get an opportunity to make a run for Matilda. With the majority of the camp between him and the girl, it wasn't likely. However, as the Comanches drove Maybry and his men back, Logan realized his chance to get her back was lost. He and Amos met up with the other Rangers and they all headed back over the ridge to where the horses were. They mounted and skirted wide around the camp, trying to get near to where they knew Matilda had been taken, but it seemed that there were groups of Comanches waiting in the thickets surrounding the camp. They were continually driven further out away from camp until there was no way they could get any closer. Boales turned the Rangers back the way they had come and didn't stop to rest for several miles.

"Damn that Maybry's hide!" he said, slapping his hat on his thigh when they did stop. "Damn him to hell!" He knew the Rangers could have gotten Matilda Lockhart, and any of the other children that might have been there out of the camp, if not for Maybry's fiasco. Boales, a very levelheaded man, was angrier than any of the troop had ever seen him before. Morale was low. Everyone was sad to see their chance slip away that morning, knowing the Comanches would never allow them to track the group hiding Matilda Lockhart, and to try now was a good way to find arrows sticking out of your body, so they headed back to Bastrop. The trip back was much slower, and the men were terse and quiet as they rode along. Failure wasn't something they much cared for, and hadn't been experienced since Lame Badger had slipped out of their grasp, but at least, he had paid for that.

Yellow Wolf surveyed the bodies of the dead that littered the camp. He and Two Crows helped the wounded Comanches to Black Elk's lodge. The wounded White Diggers were scalped and then burned to death. This was traditional with many tribes, including the Buffalo Eater Comanches. After the dead and dying were tended to, Yellow Wolf called a council meeting. He was angry that the White Diggers had raided the camp, angry that the children had focused attention on them, and deep down he was angry that the White Diggers hadn't gotten their children back, although he didn't make that part of his anger known. He vented his anger on Runs Like a

Bear and Snow Woman, though she was not in camp. It was suggested they raid some of the settlers close by, but the council, including himself, decided against it. They had been living peaceably near some White Diggers and didn't want more trouble. Though he hated them, he knew there were too many to drive from the plains alone. The Buffalo Eaters would need to band together with other camps and tribes. It was decided that he would go meet with Buffalo Hump and discuss a large-scale effort. As he readied his gear for the trip, he thought about the misery that was undoubtedly to come. He knew the trouble was probably inevitable, but he was sure Runs Like a Bear was responsible for hastening it. His band could have had at least ten years of peace before taking the path they were on now. Yes, Runs Like a Bear was responsible for much woe that would come, and Yellow Wolf decided not to allow him an opportunity to make it worse. When Yellow Wolf was ready to go, he rode to meet Two Crows.

"We will take Runs Like a Bear," he said looking solemn. Two Crows nodded as he mounted his horse. He knew that Runs Like a Bear must greet his ancestors this day in payment for the lives of the innocents that had suffered because of his foolishness. They rode to the lodge of Runs Like a Bear and sat on their horses not saying a word. After several minutes, Runs Like a Bear felt there was someone outside his lodge and stepped out slowly. He looked into the faces of Yellow Wolf and Two Crows. He did not like facing them both like this. The old familiar knot of anger, this time mixed with dread, wrenched at this stomach as he stepped out and walked toward the two fierce men.

"We ride to council with the Honey Eaters. Taking the White Digger's children has made this necessary. You will go with us," Yellow Wolf said, without room for discussion. Runs Like a Bear looked nervously back and forth between Yellow Wolf and Two Crows. Both wore expressions that were impossible to read. Runs Like a Bear knew this would be a defining moment in his life. He started to protest, to tell Yellow Wolf that he would not be ordered like some woman, that he would not go, but when he gazed into those hard, fierce eyes his anger bled from him and he was filled with fear. His resolve evaporated, and without a word, he got his horse and weapons and fell in beside Two Crows. The three rode out of camp side by side. When they had gone no more than about five miles, Two Crows stopped and looked down at his horse's right front hoof as if trying to see a problem. Runs Like a Bear's anxiety had diminished slightly, and he rode up beside Two Crows peering at the hoof also. He was caught completely unaware by Yellow Wolf, who had ridden up behind him on the opposite side. Runs Like a Bear looked questioningly at Two Crows, who had an inscrutable look on his face. Runs Like a Bear realized too late that his life was ending. Yellow Wolf's knife slipped between his ribs and sliced his heart open before Runs Like a Bear even knew his body had been pierced. He was dead before he hit the ground. Yellow Wolf and Two Crows dismounted and prepared him for his trip to the other side, where he would meet his ancestors. He was a troublemaker, and they did not like him, but he was still a Comanche warrior of the Kutsut~~uu~~ka camp. He deserved an honorable ritual of passing.

When they finished the burial rights for Runs Like a Bear, they rode on several more miles and made camp. They rested and talked until dark, then slept. At first light, they mounted up and continued the long trip to Buffalo Hump's camp.

❧

When the Rangers rode into Bastrop there was a crowd waiting. Anxious, expectant faces greeted them as they rode silently through the little town. Andrew Lockhart's wife, Catherine, stepped into the street, tears in her eyes.

"Did they get her?" she asked, her voice breaking with emotion. "Did they get my baby back? Tell me you got her away from those devils," she said, stepping out and grabbing hold of Captain Boales' leg. He reined up and looked down at the pitiful woman's face. His heart reached out to her. He hated this part as much as having to ride away from Yellow Wolf's camp without the children.

He shook his head sadly. "I'm sorry ma'am," he said quietly. "We were forced to leave without getting any of the children back." There was a loud moan from Helen Putman, who stood in front of McCutcheon's General Store. She was holding the hitching rail with both hands and began to sob, then collapsed onto the ground. People ran to help her and Catherine Lockhart burst into tears. "No!" she wailed. "No! It's not true! Andrew wouldn't leave her! He wouldn't! He wouldn't leave our baby!" Her fists were doubled and she was beating on Captain Boales leg. He continued to look down at her sadly, but didn't stop her.

"I am sorry ma'am, but Yellow Wolf's Comanches were too well organized and too many. They were at least four hundred strong. Many of the men that went with Colonel Maybry were likely killed or wounded." There was a loud gasp and cries of "No!" from the crowd. He looked around at the stricken faces of the crowd. "We have all suffered a terrible loss, you best look to the ones that make it back, they're gonna need it." He looked down at the sobbing woman one more time, then kicked his horse up, and the troop rode on to the Ranger Barracks. Logan was angrier than anyone had ever seen him. Inside he raged, but outwardly, he was silent and calm. Still, to Will, and those that knew him well, he was a smoking powder keg. Will and Lucinda knew enough to let him be, to let him think about it for a while, maybe cool down a little. He worked around the house, was pleasant to Lucinda, and played with the baby, but inside he seethed with rage.

The day after their arrival back in Bastrop, Will was on his way to his father-in-law's blacksmith shop to have a new bridle modified. Seemed his horse didn't like the shape of this new bit so it chomped at it and began throwing his head around. Will liked the horse well enough, but he couldn't abide a head-tosser, so it was either change the shape of the bit and see if that helped, or get rid of the horse. As he rounded the corner near Mr. Pensana's blacksmith shop, he nearly ran headlong into Colonel Maybry. When Maybry realized whom it was he had almost collided with, he became very gruff and tried to shove Will aside. Will, being a quick thinker, and angry about the whole affair of the last few days, countered and held his ground. He wanted to make sure Maybry knew he could not be shoved about. Then he calmly stepped aside to let Maybry pass.

"You should watch where you're going there young fella,'" Maybry said, blustering a bit. "You could hurt someone runnin' around so haphazard like." Maybry stroked his mustache as he blustered.

Will narrowed his eyes and Maybry got nervous. "I do hear what you're a sayin' Colonel Maybry, but I believe you have more to be careful of than I do, sir," Will said calmly, never taking his eyes off Maybry. "There's folks here that don't see you as the hero you might think, not after the mess you made, and the lives you cost at Yellow Wolf's camp." Will stood very still with his thumbs hooked in his belt, hand close to his pistol. If Maybry wanted to settle a score Will was ready, and settle it he would.

Maybry's eyes widened and his face got red. At first Will thought maybe he was getting sick, but then Maybry stamped his foot and started to shake his finger in Will's face.

"Look here boy!" Maybry finally gasped through his anger. "I only did what needed doin'. Why it was certain folks couldn't count on the Army or you…Rangers" he fairly spat the word out as though it were something vile in his mouth. "It's too bad some of the fellas' that went didn't come back, but that's the nature of war boy," he said, a little too sanctimoniously for Will's taste. Will's hand shot out and grabbed him by the throat then slammed him against the front of Broward's Café. The people eating inside jumped as Maybry hit the wall outside.

"Listen here you old fool!" Will hissed, his hand was on his pistol. If not for the people inside trying to eat a peaceful breakfast, he would have been tempted to shoot Maybry, then and there. "You may have been a good soldier in the past, Lord knows you was at some time 'cause you was with us at San Jacinto, but mister, you cast all that good away when you riled folks up about the Comanches stealin' those children." Will was getting angrier and began to get red in the face himself. "But to run up into that camp with farmers and settlers without so much as a once over to see how many Comanches Yellow Wolf had there was the stupidest, most irresponsible thing you could have done." Will got right up in Maybry's face. "And if you ever do anything that stupid, or talk down the Rangers again, I'll personally come find you and we'll finish what we're about here today." Maybry was afraid, but he must have thought Will would turn him loose then because he started to relax. But Will wasn't finished; he jerked him up to attention again. "You're personally responsible for those children still bein' captives, and on top of that, now they've been moved and we don't have any idea where they are. So when you go to shootin' off your mouth about how you only did what needed doin', you remember it was the Rangers that figured out where they were and surveyed the camp. Hell man! We knew where Matilda Lockhart was the moment you came riding into camp shootin' and getting men killed. Logan and Amos were only about five minutes from stealin' her back without a shot bein' fired. Once we had her, she could've told us where the rest were at." Will shoved Maybry to the side, and Maybry stumbled, but caught himself against the wall. Then, while rubbing his reddening neck, he looked at this angry, tough young man standing with his hand on his pistol, ready to kill. "We may never get 'em back now, you old fool," Will said without moving. Maybry rubbed his neck and stumbled backwards, trying to get away from this maniac. When he was several steps away, he turned and hurried down the street the way he'd come and then out of sight. Will continued to stand there with his hand on his pistol, debating whether to go ahead and shoot the old fool or not. He was so angry his breath came quick and hard. He turned to go on to Mr. Pensana's and stopped dead in his tracks. There was Logan standing in the middle of the street eyes wide and mouth open. He had never seen Will that close to cold-blooded murder before, even someone that deserved it as much as Maybry. Will was still breathing hard and felt a little embarrassed that Logan had seen him lose his temper. He couldn't think of a thing to say as he walked into the street. Logan must have known exactly what he was thinking, because he just grinned and said, "Don't worry about it. I think you said it all right there." He threw his arm around Will's shoulders and they started down the street together until they noticed the people eating at Broward's staring open mouthed out the front window.

"Damn, if I'd known I had an audience, why I'd a used more proper English, maybe I coulda' become one of them theater actors," Will said with a laugh.

Logan looked sidelong at him. "Don't think the other actors would like havin' you threaten 'em with your pistol and choke 'em while recitin' Shakespeare."

Will laughed out loud. "Maybe not Brother, maybe not."

Logan and Will were both wondering if Rangerin' was what they should be doing. They had planned to start a cattle ranch, and to date hadn't gotten very far with that plan. In the fall of 1838, Mr. John Ward, a representative of the Republic of Texas, rode into Bastrop to find Logan. Plans were being set into motion to build a new and official capitol, and the settlement of Waterloo had been decided upon for the spot. The plans for development of the area around Waterloo were well underway, and it was decided that the land given to Logan for his service in the Battle of San Jacinto was exactly where they needed to build this new capitol, so Mr. Ward had been dispatched to see if he might be able to strike a bargain with Logan. The bargain was easy. Since Logan was a very patriotic and community minded man, he simply offered to trade the new government for a like parcel. The new Republic was quick to act and offered a tract of land near a small settlement sixty miles west of the new capitol. Logan accepted, and the town of Austin was quickly established.

Ever since the Putman and Lockhart children had been taken, and the battle between Maybry's men and Yellow Wolf's camp, relations between the Texans (as they called themselves now) and Comanches had been strained to near their breaking point, and in March of 1840, they finally snapped.

Several times over the course of the previous year, some of the other camps had made bargains with a Colonel Fisher in San Antonio about ransoming back some white captives they had in exchange for paint, gun powder, and blankets. Twice, traders were sent with the items the Comanches wanted. The first time, the traders gave the Comanches blankets infected with smallpox and there was an outbreak that ran through two of the camps, nearly wiping them out. This angered Buffalo Hump so greatly that he had the traders hunted down and killed. The second group of traders was sent along with a small escort of armed men, but the Comanches feared more treachery from the traders, and killed the entire group, then burned all of their supplies long before they reached any of the camps. However, it was Blue Duck that set everything in motion. He went to see Commissioner Hugh McLeod under the guise of a truce in order to bargain for the release of the captives. He had no captives to bargain for, but that didn't matter to him, being the opportunist that he was. In Blue Duck's mind, they were too much trouble. Besides, it was his custom just to kill them, but the way he figured it, if the White Diggers were willing to send lots of trade goods, even diseased trade goods, they must be very wealthy, and he could trick them out of some goods that weren't diseased. He reckoned the White Diggers wouldn't risk having diseased goods in their own settlement. He figured that, if he went to go get the trade goods in the White Diggers settlement, he'd be OK. He thought it was a good plan, but when Commissioner McLeod sent word out to most of the other camps to join in the peace talks, Blue Duck lost his opportunity. He became furious and retaliated, torturing and killing at least a dozen settlers, so it became critical to Commissioner McLeod and Colonel Fisher to move the peace talks along as soon as they could. The two men agreed that the Comanches held at least a dozen captives, and they had to return all these captives, and any others they might have, at the onset of the peace talks. To the Comanches this was a simple matter, but one that was to be the downfall of the whole truce. All but two of the twelve captives had already been traded off to other tribes or camps, and therefore the Comanches were finished with them. In their eyes, the two captives they did still have were all that could be returned at the peace talks. McLeod and Fisher had reckoned on the possibility that the captives wouldn't be released, or the Comanches would attempt some form of trickery, and as such had stationed armed soldiers out-side the courthouse where the talks were to take place.

Almost sixty Comanches arrived in San Antonio that day, which included twelve Chiefs of the various camps, along with twenty-five of their best warriors and their families. Everything started well. Before the talks began the Comanches and some of the white settlers engaged in several games of marksmanship, such as shooting at coins, with the Comanches using bows and the settlers using their rifles and pistols. It turned out to be pretty even, but it was obvious the Comanches had the advan-tage of speed. They could shoot many more arrows in the time it took the settlers to reload, but as far as sharp shoot-ing went, the settlers held their own. The tension had dropped considerably when the peace talks began, and the Comanche Chiefs were optimistic that peace could be made. However, Commissioner McLeod demanded that all thirteen of the captives on a list provided to him by Colonel Fisher be returned before the talks could go any further. The Comanches were puzzled, because they only had two captives. The rest were not theirs to give back. They were with other tribes that were not at the peace talks. To prove their sincerity they sent for the two captives they did have, and when the two were brought into town, everyone that saw them gasped. One was a small Mexican boy that was taken from his family a little south of San Antonio. His mother was sent for immediately. The other was Matilda Lockhart. Both were ragged and filthy, but Matilda was in far worse shape.

She was obviously the victim of extreme abuse. She was listless, except when anyone, whether Comanche or white, approached, then she would become frightened and cower. There were bald spots on her head where handfuls of her hair had been jerked out, and probably wouldn't grow back. When several women examined her later, they reported that there was not a place on her entire body larger than a hand that didn't have scars from burns, beatings, or cuts. She appeared almost broken. Snow Woman had kept her for most of the time she was captive, and had taken revenge on her for the death of Runs Like a Bear, beating, burning, and otherwise torturing her until Yellow Wolf had finally put an end to the screaming. He took the girl from Snow Woman and sent her to another camp, then banished Snow Woman back to her brother's camp. Banishing her was an insult that could lead to trouble later, but Yellow Wolf didn't care.

Matilda's condition incensed the Texans, especially Colonel Fisher, and when Matilda told them the Comanches were liars, a statement of general character, they both demanded that all the rest of the captives be sent for and returned immediately. The Comanches agreed and started to leave, but Commissioner McLeod stopped them, saying that six of the Chiefs and their families would have to stay as prisoners until all the captives were returned. This was something the Comanches could not do. They could no more abandon one of their Chiefs to the whims of an enemy than they could one of their children. It was something they were sure even the

White Diggers could understand. When Fisher insisted, the warriors gathered around the chiefs. Fisher gave the order and the doors and windows of the courthouse were thrown open to reveal soldiers outside with rifles aimed at the Comanches. It was a trap, and the Comanches tried to fight their way out. They pulled their knives and drew their bows, but were cut down when Fisher gave the order to fire. In the end, all twelve Chiefs were killed along with almost all the warriors and even some of the women in the group. Only one warrior and one woman escaped. The woman happened to be standing outside the building and ran when the doors were thrown open and the soldiers took aim. The warrior fought his way to a window and jumped out into the street.

CHAPTER 9

THE COUNCIL
HALL MASSACRE

Logan was up at his usual time, before dawn and was sitting on the porch with Will drinking coffee, as usual, when Lucinda got up. She greeted them both and offered breakfast. Logan said he had to get an early start and would just take some bacon to eat on the way. Lucinda shook her head in disapproval. Logan had heard of a man named Barlow in San Antonio that was contracting for cattle. He and Will were still trying to pursue their ranching venture, and he was determined to go find this man and secure a contract. It was a two-day ride to San Antonio and he wanted to get an early start. Will protested, saying he should go along, but Logan insisted he stay and start the roundup. Logan expected they would need to get any cattle they could roundup to

San Antonio as fast as possible, in order to get the best price possible.

The trip itself was uneventful, to say the least. He traveled long days, but didn't see another soul until he was just outside San Antonio. It was still early in the afternoon when he got down near the Market Square. He figured to stay in a hotel, and hoped to find Mr. Barlow. Almost everything that happened in San Antonio happened in the Market Square. He rode in from the northeast, and as he rounded the corner by the Council House, he heard gunfire. He reined up his horse and tried to see what it was about. Men and women were running in all directions; a Comanche had been shot down. Everything seemed to stand still for a moment as if frozen in time, and then pandemonium broke out. Logan didn't know what was going on, so he jumped off his horse and ducked into the front door of a hotel. Crawling over to the window, he sat peering out into the confusion that controlled the street outside. The sound of the gunfire took him back to the battle of San Jacinto. As the gunfire continued, he saw faint flashes of the old memories around the outer edges of his consciousness, struggling to get in. It was as if he were seeing something out of the corner of his eye. He jerked his head to the left trying to catch whatever it was, but all he saw was a man on the floor. He was laying face down holding his hat onto his head as if a strong wind was trying to blow it away. The man didn't move when Logan slid over to the window next to him. The gunfire and shouting were heavy in the street. He heard several women scream and men cursing.

"You hurt?" Logan asked. The man shook his head, but didn't look up, he just clutched his hat with his eyes shut tight, terrified. Logan watched him a moment longer to make sure he was OK. "Are we bein' raided by Indians?" Logan asked trying to get a better look out into the street.

The man shook his head. After a moment he sputtered, "Peace talks."

Logan's eyes went wide as he stared at the man for a moment. "Don't appear to be workin'," he said, more to himself than to the other man as he turned back to the window. The man glanced at him with a frightened look on his face. Logan continued to peer out into the street. He was reluctant to go out since he really had no idea what was happening. After several minutes, the shooting and shouting diminished a bit, and the shots that rang out were more erratic. Several times he saw Comanches try to dart across one street or another, only to be gunned down from somewhere out of his line of sight. A soldier slipped around the corner of a building across the street and stooped down as if to inspect one of the bodies lying crumpled on the boardwalk, but before his hand touched the man there was a whizzing sound, and the tip of an arrow was sticking out the center of the soldier's chest. There was a surprised expression on his face as he looked down at the metal point, then his eyes glazed over and he sat back on his heels. He sat like this for several seconds before toppling to the side, lying next to the Comanche he had just killed.

There was a thick cloud of bluish white smoke surrounding the Council Hall. Shouts were coming from inside, and occasionally a Comanche would be seen trying to run somewhere. All but one were shot down by the people of San Antonio.

"What's your name mister?" Logan asked, trying to take the man's mind off the erratic sound of gunfire. The man was shivering. "Mister!" Logan shouted. The man's head snapped around to him, there was terror in his eyes. "What's your name?" Logan spoke more quietly to calm the man.

"B-B-Barlow, Ezr-Ezra Barlow," the man said, his voice breaking.

"Calm down Mr. Barlow. Everything is going to be OK. Doesn't seem to be too much of a dust up." Logan was trying to sound reassuring. He wasn't sure if he did. He personally didn't feel reassured. The sound of gunfire died down almost completely, only a couple more shots were heard off in the distance. Barlow seemed a little calmer; at least he'd stopped shivering. Logan got to his feet slowly and stepped outside to see what the situation was. Other people were venturing out, and most were armed. There was a troop of soldiers at the Council Hall picking up the wounded soldiers and carrying them inside. Another group was carrying dead Comanches outside and laying them in the yard. Logan looked on in disbelief. He recognized at least five as important chiefs that Sam Houston had made peace treaties with when he was President. A group of Comanche women and children were lead from the back of the Council Hall to the jail-house on the corner and locked up. Logan went over and began looking over the bodies of the Comanches as they were brought out.

"How many were killed?" he asked one of the troopers.

The trooper grinned. "Got ever' damn one we think," he said, with a certain amount of satisfaction in his voice. "All but the squaws and kids. Ought to finish it and shoot them too. You know what they say; nits grow into lice." Logan had to restrain himself. It was this kind of thinking that was responsible for the situation in the first place. He turned without a word and walked slowly back to the porch of the hotel where Mr. Barlow stood with his mouth hanging open.

"Mr. Barlow, you're the man I came to San Antonio to see about a cattle contract," Logan said as he stepped onto the porch. Barlow just looked at him and blinked. Logan went on "I don't think now is a good time to talk about it, but I'll get a room in the hotel here and we'll have breakfast tomorrow at six thirty and talk about it then." He held out his hand.

Barlow continued to stare and blink. As he took Logan's hand he said, "Yes. OK. Uh…yes that'll be fine." He wasn't really sure what he was agreeing to, but he shook Logan's hand anyway. Logan went into the hotel, checked in, and went to his room. He didn't feel much like eating supper that night, so he just stayed in his room.

The next morning Logan was in the café next door to the hotel drinking his second cup of coffee when Ezra

Barlow walked in and sat down at the table. He looked as though he hadn't slept at all, a fact that Barlow confirmed.

"I don't know if I can do business here if this is the kind of thing that occurs," he said, still sounding rather shaky.

Logan looked over the top of his coffee cup. "It's surely not a common thing, but we are in the Comancheria," he said. "This is beautiful country hereabouts, but it can be dangerous at times. Last evening happens to be one of those times. Let's have some bacon and eggs. You'll feel better with some grub in you." Barlow nodded absent-mindedly. A very pretty young girl came over to see what they'd have to eat. They both ordered a simple breakfast of bacon, eggs, biscuits, and coffee. Barlow seemed to be coming out of his funk a little because he remarked at how pretty the girl was. Logan looked at her again and had to agree. She was very pretty. He imagined that in a few years she might very well be the prettiest girl around.

When she brought the food over Barlow stopped her and said, "Miss, I hope you don't think this too forward of me, but I feel compelled to tell you how pretty you are." She blushed bright red and stood at a loss for words. "How old are you child?" he asked.

Her face was bright red as she answered "I'm eleven, sir," she said, while looking down at the ground, not sure what to say or do.

Logan tried to ease her discomfort. "What's your name, Miss?" he asked. She turned to look at him and suddenly seemed spellbound. "Miss," he said, snapping her out of it.

She shook her head as if to clear the cobwebs from it. "Mariel," she said, still blushing. "Mariel King."

"Well, Miss King, you're doing a fine job here, and we don't mean to make you feel uncomfortable." Logan said, trying to put her at ease. She seemed to relax a bit.

"No sir. It's okay sir. I-I mean, I'm fine," she stuttered.

"Mariel!" a woman's voice called out from the back. "Mariel! We've got other customers. Come get this food out before it gets cold." Mariel blushed and hurried to the back, where Logan and Barlow could hear a brief muffled argument. They grinned at each other and dug into their runny eggs and thick sliced bacon with relish. Mariel was back with hot coffee every few minutes, asking several times if their food was okay. They said it was and continued to talk business. At the end of the meal, they agreed that the eggs were perfect, the bacon was tasty, but the biscuits were some of the best either had tasted. When Mariel came back to take their money they told her so, and asked her to compliment the cook for them.

"Oh it's my mamma cooking in the back and she does do biscuits well." Mariel said as she went to make change. A few moments later, a slim, rather handsome older woman came out and walked over to their table.

"Gentlemen," she said, wiping her hands on her apron. "I hear you have something to say about my cooking." She stood confidently before them. Barlow was taken slightly aback, but Logan was nonplussed.

"Yes ma'am, we do," he said seriously. She just stood looking down at them. "The eggs were runny, just the way I like 'em, the bacon was thick and tasted well cured, and without slighting my wife, who I will say without question makes the best biscuits I've ever eaten, these were right up there near her own, for sure and for certain," he finished, grinning. Barlow gaped slightly at Logan. He wasn't used to such bluntness, but apparently, Mrs. King was.

"I thank you for the compliment sir, but I would have expected nothing less. You're a gentleman to say so, though, and I do appreciate it. I hope y'all will come back and eat here more often." She pointed over her shoulder with her thumb, adding, "I've rarely seen Mariel so attentive waitin' tables before." Logan blushed a little himself at that. Barlow almost choked on his coffee.

"Mamma!" Mariel shrieked from the back. Mrs. King smiled and gave them their change.

"Y'all come back now, hear," she added in a distinctly southern accent that was becoming very common around Texas. Logan and Barlow put the final touches on their agreement. Logan would supply Barlow with two hundred head of cattle, as long as Barlow didn't have to come to Texas again unless absolutely necessary. When he found out Logan was a Ranger he added that if he did have to come to Texas, Logan would have to ride northeast to Fort Smith, Arkansas and escort him down personally.

They shook hands, and as they walked out the door, Mariel called out "Goodbye!" from the back of the room.

Both men stopped and tipped their hats to her then left. She stood against the back wall, hands folded in front, smiling.

Logan was on the alert all the way to Bastrop and only spotted some dust off in the distance one time the whole way back. It was too far away to tell if it was buffalo, Indians, or who knows what. He kept out of sight, took his time, and made it back in two and a half days. Lucinda and Will were both worried. Logan assured them he had never really been in any danger during the little bit of a dust up, as he called it. When he and Will were alone he relayed the story with as many details as he could recall.

Will was shocked. "They killed them all?" he asked in amazement. Logan nodded.

"I recognized five of the chiefs from a treaty they signed with Houston, and I know there was at least that many more Chiefs I didn't recognize," Logan said. He could tell by the ornamentation, which was stripped from them for souvenirs by the thoughtless soldiers. They obviously didn't understand the respect those fierce men had earned. Some word had come from San Antonio right after it had happened, but the details were sketchy to say the least. Will had even heard that five hundred Indians had ridden down out of the hills and tried to butcher everyone in San Antonio, but they had been repulsed by the heroic Colonels McLeod and Fisher. Logan just shook his head and looked disgusted. They rode on over to the land they had been given for their service at the

Battle of San Jacinto and were met by four other men. Two Texans and two Mexicans, who had agreed to help Logan and Will round up the wild longhorns that were so plentiful there. They had all agreed to round up as many as they could and then divide them up. Since it was Will and Logan's land they would take six of every ten, and each of the other men would get one. This worked well, as they gathered more than five hundred head and drove them into a water trap, a heavily built brush and pole fence built around a pond that was closed off when they were all inside. In the end, Logan and Will had three hundred head to sell and the other men had fifty each. It was a good week's work, for all.

In June of that same year, Logan's status among the Comanches would change, as would his relationship with Yellow Wolf.

After gathering another small herd of cattle, Logan was again going into Bastrop to talk to a local buyer for the Army. As he approached the town, he came onto a group of about twenty painted Comanches stopped just outside the edge of town. Logan had picked up a few words of the Comanche language, just enough to make himself understood, if accompanied by some hand signs. Their attention was fixed on the town and he caught a couple of the hand signs that indicated several of the group would go around to the other side of the little settlement. When they turned to go and spotted Logan, there was a distinct look of guilt on their faces. The kind that conspirators get when caught. The thought of Comanches plotting to do harm to Lucinda, Will, Rebecca, and all the others in the town instantly filled his head with swirling images. Images he didn't want swirling in his head. This enraged Logan and without thought he kicked up his horse to a dead run, straight at the group. Most horses would have shied off or stopped before running headlong into something, but the big buckskin of Logan's had been well trained on the trail. He and Logan had gained a trust of one another not often found even among men. The big horse never slowed or missed a step. The few that saw him coming tried to get out of the way while whooping to warn the others. The horses that saw what was happening began to dance around the group. When they did, the three Comanches that saw him were soon caught in the middle of the group, and as the horses continued to dance, confusion set in. More horses danced and jumped. One young horse even bucked several jumps. In the end, none were able to purposely move out of the way as Logan and the big buckskin crashed headlong into the group. Logan rolled clear as his horse, and four others, hit the ground. He was on his feet almost instantly and grabbed the first Comanche he saw. He was about to deal him a mighty blow when he recognized Yellow Wolf trying to get clear of the pile of horses and Comanches. He shoved a big Comanche and Two Crows aside like dolls and waded through the tangled mass of arms, legs, and horses. He grabbed Yellow Wolf by the throat lifting him until his feet were up off the ground and they were eye to eye. He reached down in one fluid motion, grabbed

Yellow Wolf's knife, tossed it away, and then had his own big knife out and at Yellow Wolf's throat.

The other Comanches were dumbstruck. They had never seen anyone so brave or so foolish as this. Either way he was crazy, and none wanted to cross blades with him. They all stood stock-still. The horses got to their feet coughing, but also stood still. Logan's stare never wavered, nor did he glance at any of the other Comanches, who stood unmoving behind him, watching the scene unfold before their unbelieving eyes. He was fully expecting to be overwhelmed, but he refused to break eye contact with Yellow Wolf. He had figured the rest would be on him in an instant, and had already decided that he would take as many with him as he could, but when no one made a move, he began trying to think of something to say. He hadn't really thought that far ahead.

Finally, out of embarrassment at his own rashness, he growled "Aw, hell." Then, pulling Yellow Wolf closer, so their faces were only inches apart, he hissed in a low and truly evil sounding voice, "I know you can understand what I say, but I'll speak real slow and clear." Yellow Wolf began to turn red in the face so Logan eased his grip just a little to allow him to breathe. "There's been enough killin', on both sides. No more!" He spoke quietly with a look that was undeniable. "If there's to be more, let it be here, let it be now, just you and me." He stared into Yellow Wolf's eyes as if his stare would pierce him through.

Two Crows began to translate what he said, but Yellow Wolf flashed a brief look that told Two Crows he needn't bother. Yellow Wolf understood the big man's words very well. Logan noticed there was no fear in this man's eyes. There was anger and hatred for sure, but, by the man's own Gods, this Comanche wasn't afraid, even though he hung on the edge of death. He couldn't tell what Yellow Wolf was thinking, but he figured Yellow Wolf hated him more right then than any man alive. He held Yellow Wolf's stare a while longer, then turned his gaze upon the others, still frozen in place, "You all might kill me here and now, but I'll take many of you with me. Which of you will join me on the other side?" Two Crows translated this part and they all looked at each other. It was clear no one wanted to be included in that group. "My family and friends are here and I will not let you attack them, not without a fight with me first. If you attack here at any time I swear on *my* ancestors that I'll find and kill you all." He waved the big knife at them. They all took a step backward. Every one of them had heard the story of this big man and his Piapuha Nahuu, his big medicine knife, and his killing many Mexicans at the buffalo swamp before dying and then crossing back from the other side to live again. They honestly had begun to think he could not die. Even Two Crows, unflustered by most things, stood a bit further back. Logan turned and peered into Yellow Wolf's eyes. He expected to see anger and hatred seething there, but neither was, and he was not prepared for what he saw behind those intelligent dark eyes. It was respect, even awe. How could this be, he had this man on the edge of death, and yet Yellow Wolf showed him respect. He held him a moment longer and then carefully set his feet on the ground and stepped back. Yellow Wolf stood tall and did not cower as lesser men might have, nor did he rage, or try anything stupid. He simply nodded slowly, turned, and picked up his own knife, sheathing it as he stepped back in front of Logan. It was important that he show no fear of this big fierce warrior with the big medicine knife. After a moment, he turned, mounted his horse, and spun it to face Logan.

He raised his hand palm out. "Will not come here," he said flatly, looking deeply into Logan's eyes. After the other Comanches had mounted, they all turned and followed Yellow Wolf to the northwest, back in the direction of their camp on the Brazos River.

Logan heard horses coming hard and fast from the direction of town and turned to see Will, Amos, Little John, and several other men riding toward him. He held up his hand and they broke their stride and slowed a little. All had their pistols or rifles out when they got there. They were all looking back and forth between Logan and the Comanches riding away in the distance with amazement on their faces.

"What was that all about, Brother?" Will asked, as the others gathered around. Logan was a little embarrassed at being so rash.

"I guess I got mad and acted...stupid," he said, feeling his ears starting to get warm. He turned away and went to fetch his horse so they wouldn't see his red face. He checked the cinch, lifted all his horse's feet, and ran his hands over the animal's legs to make sure it was still sound after slamming into the other horses so hard. The horse rolled his eyes at Logan as if to ask, "Would anything else that stupid be required." Logan saw the anxious look in the buckskin's eyes and rubbed his nose, comforting the big horse. He almost laughed, thinking about what had just happened, and he might have, if it weren't such a serious matter, and if the other Rangers hadn't been there. When he turned back to face everybody they were all just sitting on their horses, staring, looks of amazement still glued to their faces. He stopped dead in his tracks.

"What?" he asked, trying to look innocent. He was sure they would think he was touched in the head for doing something so outrageous. He could only hope they hadn't seen all that happened. From the looks on their faces, he had no such luck. He tried to just mount up and ride on into town, but Will would have none of it. He rode up and stopped Logan, and in the end Logan had to give them at least a brief description of what had occurred. Still they pestered him with questions until finally he kicked his horse up to a lope and rode on into Bastrop and Lucinda's open arms.

He knew the Comanches would retaliate for what had happened at the Council House in San Antonio. Within days, people had begun to call it the Council House Fight. Logan saw it as something different and couldn't shake the feeling of shame he felt at what had been done there. He was rethinking his service in the

Rangers. Since it was the middle of the summer, he had decided to resign at the end of August and work at ranching full time. He knew this would please Lucinda greatly, although they would miss the Ranger's pay, irregular though it was.

However, Buffalo Hump would soon change Logan's plans, yet again.

❦

Comanches from all around mourned the loss of the Chiefs that were killed at the Council House. All were enraged and vowed revenge. They covered themselves in ashes and cut their arms, chests, and hair. Tribes and camps all over the territory danced, prayed, and called on every spirit leader for guidance. In the end it was Buffalo Hump and Yellow Wolf that provided the outlet they all sought. The two war chiefs held council, off and on, for more than a month and settled on a plan to set their people on a path into the future. A future many wouldn't survive.

It wasn't until the middle of June that the plan was finally set into motion. It was the hottest time of year, and 1840 seemed especially hot and humid. Yellow Wolf knew the lazy White Diggers didn't care for the hot weather and would spend as much time in the shade as possible. He knew they would be waiting for the inevitable break in the weather, putting off all manner of chores for the next month or two. He and Buffalo Hump figured they could take many of the White Diggers by surprise. Preparations had begun in earnest two months previously and had continued in secret until all was ready. In the warm glow of predawn, in the first days of August 1840, Buffalo Hump, and more than a seven hundred painted warriors outfitted with new weapons and fresh supplies, rode out of The Honey Eaters' camp and headed south to the coast. Now the White Diggers would pay. They did not hurry, but rode with determination. They arrived at Yellow Wolf's camp to find more than three hundred Buffalo Eaters mounted and ready to exact payment for the disrespect shown by killing and defiling their most revered chiefs. There was a tremendous war cry as they rode out of camp toward the south. The younger boys that were eager to go, but left behind, ran along beside them as far as they could. In the end, there was only a great cloud of dust to mark the beginning of their journey. By nightfall, they had raided more than a dozen farmsteads and killed all they found: men, women, children, and most of the animals. They only kept a few of the better horses. Yellow Wolf was glad to be striking a blow of such proportion at his enemy and was certain of the success of the raid.

Several days, and more than two dozen farms and ranches later, found them within five miles of Victoria, a small town near the coast. Here they came upon a man named McNuner, a Doctor Gray, and a young boy. The boy was able to get away from the group, which was a considerable feat in itself, but Mr. McNuner and Dr. Gray were not so lucky. They were killed and then hacked apart. As the raiders got closer to Linnville they became more brutal in their attacks. It was no longer enough to just kill and scalp these hated White Diggers, now they began to hack them up and decorate their horses with some of the body parts. By the time the group reached Victoria, the wounded boy had already raised the alarm and the fifty or so men there could not be taken by surprise. For four days, the Comanches surrounded and harassed Victoria and Linnville, killing any of the residents still trapped inside the town limits. When finally they did leave, it was with every horse and mule in the area along with numerous wagons loaded to the top with expensive goods. In all, this group of warriors had killed several hundred Texans and was leaving with many thousands of dollars' worth of goods from the two towns as well as most of the stock left at the nearby farms.

There was great joy in the group, many coupes had been counted, and many enemies killed. They had the scalps to show for it. Travel was much slower going back north, but they did not try to hurry or hide. Let the White Diggers try to attack the group and their bones would lie in the sun along with those from Victoria and Linnville.

Logan and Will heard the news of the great raid from a young boy sent out by Captain Boales to fetch them. The two were once again out on Logan's ranch on the Colorado rounding up cattle for another drive to Arkansas. They had just finished dropping the brush and timber gate of their trap in place on about a hundred head of cattle when the boy arrived and spouted out the news. Logan and Will quickly gave orders for the four men helping to get the cattle settled and then ride the perimeter of the trap and double check for openings. These were wild Texas longhorns and they were truly difficult to manage. The longer you kept them in an area, the more difficult they became. Many had never seen a human before, and none wanted to see another, except under hoof, it seemed. Logan and Will rode hell bent back to Bastrop, just a few miles away. The mustangs they were riding took the trip in stride, and they made it just as it was getting dark. Logan and Will went straight to the Ranger barracks. Captain Boales was there making preparations to leave with the rest of the troop. He planned to meet up with Colonel Burleson, who had requested they join up with him at a place to the north, near the Brazos River. They would leave within the hour. Logan and Will started to their homes, but Logan stopped his tired horse and looked up at the starry sky.

"What's the matter, brother?" Will asked, stopping to watch Logan and see what he was up to. Logan sat for a moment longer looking up.

"Is this the right thing to do?" he asked, still gazing upward. Will looked puzzled.

"What do you mean?" he asked, turning his horse to face Logan.

Logan sighed, saying, "Do you think it's right to go ridin' off with blood in our eyes to kill more people because they killed some other people?" he lowered his gaze to Will, "I mean, where does it stop? When we're all dead?" There was trouble in his dark eyes and his knotted brow. Will was surprised, and not the least bit happy about what he was hearing from his lifelong friend.

"They killed dozens, maybe even hundreds of people," Will said, with some spark in his voice. "Every one of 'em farmers or ranchers." He took off his hat and wiped the inner band with his bandana. "We can't just sit by and let them get away with that sort of thing!" He was becoming agitated and spoke more forcefully. "Hell fire man, those folks weren't their enemies!" he practically shouted. Logan was surprised. Will was the most levelheaded man he had ever known. He had rarely seen him react this way. "I agree, they weren't the Comanches enemies, but I understand why the Comanches wanted to raid and kill: Revenge. Revenge for the dishonor of their great chiefs. We wasn't invited here you know. We've all crowded into land they've held for hundreds of years and just pushed 'em out and slaughtered their buffalo by the thousands for no better reason than to take their hides. Top that off with what happened at the Council House, and Brother I can't blame them for hating every last one of us." He was speaking slowly and quietly to try and offset Will's agitation. He hoped it might calm Will. It didn't. Will threw his hat on the ground and dismounted.

"Damn it Logan! You can't possibly say this was OK!" he shouted. Logan just sat and looked down at him. Will picked up his hat and beat it against his leg to dust it off. Finally Logan spoke again, "No, it wasn't OK. It was the most wrong thing they could have done, but doin' the same back to them is just as wrong." His look was pleading. He wasn't arguing with Will just to get him to agree. He was pleading with his best friend to see what he was thinking and feeling, to understand. "More killin' won't solve the problem. In fact, it'll make it worse. You know it will." He dismounted so that he and Will were at eye level. "I've thought about it all the way back from the ranch…. I'm not goin' Will." He stood squarely facing his friend. Will looked at Logan and said nothing for a long time. Finally, he turned, put his hat back on, and mounted up.

Turning his horse to face Logan he said, "I understand what you're saying Brother, but I just can't agree, leastways, not right now. Maybe this is a mistake, maybe I will see it different later, but right now I just want to kill Comanches." He leaned over his saddle horn. "I hope you can live with this decision," he said, turning his horse and heading for his house. He stopped and looked back at Logan still standing beside his own horse and added, "I hope I can live with mine too." A moment later, he kicked up his horse and was gone. Logan felt empty inside. He and Will had never disagreed on anything in their entire lives. At least that he could remember. This was the closest they had ever come to a fight, and he felt hollow and sad, as if some part of his body had been cut away. He sat down on a nearby log and thought for a while. After making up his mind about what he needed to do, he mounted up and turned back toward the barracks. He had to go tell the Captain he wasn't going.

When Logan broke the news to the Rangers, Captain Boales was surprised, the rest of the Rangers weren't, saddened, but not surprised. Will was not there. Lucinda was delighted, but remained slightly subdued. She knew how hard it must be for Logan, especially after hearing about his disagreement with Will. Deep down she was thrilled. Logan sat out on the porch watching the moon set that night. He didn't crawl into bed until just before sunrise. Nevertheless, at sunrise he was up, coffee was brewing, and he was ready to start ranching. After breakfast, he rode out to see if his hired help was still to be found. He expected most any man that could carry a gun would be riding out to try and intercept the Comanches. To his amazement, all four were waiting for him, horses saddled and rolls packed. They seemed to know him better than he realized. The five men rode solemnly to the west away from trouble. Rounding up longhorn cattle, which were some of the meanest, wildest animals on the plains, was not an easy task, and was dangerous beyond description. Richard Chisholm, a well-known rancher of the area, had stated on more than one occasion that because they were easier to roundup and manage he surely would have stocked his ranch with buffalo if there weren't so damned many longhorns in Texas. During this roundup, the men had been drawn further south than they normally worked. They finally made the water trap between the Blanco and Guadalupe rivers, and while there found numerous larger groups of the big four legged devils. Three times they were forced to shoot and kill rampaging bulls that were trying to gore, trample, or stampede the men and other cattle. They spent five days rounding up the wildest, craziest, meanest animals any had ever seen, and the trap was set and stocked. One of the old cows tried to break out of the trap twice. Logan could see she would be a problem that they didn't need, so he cut her out and turned her loose. Two days of rest put them on the trail to fulfill another new contract to supply cattle to several other ranches in the northeastern part of Texas and Louisiana. There were three brothers named Orgain that were working cattle on land they had been granted near a small town called Shreveport, where the Texas Trail crossed the Red River. The Orgain brothers were interested in the large herds found in southern Texas. They were looking to buy between two hundred and five hundred head every four months, and Logan had to prove he could supply them. Logan's plan was to drive the herd east to Ishom Goode's ranch near Lockhart, and then turn north to Bastrop. There they would stop for two days and round up the stragglers, then turn northeast toward a small limestone lake with good grass where they could stop for a couple of days before crossing the Trinity River. After that, it would be a straight run right on up to Shreveport.

Will's ears were ringing as he rode away from Logan. He had never felt this particular feeling before, and didn't know what to make of it. He rode home quickly and began gathering his travel pack. Rebecca could feel the tension the moment he walked in the house. She watched him for a few moments and then walked over and put her hand on his shoulder. That usually did it for Will, and it did it this time too. He slumped; his shoulders sagged as he looked into her eyes. She could see the trouble there and was silent. Finally, Will opened up and explained what had happened. Rebecca stood quietly and listened. When Will finished, she put her arms around him and looked up into his steel grey eyes,

"I don't need to say that Logan is a grown man, or that you can't choose what he should do. I won't say he's wrong and you're right or the other way around. It really doesn't matter. What matters is that you understand that Logan is still your best friend, and admit to yourself that he may be right." Will tensed up at the last part, but still held her tightly. After several minutes, he finally stepped back with his head lowered. "I know all that," he said lowly.

Rebecca smiled slightly. "I know you do, but sometimes a person just needs to hear it anyway." She brushed the dust from his shoulders, trying not to make him feel uncomfortable by holding his gaze. "Anyway, it was bound to happen. Two stubborn mules like the two of you, ridin' together all these years, spendin' all your time together, goin' through what you've been through together. Couldn't expect anything less." Will's tension had eased noticeably. "Besides, you'll have plenty of time to shake hands and make up when you get back. By the way, where are you goin' this time?" she asked, catching his gaze and holding it.

Will shuffled his feet and started in on one of his "thimble sized" explanations, as Rebecca called them. Whenever Will would try to get away with giving her the briefest of explanations she would patiently wait until he was done and then say,

"Well, that don't tell me anything, William Magill. Why, that story'd fit in a thimble with enough room left over for a mule, now you tell me the rest of it." Will would usually look sheepish and start over, sometimes being just as spare with the details. After two or three tries, Rebecca would usually give up and let him be on his way. She knew he loved her and was probably just trying to save her worry whenever he did that. This time it was different, perhaps it was because Will was going off without Logan for the first time since Logan was five years old.

Will kept eye contact with her while he told her about the raid and that most of the Rangers, men, and soldiers in the area were getting ready to ride north to intercept the Comanches. She blanched slightly at the thought of a thousand Comanches rampaging across the territory, but kept her composure. She had learned early on it was no use to try and dissuade Will Magill from any course of action he had set his mind to. He gathered his travelin' pack and had his hand on the door when Rebecca took his arm.

"Don't you think you can walk away from me this time without holdin' me tight before you go." Will, not being one to fully comprehend a woman's emotional needs rose to the occasion. He dropped his pack, put his arms around her, pulled her close, and kissed her long, before gazing into her eyes and telling her that he loved her. When he finally left, Rebecca wept. Will Magill had never been quite so expressive before going off Rangerin, as he called it. She was worried. What if something happened? She took some consolation in their having parted sweetly.

Will joined the other Rangers and they rode south to meet up with Colonel Burleson at Ishom Goode's ranch near Lockhart. By morning, they were drinking coffee with Ishom and several of his hands, who were preparing to ride out as soon as Captain McCullough arrived, as were Captain Ward and Colonel Burleson. It was decided that the troops should split up and scout out no more than fifteen miles for the Comanches and then send riders for the rest of the troops who would wait at Goode's ranch. The three troops were gone in different directions before the breakfast fires had smoldered out.

Will was glad Burleson's troop wasn't staying in camp at Goode's. Being a man of action, he didn't wait well. They rode west toward the Guadalupe in a zigzagging pattern, moving relatively slowly, for them, looking for any sign of the Comanches. Will was sure that if they came across any signs they wouldn't miss them. After all, how sneaky could a thousand mounted Comanche warriors be? By nightfall, they had covered an area fifteen miles long and fifteen miles wide, and felt pretty sure they had seen every jackrabbit's track in it, and nary a Comanche sign. They camped for the night, heading back toward Goode's ranch at sunup. About three miles out from Goode's, a rider caught them and told them the Comanche's had been spotted and were headed for a crossing on Plum Creek. Burleson sent the rider back with word that they were only five miles out, and coming double-time. The rider bolted at a dead run and the troop followed quickly. As they reached the spot on Plum Creek, they could see that Captain McCullough and Captain Caldwell had positioned their troops and were preparing to rush, what appeared to be, every Comanche in Texas. They joined up quickly and discovered that command of the entire action had been turned over to General Felix Huston, who was, as yet, untried at fighting Comanches. Huston wanted to defer the command back to the individual Captains, but they would have none of it. He was their superior and that was it. The force divided into three troops, with Ward's men taking to a line of trees off to their left. They would take advantage of their muskets and long rifles, while McCulloch and Burleson took their troops straight at the Comanches. Huston gave the signal, and the skirmishers started toward the Comanche warriors, who sat on their horses in a line a quarter mile wide, painted for war.

Yellow Wolf felt the raid on the White Diggers' big village by the ocean was more successful than he had hoped for. Only two of their warriors had been killed during five days of raiding and looting. Now they had many horses and wagons loaded with all the things the White Diggers had. This was good. At first, he thought that to get it back the White Diggers might agree to leave, but he knew in his heart the only way the Diggers would leave was on the wind. He knew they would have to kill them all or be killed themselves. As they headed north, they were constantly harassed by a small group of White Diggers. It was never enough to stop them, but it was slowing them down. Yellow Wolf approached Buffalo Hump and offered to take some of his men and hunt these fleas on their hide and kill them so they might travel in peace. Buffalo Hump did not think this to be wise. They had already killed many of the whites, and he felt it was important for them to get back to their camps as soon as possible. The whites would probably be coming for revenge. They pressed on, trying to move the massive group of horses, mules, wagons, cattle, and other stock. Movement was slow, but Yellow Wolf was pretty sure they didn't have to worry too much about the small group harassing from behind. Then, four days after they left the coast as they approached a small stream, a larger group of the White Diggers appeared and made threatening movements toward them. Yellow Wolf was not worried. His medicine man, Black Elk, as well as the medicine man from the Honey Eaters camp had danced, sang, and woven very powerful medicine over all the warriors. The medicine men had told them all to make new war bonnets, the headdresses they wore into battle, to protect them, and they suggested different parts of the Buffalo. Some had headdresses made of Buffalo heads, some wove the tails into their own hair and the manes and tails of their horses. Some made shields from the dried hides that were very powerful and would make bullets and arrows bounce off. Their power had been proven several times as warriors ran directly into the line of fire and faced death to count coupe on the White Diggers, bullets flying from their bodies as if they were invincible. All had seen this and all believed.

As the pitiful little group of White Diggers rode out onto the plain Yellow Wolf almost laughed. He spread his warriors across the other end of the plain behind the train of wagons and pack animals. The line of warriors seemed to stretch from one side of the prairie to the other. They sat and waited while the train of goods taken from the whites moved away behind them. Then as the line of White Diggers began to move toward them shots rang out from the trees. Bullets hit and bounced off the shields of several warriors. Bullets hit the breast shirts of two warriors without injury. This incited the warriors into a frenzy. They began dancing their horses out of line, trying to attract the bullets of the White Diggers. Then, the small line of soldiers began to run at them and still they waited. All wanted close battle to count coupe before they killed this enemy. A rider came to Yellow

Wolf at this moment. He was called Long Shirt and was one of Buffalo Hump's cousins and closest advisors. He quickly told Yellow Wolf that the Honey Eater's medicine man had dreamt of this day and there would be no battle here. Buffalo Hump wished them to simply follow behind the main group and keep the White Diggers from stopping their movement. Yellow Wolf kicked his horse round to face Long Shirt, fire in his eyes. This was something Yellow Wolf would never accept easily. He was Yellow Wolf, War Chief of the Buffalo Eaters camp. Accepting a challenge to battle defined who and what he was. Yellow Wolf would not normally have paid any attention to such a request from Buffalo Hump, and he would have likely killed Long Shirt without remorse for suggesting such a thing, but this time it had come from the medicine man. He knew better than to ignore the spirits that gave powerful men the visions that directed the lives and deaths of his people. He did not like it, but he called for the line to hold their position. He would not give the order to charge the tiny band of White Diggers and kill them all. The other warriors were puzzled, but none dared act without Yellow Wolf's command. Many continued to dance their horses around taunting the onrushing soldiers. Several warriors were not pure in thought and were shot from their horses. He directed a short section of his line to move out and meet the soldiers. He wanted to break their charge. About fifty warriors dashed out and charged full speed at the oncoming soldiers.

They broke the soldiers charge while Yellow Wolf commanded the rest to retreat behind the pack animals and wagons. There were groans of disapproval, something he normally would not tolerate, but he could not punish them for speaking his own mind. There was a small, quick, and fierce battle pitched between the retreating soldiers and his warriors. Several that wore the Buffalo Head medicine hats were very brave and rode right into the mouths of the Diggers guns unharmed and counted many coupes. One warrior's horse had been shot from under him because he had obviously not painted or adorned it properly, but he himself was unharmed even when he ran back on foot, bullets flying up all around him, to retrieve the new bridle he had taken during the raid. He made it back to the safety of the Comanche line, but had several red spots on his back where it was believed bullets had hit and flown from his body. He was called Munatsahkiapu (Cut Nose) because of a deformity he was born with. Comanches would cut the noses of any that committed serious offenses against any Chief or the entire camp to mark them forever. Even though Munatsahkiapu had never committed the offense in this life, it was believed he had offended some malevolent spirit before this life, and so his nose had been cut in his mother's womb. He was not shunned, but neither was he accepted, until now. He bore the proof of his bravery and the protection of powerful spirits. His life would change drastically hereafter. He then became known as

Nabaka Ke Peeka, (The One Bullets Could Not Kill) and was respected by all, and many songs were sung of him.

Will sat on his horse looking across the plain at the long line of painted Comanches. There didn't seem to be any way this would turn out good, for anyone. The Comanches outnumbered them five to one, but this was a group of Texans made up of determined men, most of whom had battle experience against Mexicans, Comanches, bandits, or all three. He knew that in a pitched battle they didn't stand a chance. The only thing they could hope for was to take as many Comanches out of action as possible, so that any troops going up against them later might have a better chance. As he sat there, he couldn't help but think about Logan and their last encounter. Maybe Logan was right. For the first time, he felt he really saw the situation clearly. The Comanches truly had been the Lords of the Southern Plains for more than two hundred years. That certainly was long enough to take their claim seriously. Maybe the white man didn't have much right to crowd in and take over land that the Comanches considered their own. He tried to put himself in their moccasins, and could see how they might hate the white men. When they did start their charge at the line of painted warriors, Will doubted his right to be in this fight, but it was too late. They were already running hell bent for certain death. He hoped he had made Rebecca understand how much he loved her. He wished he could go back and spend every day showing her. He also wished he could tell Logan that he had done the right thing. This wasn't a fight they should be in, and then the first shots rang out. He rode with his rifle in hand, but didn't waste any bullets from that range. He waited, and when he was close enough, he shot the horse out from under some unlucky Comanche, watching him roll over and over. Covered in dust from head to foot, the Comanche jumped to his feet, ran toward Will, and slapped him on the side as Will rode by at full speed. Suddenly, Will had the solution, he would count coupe on the Comanches. He rode straight at a wildly painted warrior, and just as he got there, he ducked the war club and slapped the warrior on the chest. He sat upright and headed for the next. He didn't know how many times he might get away with that, but he kept riding. He slapped two more before the line of soldiers broke and began to retreat back to the trees. On his way back, he saw the warrior whose horse he'd shot. He felt bad about shooting the horse. It looked like a good one. He was running back toward the Comanche line with what appeared to be a new bridle in hand. As Will approached, the warrior braced himself for a fight. Much to the warriors surprise Will appeared as though he would ride right on by. At the last minute, Will grinned, leaned out of the saddle, and slapped the warrior on the shoulder, then rode on. As he did this he heard the distinct "thunk, thunk" of bullets hitting home. Will expected to see the warrior drop, but instead he turned, raised the bridle in the air and let out a whoop, then turned again and ran to the Comanche line, seemingly without injury. If Will hadn't seen it with his own eyes, he wouldn't have believed it.

Back at the tree line, the troops were all gathered, waiting for the order from General Huston to attack the Comanches again, but this time all out. It didn't come. Huston, inexperienced in this type of warfare, didn't give the order. Instead, he called for a general regrouping back at Plum Creek and they all watched as the Comanches disappeared over a low hill.

When the troops reassembled on Plum Creek, Ben McCulloch was ranting that they needed to pursue the Comanches and kill all they could before they got to the mountains. Huston was unsure, and didn't seem disposed to continue the fight. There was much discussion, and after many heated words, Huston gave the order for Captain Zumalt, known as "Black Adam Zumalt," and Ben McCulloch to take some men and follow the Comanches. The rest of the troops were ordered home.

After the soldier's charge was broken, the Comanches began to leave the area, picking up the bodies of the impure that had been killed while all continued moving to the northwest. The White Diggers kept behind them for the remainder of the day, harassing and retreating, but they posed no real problem for the progress of the Comanches. After dark, the Comanches stopped, set up a very limited camp, ate some food, and after moon set, slipped away into the night. The lazy White Diggers slept on without a clue that a thousand people, and more than three thousand animals, had moved past them in the dark of night. Come morning they were many miles from the White Diggers' camp.

Logan thought long and hard about his decision to quit the Rangers on the trip to Shreveport and back. Although it was probably the best thing for him to do for Lucinda's sake and for the sake of his ranch, he wasn't sure it might be the best thing to do, all things considered. What if the raid on Linnville caused a general outcry for more blood—Comanche or Kiowa blood? He felt there was a very good chance of it. Perhaps he would be in a much better position to help if he was riding on the side of the Rangers. He thought repeatedly of the look in Yellow Wolf's eyes the day he had choked him. This was not a mindless beast, as many a white man would have him think. He was intelligent and courageous. He would have to sit with Will and talk about it when he got back.

CHAPTER 10

THE BUFFALO EATERS CAMP

When Logan got back to Bastrop, Lucinda was there waiting as always, but she seemed a little reserved. She greeted him warmly enough, but he could tell there was something just under the surface, bothering her. As he was unpacking his travel bags, Lucinda bustled by quietly. The third time she bustled silently past him he reached out and took her hand and turned her to face him.

"All this quiet's getting' pretty deafening here," he said, looking serious. A look of pain flashed briefly across her face like a cloud's shadow on a breezy day. She looked long at the man she had loved from the moment she saw him. Silently, a tear rolled down her cheek. Logan hated the thought of Lucinda ever being sad enough to cry and his heart ached, but he stood and waited. Finally, she threw her arms around him. "I just don't want to lose you!" she sobbed. Logan was taken by surprise.

"Lose me! Why would you think you're gonna lose me?" he asked, lifting her chin to look into her face. She buried her face in his chest and sobbed even harder. He just let her get it out and held on to her. Finally she looked up, tears streaking her face.

"Of all the things I've had to do in my life, including burying my own mother on the trail out here, and watching you go out time and again, knowing you might not come back, this is the hardest." The baby, Eliza, started to fuss, but Lucinda stood her ground. "With all the worry and heartache of watching you go out after the worst men in the territory, I never would have thought I'd say what I'm about to say." He studied her face to see what it might be she was about to say. She walked over to the crib and lifted Eliza out, then came back and handed her to Logan. Eliza cooed in her daddy's arms. A look of resolve came over Lucinda's face then anger flashed there. "I'm not sure quitting the Rangers is the right thing for you to do," she said, stepping back from him, holding her small hand to her mouth, her eyes wide. Logan was shocked. It was the last thing he would have expected her to say.

"Why do you think that?" he asked, truly dumbfounded. Although he had been thinking the same thing, he was sure he would have to run for cover when he told her, but here she was, saying exactly what he was thinking. He almost felt as though he should look around to see if a deadfall was about to hit him. Instead he looked long into her face and eyes, then took her in his arms once more and held her and the baby tight even though she tried to struggle a little. After a moment, she went limp, sobbing again. He held her for a little while longer, then said, "I thought about it on the way to Shreveport and back, and I think maybe you're right, but I never thought you'd see it." She jerked free of him with fire in her eyes, and for the first time since he could remember he was afraid.

"Dammit Logan, I'm not stupid. I can see what's happening here and I know how you feel about it all, but I think you can do more good in the Rangers than out. At least you'll be involved in things as they happen instead of caught up in what happens after." Logan was surprised by her flurry of anger. He reached out and took her hands again, gently. "I'm sorry if I ever gave you the impression I thought you were stupid, 'cause I surely don't. I think you're the smartest person I know. I think you're smarter than I am by far and I'm amazed that you picked me in the first place." She looked puzzled. "I loved you the first time I saw you, and made plans on how I'd win you, but it didn't take long to see that my plans meant nothin'." Lucinda blinked wide-eyed at him. "It was you who chose me, and even now I don't understand why. I'm gone as much as I'm home. I can think of a dozen fellas'd probably be better providers than me. I know this is a hard life and a hard place to live, but you're right. I need to be where I can help make some of the decisions about how we treat the

Comanches." He stooped slightly so he could look more directly into her eyes. He could see fear, relief, pain, and happiness there. Then he held her again. She buried her face in his chest, but this time she wasn't crying.

"I think you should try and make peace with the Comanches," she said, still resting her head on his chest. "After all, you and Yellow Wolf seem to get along so well. You choke him; he doesn't kill and scalp you." Logan hadn't told her about threatening Yellow Wolf and he was sure Will hadn't either. He tensed and it gave away his surprise. "Did you think I wouldn't hear about it? Everybody in town has heard the story of the 'man with The Big Medicine Knife' that choked Yellow Wolf." He just held her and stroked her hair. After a moment, she pushed back and looked up into his eyes. "And who are these other men who are better providers that you know about? I guess I should know too, just in case you ever do anything like that again?" She had a look of mock anger in her eyes. He pulled her to him and held her head against his chest, smiling.

❧❧

On the second day after the small battle, Yellow Wolf's group broke off from the rest of Buffalo Hump's warriors and went to the east to set up a new camp. Four days earlier, Yellow Wolf had sent two warriors to the west to gather the rest of the camp on the Guadalupe, near San Antonio. He had decided to move the camp to the northeast, onto the Brazos River. They had many horses, mules, and wagons. The horses they could trade, the wagons they would burn in celebration, and the mules they would eat. Two days after the Buffalo Eaters separated from the Honey Eaters, they came to a wide prairie above the Brazos. They had seen signs that showed much game on the way in and the river was wide here. It would be difficult for an enemy to sneak up on the camp with so much open prairie to cross. It was a good place. He could be happy here, for a while. At least until the White Diggers came again.

While the camp was being set up, he sent out scouts to see how many of the Diggers were near and if they might be a threat to be rid of quickly or could the camp enjoy some peace for a short time first. After the scouts rode out, the rest of the camp settled in for a day of rest. The coming celebrations would last for days. There were many gifts in the wagons to give, many mules to eat, and many horses to trade. The camp slept for the remainder of the day and that night. In the morning, preparations began in earnest. Yellow Wolf and Black Elk looked over the wagons and tried to figure out what many of the things there might be used for. Black Elk seemed very knowledgeable and suggested that most were obviously used to conjure up some type of spirit and were therefore to be used as adornment. They spent most of the day going through everything and looking the horses over. Yellow Wolf picked out ten of the best horses for himself and gave five others to Black Elk for dreaming such a good raid. He was definitely worth it. No other medicine man was as worthy of honor that day as Black Elk.

The scouts had all come back in the late afternoon and told Yellow Wolf that there were only a few White Diggers in the area, and the ones that were there were poor and spread out. They would pose no threat to the Buffalo Eaters, now or later when it was time to kill them. That same afternoon the rest of the camp arrived from the Guadalupe.

Many fires were lit and five mules were cooked throughout the day. There was flour in the wagons, and the women mixed it with water and buffalo fat and cooked it on hot rocks. Yellow Wolf thought it odd tasting and didn't eat much of it. He even ate sparingly of the roasted mule. After all, it wasn't buffalo. The fires were kept going all night, and groups of men went from one lodge to another celebrating, each recounting stories of bravery, telling again and again the number of coupes counted and enemies killed. There were several new songs sung about the bravest. Yellow Wolf and Two Crows heard one about The One Bullets Could Not Kill. They both smiled and raised their eyebrows. It was fitting; he had done deeds of daring and bravely counted coupe. Neither could say how many enemies The One Bullets Could Not Kill had actually killed, but it really didn't matter. Yellow Wolf and Black Elk assembled the revelers to give gifts and to show what the objects were used for. Many horses were given and traded around. Within the next three hours, all the loot had been given out as gifts. Everyone in camp had gotten something, even those who had been left on the Guadalupe that had just arrived that day. They all strutted around with their new adornments, knives, mirrors, pots, and many other things. When the first faint streaks of red began to show in the sky, the celebration wound down. It would start up again in the evening, though not with the energy of the previous night.

Logan went to Will's house and found Rebecca baking bread and feeding the baby. She looked up and smiled, then gave Logan a hug and handed him the baby. He sat down on a chair and bounced Will and Rebecca's first born, Mary Naomi, on his knee. She giggled and bounced and giggled some more. Rebecca finished taking the bread from the oven and laid the loaves out on a cooling rack, then turned and took the baby from his lap.

"Will's out back soapin' down his saddle." He looked up at her trying to read her eyes, hoping he could see in them what might be in store when he talked to Will. There was compassion in her eyes. "Well, go on! You two gotta make up sooner or later, and the way he's been mopin' around here, sooner would be better." She nodded toward the back door and Logan could see Will sitting in the shade of a tree with his back to the house. "You better hurry up, if he soaps that saddle one more time he'll likely slide right

off the first time he tries to ride it." Rebecca stood looking out the back at Will, baby Mary perched on her hip. "I
swear you'd think you two were married, the way you act
sometimes." She mumbled as he started for the door. He
was a little taken aback, but didn't stop.

His shadow gave him away as he approached Will.

Without turning to look up, Will said, "Well Brother,
are we goin' to try and make peace or just sit around
here hunkered down like everyone else and wait for the
Comanches to come back?" He leaned over and looked
at a spot he might have missed.

Logan stood quietly, grinning at his friend. His statement only reaffirmed how much alike these two really
were. Without discussion, Logan knew Will was talking about making peace with the Comanches and not
himself.

"Reckon Yellow Wolf's the one," Logan finally said, as
if they had only recently been interrupted in the middle
of this conversation.

Will did a double take. "Yellow Wolf?" he asked, plainly
surprised. "Are you sure he's the one and not Buffalo
Hump?" Logan grinned. He'd finally done something he
thought might not be possible; he'd surprised William
Magill. "I mean, what with all the chokin' and theatenin'
in your past he might not be real anxious to stop his three
or four hundred warriors from proving you *can* be killed."
Will threw his rag over the hitching rail and stood up to
face Logan "Hell's bells man, your hair could be hangin'
from his lance five minutes after we get there." He stood

looking up at his friend, and could see the resolve in Logan's eyes.

"He's the one, Will. I had him this close to death." Logan held out his thumb and forefinger for emphasis. "And you know what I saw in his eyes?" Will stood a second and then cocked his head slightly as if to hear it more clearly. Logan paused a moment. "It wasn't fear and it wasn't hate." Will saw that Logan wholly believed what he was saying. "It was respect and courage. He's a smart one, 'ol Yellow Wolf." Logan walked over and sat in one of the two chairs under the tree. "There were a lot of things he could've done that day after I let him go, including have me killed and scalped, but he didn't. He looked me straight in the eye without fear and showed me respect. He surely earned mine that day." He reflected on the encounter momentarily before adding, "Yep, he's the one." Will sat down in the other chair and looked out across the empty lot at the line of trees surrounding the little house. Logan hesitated slightly then continued. "I know you hate what's happenin' here as much as I do, but I'm not askin' you to go with me. Matter of fact I don't think you should." He watched for signs that maybe he'd misjudged Will.

Indeed, he had. Will started as if he'd been stung. He just looked at Logan and his mouth actually hung open. Logan squirmed in his chair a little.

"Don't even think you can go riding off across the country to do this alone. Why, Lucinda and Rebecca both'd have my hide peeled and stretched before you got outta sight," Will said, as he stood and picked up the saddle and headed for the small tack shed attached to the back of the house. "Why, I don't think I could live with myself if I let you wander off by yourself across the prairie lookin' for four or five hundred Comanches that would just as soon kill you as look at you. No sirree, that there is somethin' I wouldn't want to miss." There was sarcasm in the last part. He tossed the old saddle onto the rack in the shed and closed the door, and then turned to look at Logan, who sat staring down at his feet. Rebecca came out of the house with two cups of steaming coffee and handed them both to Will. She looked from one to the other and shaking her head, walked back into the house. They sat for a while drinking coffee and talking, as if never a cross word had passed between them. They made plans to leave in three days. Logan stood up, tossed the last sip of coffee out, and left for home.

Life on the Brazos was good. There was plenty of game, and The Buffalo Eaters were able to go north within a month after the raid on Linnville to hunt the great shaggy beasts that provided so much of their life's fiber. More than half the camp went for many days, and came back with enough buffalo meat and hides to last the winter. The Buffalo Eaters were wealthier than any could remember.

Yes, life was good, but how long would it last? Yellow Wolf and Two Crows spoke of this several times while hunting. Things in life are always temporary. Wealth, happiness, sorrow, despair; all are temporary.

Shortly after they had returned from this hunting trip, word came to Yellow Wolf that two White Diggers were heading their way without any apparent fear. Yellow Wolf knew who it was. Many warriors came to see if he wanted them to go and rub these two foolish men out. Yellow Wolf did not need any warriors to rub out two of the diggers, and especially not these two. He ordered all his warriors to remain in camp except for the three pairs of scouts that he sent in other directions, just to be sure this was not a trick to capture their attention. He and Two Crows mounted their best horses and rode out to meet these two foolish men.

Three miles out, they saw the two white men far across the prairie, each leading a packhorse. Even at that distance, they both knew who it was. What could these two want? They rode forward cautiously, looking around for any sign of a trap, speaking quietly about why these two would come to the Buffalo Eaters' camp. By the time they had crossed the wide plain they had agreed that neither knew, and since Comanches never guess at anything, it remained a mystery.

As the two parties approached one another, the big man held up his hand, palm outward, in a sign of openness and peace. Yellow Wolf held his hand out in a similar fashion. They rode to within ten feet of one another and stopped, looking each other over.

Logan said, "We have come to talk about peace with the Buffalo Eaters." He sat tall in the saddle. Yellow Wolf remained expressionless. The fact that he had not ridden away or tried to kill these two was proof enough that he would listen to what they had to say. This however was not the right place. Any talking of importance always took place in Black Elk's lodge with a lit pipe to bind genuine intentions. Two Crows knew this and with a brief hand signal told them they would go to the camp. Without further acknowledgement, Yellow Wolf turned his horse and began riding back toward the camp.

They rode in silence, and as they approached the camp, several of the older warriors rode out to meet them. No word was spoken by Yellow Wolf or Two Crows. The other warriors rode directly to Logan and Will. All had menacing looks on their faces and two even attempted to stop them by riding directly in front of their horses. Logan and Will were both prepared, and as the Comanche warriors approached, they kicked up their horses and shouldered their way through, forcing the war ponies to hop and dance out of the way. Without looking back, Yellow Wolf smiled slightly as they rode on. They stopped at Black Elk's lodge, but did not dismount. Doing so without an invitation would have been bad manners. Only Two Crows dismounted. He cleared his throat and went in. Shortly he and Black Elk both stepped back out into the sun. Taller than Will, but not quite as tall as

Logan, Black Elk was an imposing figure. His eyes were very piercing and his handsome face told all who looked upon it to speak truthfully, for he would know the difference. He wore the horns of a very large buffalo in his headdress. He moved forward and looked the two men over carefully. He had heard of the warrior with the big medicine knife. Finally he stepped back and indicated that they should come inside. Two young boys appeared from nowhere, at Yellow Wolf's signal, and took the reins from Logan and Will. They would hold the horses there. Logan and Will were both sure that no matter what else happened, those two boys would keep horses and gear alike secure and untouched.

All five men stooped into the dim lodge. It was smoky and smelled of cooked meat, fur, and sweat. The combination was very earthy, but not unpleasant. Both Logan and Will found it vaguely familiar, somehow. Black Elk indicated that they should sit beside a small fire pit. It was used for light and warmth, while another pit set to the side a few feet was used for cooking.

It would have been improper to offer a pipe until the strangers stated their intentions, so all five sat in silence. After a rather long time, Two Crows finally spoke up.

"You must speak your heart," he said to Logan. Logan sat silent for a moment longer.

"We have come to speak with the Buffalo Eaters about peace," He said, looking first at Yellow Wolf and then at Black Elk. Two Crows did not translate so Logan and Will assumed all at least understood his words. They sat as if measuring him up, yet again.

Yellow Wolf spoke. "Why you come here?" Logan and Will looked at each other puzzled. "Not wanted," he added. Logan understood.

"We came here to raise families and cattle," he said, and after a pause added, "We didn't come to fight Comanches, Kiowa, or Apaches." Black Elk turned to Yellow Wolf and said something Logan couldn't understand.

Yellow Wolf thought about it and said to Logan, "Why come here, why not other place? Why not leave?" His expression was one of open curiosity. With all that had happened, he was truly curious as to why these White Diggers didn't just leave. The Buffalo Eaters and Honey Eaters had proven that the White Diggers could not stand against the Comanches. Logan thought long; he knew his words must be picked well.

"We know the Comanches are the Lords of the Southern Plains and want to be friends with them. We know we crowd into your land without asking. My people are rude for not speaking with the Buffalo Eaters and the Honey Eaters, and all the other camps before coming onto this land." Yellow Wolf didn't understand the word 'rude' and asked Two Crows about it. The briefest shadow of a smile swept over his face. Logan went on, indicating him and Will. "We didn't know better. We are asking Yellow Wolf if we can live on this land in peace." He let them chew on this for just a brief moment then added, "We believe we can live beside the Comanche without war, but we will not go, except on the wind." Will's head snapped around to look at him. It was risky business, implying a threat to any Comanche, especially this one. He watched their expressions for any clues as to what they were thinking. They were inscrutable, one and all. "We have brought gifts to show Yellow Wolf we speak the truth." All three sat without movement or expression. Logan wasn't sure what to say. "We only want to round up the wild longhorns and raise our children here, in peace." Yellow Wolf sat for a moment then leaned toward Black Elk and talked slowly in Comanche. They kept it up for a few moments, and then Two Crows added something.

When they had finished, Yellow Wolf asked, "You speak for other White Diggers?" Logan and Will were not sure what he meant by White Digger. Two Crows explained it so they understood that *they* were White Diggers.

Logan locked Yellow Wolf's gaze, he said simply. "No" The three just sat and stared at Logan. "I don't speak for any, but myself and my brother," he indicated Will. Not one of them looked away from him. The three Comanches talked at length and finally Two Crows turned to them.

"It is decided that the Buffalo Eaters will not make war with Piapuha Nahuu or his Tami. Your children may live here also. You will give gifts of the cattle meat in winter if Yellow Wolf so asks and you will not make war with any Comanche. Yellow Wolf and Black Elk do not speak for any other camp, but in the Buffalo Eaters camp you are friends." Logan was curious and asked what Piapuha Nahuu meant.

"It is the name all the Nʉmʉnʉʉ call the big warrior with the big knife. Piapuha Nahuu, it is Big Medicine Knife." Two Crows indicated Will and added, "this one is Tami, the Smaller Brother." Will and Logan sat a moment trying to memorize the names Yellow Wolf had told them. All three sat for a moment longer and when it became apparent the White Diggers didn't know proper etiquette Two Crows added "Gifts now, smoke after." Logan held out his hand as if to shake, all three sat looking at it. Yellow Wolf reached out and grasped his forearm, then Black Elk, and finally Two Crows. All three repeated it with Will. Will stood and went out to retrieve the gifts they had brought.

Knowing that the Buffalo Eaters had just taken many thousands of dollars in goods from Victoria and Linnville, Logan and Will were unsure as to what they might offer that Yellow Wolf would like. Little did they know that almost anything would have been suitable. They settled on several very nice bridles, many blankets, and half a dozen very well made knives. The blankets were offered first and accepted graciously. The new bridles, with finely tooled leather and silver conchos, were accepted with more enthusiasm, but the fine knives were obviously appreciated the most. Yellow Wolf stood, still holding his new knife, and held his hand out to Logan. He and Will both stood, and grasped his forearm.

At this point, Black Elk produced a very long and beautifully adorned pipe made of smooth rust colored pipestone. He packed it with a pungent leaf, lit it, and handed it to Logan. Logan took a long drag on the pipe and inhaled only slightly. His lungs felt as though he'd inhaled pure fire, but he didn't allow himself to cough. Will followed suit and then passed the pipe to Yellow Wolf, who drew long and inhaled deeply, before passing it to Two Crows. It was settled; there would be no war between them. As Logan and Will got up to leave Two Crows put out his hand to stop them. His look was mischievous.

"Now we dance," he said solemnly. Logan and Will looked at each other, and then nodded as graciously as they could and sat back down. Two Crows stepped outside and called to someone. They could hear people running and Two Crows speaking in Comanche. When he finished there was a loud whoop followed by the sound of many more feet running and much shouting. Black Elk lit the pipe again and Logan and Will settled in for a while. The celebration went long into the night with many more gifts exchanged between the elders and the more favored warriors. Two Crows was very helpful. He not only translated the words, but he also kept them from unknowingly committing any social offenses. He would nod or shake his head appropriately to let them know if a gift was expected. Several times he indicated the type of gift required. By moonset, Logan and Will had eaten enough buffalo to gorge a pack of hungry wolves, given every gift in their packs, received almost as many in return, and finally had made fools of themselves by trying to dance with people that had spent their lives expressing themselves, praying, worshipping and celebrating with dance. Neither attempted singing. It seemed they had just crawled into their blankets, when Two Crows cleared his throat outside their flap and informed them that Yellow Wolf was waiting to go hunting with them. Logan was anxious to get home, but knew better than to let on for fear of offending their newly made friends. They rolled out into the predawn darkness and gathered their gear quickly. Years on the trail Rangerin' had taught them to come fully awake at any time of day, and function as if fully rested.

He and Will got ready quickly, and Yellow Wolf seemed less gruff once they started off. Logan figured that Yellow Wolf could probably get as cranky as a stepped-on rattlesnake if he was kept waiting long. He was right.

As they mounted up, Two Crows sidled past him and mumbled, "Good you come soon. Yellow Wolf doesn't like hunting with a short shadow." They spent the next two days hunting, visiting, and getting to know many of the Buffalo Eaters. Will recognized The One Bullets Could Not Kill from the Plum Creek fight. He asked the warrior about the bullets he'd been hit with and sat for almost a full hour while three different warriors, and The One Bullets Could Not Kill, told the story in great detail from different points of view. The man recognized Will and admitted that Will had counted coupe on him. Several other warriors chimed in admitting that he had counted coupe on them also. His status in the camp was rising by the moment. Afterwards, The One Bullets Could Not Kill asked him to tell the story of The Big Medicine Knife and the battle at the buffalo swamp. Will told a version that was so embellished it would have made Logan run for cover from embarrassment if he'd heard it. Two Crows translated it and added some embellishments himself. After all, he too had seen the battle and felt it appropriate. Will figured it was good if they were awed by Logan. He knew word would spread among the other camps, and soon no Comanche anywhere would risk the wrath of a warrior that had conquered death and come back to fight again. Besides, The Big Medicine Knife was already well known; after all, he had choked Yellow Wolf. On the fourth morning Will and Logan displayed their grasp of Comanche decorum and left for home. There was no sense overstaying their welcome. Most of the camp came to see them off and watched them travel across the prairie long after they had left the camp. It wasn't often they got to rub elbows with someone who had conquered death. They would sing of this for many years.

During the first day of their trip back home, Will and Logan spoke little. Both were caught up in their own thoughts. They had gone to the camp knowing that they had a better chance of being killed on sight than being welcomed, and as such, had left feeling quite confused. There was one thing they had to admit; Comanches were not what they expected. Their fear and confusion had turned to relief, understanding, and finally happiness and actual friendship. They felt drained the first night on the trail back, and both had gone to sleep early and slept sound. In the morning, both felt they had a clearer picture of life on the southern plains.

❧

The next few years seemed to glide by for the Vandeveers and the Magills. From 1840 to 1849, Logan and Lucinda had six more children. Their second, Mary, their third (who was their first son), Logan had named William Harrison, after his lifelong friend, the fourth was Andrew, then Sarah, Emma, and Lucinda, born respectively. Logan and Will spent the years rounding up longhorns on the ranch and bandits on the range. They continued Rangerin', but would not fight the Comanches. Twice, they were able to talk Captain Boales out of a full-scale battle with the Comanches over some stolen stock. It had cost Logan twenty head of cattle and three good horses, in exchange for the three horses stolen, to keep the peace. Relations with the different tribes and camps in Texas were strained to the breaking point already; one more battle would have just caused another war. Something no one needed. In the end, they lived relatively peaceful lives. Logan, always on the lookout for any opportunity, had acquired a beef contract for Fort Croghan just west of the ranch. In 1847, Calvin Boales retired from the Rangers and Logan and Will were transferred to another troop of Rangers under Captain Henry E. McCulloch.

McCulloch was an experienced Indian fighter, and because of this, the troop spent much of their time watching and tracking the Comanches, Kiowas, and Apaches in the area. Logan and Will were both uncomfortable with this, having given their word of bond to Yellow Wolf not to make war with any Comanches. They only had two scrapes with Indians during this time, and both were with Kiowas, but they knew the day would come. So in December of 1848, they both mustered out of the Rangers.

During this same time, Will and Rebecca had been keeping pace with Logan and Lucinda, and had six more children. Their second born was James, followed by William Harrison Jr., twins Thomas and Louise, Samuel, and finally John. Life was hard with seven children each, but these were pioneers of Texas and they rose to the occasion. Houses were built, ranches were stocked, and businesses flourished. Logan and Will took an active interest in their home community, and thus were involved in all manner of public affairs. It was apparent that they would make their everlasting mark on the territory, and several of Bastrop's citizens were heard to say that Logan might someday be President of The Republic of Texas. Logan got red in the face and dismissed it as idle fantasy the first time he heard it, and would never speak of it with anyone after that.

Then in the summer 1848, Logan and Lucinda's lives were shattered by the death of their oldest son, William Harrison. He had been in the back lot playing with grasshoppers. He would chase them as they flew, and then dive onto them to catch them as they hit the ground. Being a typical five-year-old boy, he didn't pay much attention to where they lead him. Soon he ended up on the bank of the Colorado. It was wide and deep there and the banks were dotted with stones worn smooth from the flow. He hopped onto the closest and jumped to the next so he could catch a big yellow winged hopper that had flown across a marshy area. When little Will's foot hit the second stone, it slid on the smooth surface as if it were ice, and both feet shot from under him, sending him down with tremendous force. They found him in the afternoon lying next to the big stone, his blood still covering it. He was buried in the little cemetery near the house. Logan tried to spend as much time near the house as he could, for Lucinda and the other children's sake, but he had many irons in the fire, so he was hard pressed. However, he had no idea how hard pressed he would be, or how soon it would come.

Two months later, their second son, Andrew, died. Logan and Will had decided to take both families out gathering firewood for the winter and thought a picnic was in order, so they packed a lunch, some saws, axes, all the children, and then stopped to pick up Dr. Mayes for good measure. They drove the old freight wagon Will had gotten in a trade so they could get enough wood to make it worthwhile. Will knew of a small watershed not far out of town with a nice stand of oak and a five-acre grass park. It was perfect for gathering wood and having a picnic. When they got there, everybody split up into groups and started gathering the dead dry limbs that were so abundant beneath the old stand of oaks. Andrew was a serious boy, and even though he was only three, he picked up limb after limb, depositing them near the wagon for Will and Dr. Mayes to cut with the saws. They all worked hard that morning and had made a real dent in the empty space the freight wagon afforded, when Rebecca called them for lunch. Everyone had gathered around to wash up when Lucinda noticed Andrew was missing. Logan thought he'd seen him picking up limbs on the east side of the watershed, and had just started to go gather him up, when Andrew came around a big oak toward them. Logan turned to go back to the wash-basin when he heard Lucinda gasp. He spun around to see Andrew lying face down in the grass. They all ran to him and when Logan turned him over his lips were starting to turn blue and he was pale, gasping for breath. Dr. Mayes crowded in and looked him over quickly, but saw nothing.

"Get my bag out of the wagon." He said to no one in particular. Will's son William Jr. ran for it. Dr. Mayes ripped the boy's shirt open and as he lifted him to pull it off he noticed the two small puncture wounds above Andrew's left elbow. Quickly he lifted the boy's undershirt and there were four more pairs of identical punctures. Dr. Mayes' shoulders slumped. He knew that as small as Andrew was, there was little that could be done. Groups of puncture wounds like this meant only one thing, Copperheads. Andrew had unwittingly uncovered a nest and was paying the price for the disturbance. Dr. Mayes looked up at Logan and Lucinda with sorrow and pleading in his eyes.

Please don't make me say it, he thought to himself, but he knew he had to.

"Snake bite," he said. "With this many bites, it's likely Copperheads." William Jr. ran up with the bag, but when Dr. Mayes knelt beside Andrew again he saw that the boy's lips had turned even bluer. His eyes fluttered shut and he was barely breathing. Dr. Mayes knew it was just a matter of minutes. He put his ear to the boy's chest and listened for the heartbeat. It was very faint and erratic. Dr. Mayes tried to look like he was doing something to help the boy, but he knew there was nothing that could be done. Within two minutes, Andrew's breath stopped and Lucinda collapsed. Will picked up Andrew carefully and carried him to the wagon while Logan carried Lucinda. Logan knew that life in Texas was tough, but it was especially hard for him to bury both his sons.

Death was suddenly no stranger to the Vandeveer family and in October of 1849, it came to their home yet again, casting its eye on their youngest daughter, named Lucinda. Whooping cough took her at just seven months. Logan was saddened beyond reason. Little Lucinda looked so much like her mother that he had become quickly and completely attached to her, seeing her mother come out in her more and more each day. When the baby died, it was more than Lucinda could handle, and she was unable to get past it. She began to lose weight, which she could not afford, slept little or not at all, and found herself crying for no apparent reason. Sometimes weeks would go by without so much as a smile crossing her lips, and all the while she was becoming paler and thinner. Logan was worried about her and tried to talk to her about it, but she would break down and sob uncontrollably, so he decided to just give her some time. He talked to her father about it, but aside from some laudanum, which was nearly impossible to get, there wasn't much he could do to help. As a dentist, death was something he was untrained for. As pioneers in Texas, it was something they all faced more often than anyone cared for. It was a part of life here, but it was especially difficult when it hit the family.

In June 1850, Will's father, Samuel and mother, Nancy Shackleford Magill, arrived in Bastrop. It was a time of celebration for both Will and Logan, as they were as much Logan's family as his own parents.

Around this same time, while Will and Logan were just about ready to run twenty head of longhorns up to Fort Croghan, something else happened. Logan looked out across the range to see his oldest daughter Eliza riding toward them. It wasn't unusual for her to come out, but it was unusual for her to come out alone. Logan felt his anger rising, wondering who would let a young girl ride out here alone. He would see about it when he got back, and there would be hell to pay. When she got closer, all his anger evaporated. He could tell something was wrong. Her horse was lathered and done in, and her eyes red and swollen from crying.

"Eliza? What is it? What's happened girl?" he asked, sweeping her from the horse and setting her on her feet. She was distraught and started to cry uncontrollably. He held her to him and tried to comfort her. "Tell me, what is it?" he asked again, his frustration starting to mount.

Finally the sobbing began to lessen and she looked into his face. "It's Mama!" she sobbed. "She collapsed. I think she's dyin' Papa." The sobbing started again. Will began shouting orders to the hired hands while he tightened the cinches on his and Logan's saddles.

"Jose'!" he called to one of the cowboys tending the horses. "Bring that sorrel mare out, and get her ready for Eliza. Her horse is done in." The man scrambled over the fence and had the horse saddled and ready in moments. As he led her out, Eliza tried to tell them what had happened.

Between gasps the story came out "She was scrubbin' clothes and all of a sudden she stopped and she got this far away look in her eyes, like she was daydreamin', but you know Mama, she never daydreams. Her eyes glassed over then she dropped the brush and fell down on the floor spillin' the washtub all over. I sent Sarah to get Grandpa and he put her on the bed and checked her over." Eliza was shaking almost uncontrollably now and the words came out in gasps, "Oh Papa! There's somethin' bad wrong with her and I'm afraid she's gonna' die." Logan loaded her onto the long legged sorrel. It was the only horse there that could keep up with his buckskin and the Medicine Hat pony Will had gotten from Black Elk. All three raced the twenty miles back to the house nonstop. When they got to Logan's house, their horses were heaving and lathered. Will's oldest boy, William Jr., was waiting in the yard to take the horses. Logan rushed into the house and found Dr. Mayes sitting beside the bed holding Lucinda's hand. She looked wan and pale. The left side of her face was flaccid and seemed to sag, as if it would fall off onto the bed. Logan came up on the other side of the bed and took her hand.

"Lucinda. Honey, I'm here. Lucinda." There was no response. "Lucinda. Lucinda!" he was worried. Why didn't she at least look at him? Her eyes were open. Was she dead already?

Dr. Mayes laid her hand onto her stomach and stood. "I don't know if she can hear you Logan. She's had a stroke, a bad one." He took off his glasses and began cleaning them on a white handkerchief from his vest pocket. "There isn't anything we can do right now... except pray for her," he said, looking up at Logan and then over at Will. "Nobody knows much about these things. They come on hard and some folks recover as if nothin' ever happened, but some never do get over it.

The bad ones sometimes kill a body outright, or maybe later. No one can say what will happen, save for God himself." He put the wire-rimmed glasses back on and wiped the sweat from his forehead. "I've done all I can here. Tomorrow we may know more. I'll stay through the night," he said, as he went outside to have a smoke. Logan would normally have objected to putting anyone out, but this was Dr. Mayes' only daughter so he just nodded and put his hand on the old man's shoulder. Their eyes met and Logan knew what Dr. Mayes wasn't saying. It was bad. The worst he had ever seen. Logan's heart sank.

Eliza sat down beside her mother and began to cry again. "Oh Mama, please wake up. Please Mama," she begged. Logan put his hand on her shoulder and looked down at the ghost of a woman lying there. He had loved her from the moment he'd laid eyes on her, and looking down, seeing her like this made him feel like his heart was being torn out. He needed to stay strong for the children, but the pain in his chest was so bad he could hardly breathe. She had been in poor spirits since William had died and her health began to go downhill after they buried Andrew. When baby Lucinda died, her outward appearance took a shocking turn for the worse. He had lain awake many nights worrying about her. She kept telling him she was fine, but he knew she wasn't. Logan sat on the other side of the bed and held her hand late into the night. Long after Eliza had given in to exhaustion and gone to bed, he stayed and held onto her, and he did something he rarely ever did. He prayed. He prayed, pleaded, and even begged God, and any other spirit that might give him a sympathetic ear to give her back to him, to them all. None of his prayers were answered. In the early hours of the morning he dozed off, still holding onto her hand. He was startled awake when she weakly squeezed his hand.

He leaned forward. "I'm here," he said quietly. "I'm right here. We're all awful worried about you." Her eyes weren't glazed anymore. He could tell she was alert and he leaned over and kissed her.

"Tell the children I love them," she whispered so softly that if he hadn't been that close he wouldn't have been able to hear it. "And know that I love you, too." It was very difficult for her to speak, even in a faint whisper. "Always have, from the first time I saw you I loved you." Tears dripped from his nose onto her neck. "Take care of our babies," she whispered, and then she shuddered slightly and was gone. He held her tightly and cried into her hair. He was at a total loss as to what to do. He blew out the lamp and just sat for a long time, holding her hand and talking to her in the dark like he used to.

The funeral was the next day. She was buried in a small plot not far from the house.

Logan had nearly seventeen hundred acres that he ranched, but instead of living on the ranch, he had built their home in town. He hadn't wanted Lucinda and the children to be so isolated. Even though he'd made peace with the Buffalo Eaters, he didn't enjoy that arrangement with the numerous other bad men roaming the territory. There were bandits, killers, Kiowas, Apaches, and several other Comanche camps in the area, and he wanted the safety of the little town for his family.

It didn't take long for the ache in Logan's heart to drive him to make a change. Every day the house was a painful reminder of the life that had been so tragically stolen from them. So in August, he began building a new house in the small settlement out to the west, near Ft. Croghan, called Hamilton. In February 1851, Logan moved his family to the new house.

Will and Rebecca talked it over and decided that a move might be good for them too, so they built a house next to Logan's and moved in a month after he did. Rebecca tried to help Logan with the children as much as possible, but with seven children of her own, it wasn't easy. Even though she never complained, Logan knew how hard it was for her, and he was determined not to be a burden. So, he put in less and less time at the ranch. He and Will had four full-time Texian cowboys and two Mexican Vaqueros to roundup and handle the cattle, as well as the best Caballero in Texas and Mexico to tend the horses, of which they were accumulating a fair sized herd. Will did his best to pick up the slack for his friend and encouraged Logan to spend more time with his girls.

Two Crows had been on the trail for many days. He had gone to the northwest to hunt, but he wasn't hunting an animal. He was hunting a vision. For three nights before he had left the camp of the Buffalo Eaters, he had dreamt of a place looking over a small river. At first he thought little of it, but on the second night he had dreamt of taking the trail to the northwest, traveling far over the Brazos and coming to a place overlooking the small river. On the third night he seemed to be guided by a voice telling him to hurry. At every turn the voice was there: *hurry... hurry.*

On the morning after the third dream he went to speak with Black Elk. They smoked on it, and it was decided that he must follow this voice, and that it would lead him to a vision. He packed his traveling pack, a new bow, a quiver of new arrows, some special paint, and some leaf that Black Elk had given him to smoke and prepare for the vision. When he was all packed he went to tell Yellow Wolf, who listened to his story and nodded glumly. He and Two Crows were to go hunting for the fat turkeys that were so plentiful this time of year. They had wanted to eat the meat of a turkey for a while, and decided that now would be a good time. The voices in a dream could not be denied. Two Crows must go. He would have offered to go along, but Two Crows would have only refused him because he was not included in the dream.

Two Crows headed northwest and travelled quickly. Never so hard as to wear out his favorite Medicine Hat pony, but he crossed many streams and prairies in just a few days. Still he continued on. Twice while on the trail he had the same dream again, and would rise early and ride hard all day. He began to worry more and more about his pony, but the second night he had the dream the voice comforted him and told him that his pony was a blessed Medicine Hat, and would gain power from the trail of a vision. He no longer worried, and the pony seemed to get stronger every day. Finally, he crossed the Brazos. He slowed and surveyed the area, then camped under a large pecan tree. He gathered many pecans to render oil for his skin. He would burn the shells to purify his body for the vision. That night he washed himself in the Brazos and began to prepare for the vision. It wasn't time yet, but soon.

At sundown the next day, he rode up onto a small mesa and looked north where he saw the small river from his dream. He would camp here and finish his preparations. When his horse was rubbed down and smudged with sage and cedar, he began to cleanse himself. He had not eaten for the full waning of the moon and his senses were heightened. He heard things he could not normally hear and smelled things he had never smelled before. It was the night of the dark moon and he must be ready. He rubbed the pecan oil over himself and threw some of the shells on the small fire, then swept the smoke over his body to drive out anything bad that may be hiding there. He felt cleansed and his senses were very high. He prepared the pipe with the leaf Black Elk had given

him. It had an earthy odor and he could smell the mush-
room powder and cedar bark that was mixed into it. He
smoked the pipe, making sure to sweep the smoke over
his head, and then sat looking over the darkened river.
For a long time he felt and saw nothing, until all at once
he noticed that he truly felt nothing, not even his weight
on the stony mesa. He seemed to be floating above the
ground, and as he looked down, he saw as the crow sees.
His vision followed the river as if he were flying among the
trees. It was much lighter than he would have expected,
since the moon was dark this night. He flew along the
river in his crow's eye. Then he saw it; a glimmer, small
at first, but suddenly so bright it nearly blinded him. It
was a fire, a campfire. He rose above the fire and could
see many men below, men of different tribes. Some were
Comanche, some Kiowa, some Mexican, and there were
even some Apaches and several White Diggers. Suddenly
one of the men's movements caught his attention. It was
no great movement, and Two Crows couldn't understand why it would be so remarkable to him, until he saw
who this man was. He felt anger, fear, hatred, and fatigue
because of this man. He watched as the group of men
slept. Soon the sun was high and they travelled south.
He flew along the ridges and down into the river valleys
and out onto the plains again. He finally came to a village built by Mexicans and White Diggers. It was the one
they call San Antonio. The man was there, in the bright
light of the nearly full moon, working his evil, killing and
deceiving. It was Blue Duck, but he looked different. He

wore a great hump on his back as if he were trying to hide his true face and pretend to be one of the great shaggy buffalo of the plains. It seemed the White Diggers and Mexican couldn't see Blue Duck, but only the great buffalo. Two Crows had no love of the Mexicans or White Diggers, but he saw what was happening. Blue Duck was working his own evil in the name of all the Comanches. The men took captives and fled in different directions. Some went north, some west and some east. He didn't understand why he couldn't tell which way Blue Duck went, but the larger group went east. That must be the way. This would cause many women to cover themselves in ashes and cut their arms in grief. Now he understood part of the vision. As he watched below, he was suddenly wrenched backward over the ridges and rivers to the mesa above the small river.

He was startled awake and realized that he had only been gone a short while. There were still embers in his fire ring. He built the fire up a little then drank some water. He sat and cleared his head while he ate some dried meat. In the morning he would turn back southeast to speak with Black Elk and Yellow Wolf.

His return trip was just as rapid. He was back at Yellow Wolf's lodge two days before the moon was full and told him and Black Elk of his vision. Black Elk spoke of his sincerity and said the vision was true. Yellow Wolf asked Two Crows what the great hump on Blue Duck's back meant. Two Crows didn't know.

After a short reflection Black Elk spoke. "Blue Duck is hiding behind his father," he said looking solemnly at Two Crows and then Yellow Wolf. "He hopes to make the stupid White Diggers see only Buffalo Hump, not Blue Duck. He hates the White Diggers as we all do, but he fears them, and because of this, his hatred reaches inside his own belly." Yellow Wolf and Two Crows understood very well what Black Elk meant by his hatred reaching into his own belly. Blue Duck hated himself for many things, but his fear of the White Diggers was something he hated most of all. He advised Yellow Wolf to heed the vision and hunt these deceivers that would bring the anger of many people into their camp. Yellow Wolf agreed; this was something that could not be tolerated. He must try to stop Blue Duck from visiting sorrow upon the Buffalo Eaters and the other camps in the area. Yellow Wolf sent two riders to tell the Honey Eaters of Two Crows' vision. Before the sun had moved the shadows more than the span of a hand, Yellow Wolf and twenty of his most experienced warriors were ready to ride south and hunt this whelp of a devil that shamed Comanches everywhere.

CHAPTER 11

RENEGADES IN SAN ANTONE

Early in the spring of 1851, Logan's father, William, his sister Anna Baber, and his brother Zachary finally moved to Texas. Now almost all the family was in Texas. Besides the comfort of living in the bosom of a large family, it took a huge load off of Logan and Rebecca, as all three jumped right in and helped with the children.

In the same year Logan got another contract with the army to supply cattle to Fort Mason, fifty miles to the west. His cattle business was going better than he could have hoped. Will and his brother Zachary ran the business, so it required little attention from him. He had time to spend with his children and other family members, and was regularly at Will and Rebecca's playing with their children as well. He thought often of Lucinda and the three children that had died, and whenever he did he would gather his four girls together and they would spend time enjoying each other's company. Later in life his daughters would remark about what a good and loving father Logan was. Never did they feel neglected or want for anything that he couldn't provide. Logan sold the ranch near Bastrop, bought 1100 acres near Hamilton, and moved the ranching operation there. Since they lived close to the ranch now he was home every night and to the girls' delight they were constantly in his eye.

Still, something seemed to be missing in his life. He couldn't put his finger on it, but it was missing, nonetheless.

In early summer of 1851 he finally found something that captured his attention, public affairs. With the ranch running smoothly and in no great need of his constant attention, Logan began to focus on several other things. He started talking about building a church and a schoolhouse. He knew that without these two essentials the town would not prosper. He threw himself into these projects to keep his mind off his sorrows. He got involved with a petition to have the area they lived in designated a new county called Burnet County. There was much opposition to it, but Logan saw the value in doing so. Hamilton was isolated, and it would give them an opportunity to establish a resource pool that wasn't available to them otherwise. Within three months he had explained it to enough of his neighbors and gotten enough signatures that he was able to present the petition in Austin, and

Burnet County was born. He became a man possessed. He offered up all manner of assistance to any person or organization that seemed to need it. He helped Will obtain a local mill, started building a church, and was closing in on realizing his plan for a school.

Since there was no bank in Hamilton he decided that it was time they had one, so off he went to San Antonio to see if he could interest one of the three bank owners there to invest in Hamilton.

Although there were still many hostilities between the Texans and Comanches, Logan rarely felt uncomfortable traveling. It was just after sunset on a warm summer day when he rode into San Antonio. He took his normal route and approached the Council Hall from the rear and was just entering the Market Square. He thought he might come back to the square after he got settled at the hotel. He preferred to look around after sunset when it was cooler and much more pleasant. Maybe he could find something special for the children, and by children, he meant not only his children, but Will and Rebecca's, his sister Ana's, his brother Zachary's, and any number of other children in the area. He had become sort of an adopted father to many of the children in or near Hamilton whether they were white, Mexican, Comanche, or Kiowa.

As he rode around the edge of the market square a shot rang out very close by. His horse shied and Logan was almost unseated. He grabbed the saddle horn and quieted the horse, then more shots rang out. He kicked the horse up to get out of the square. The echo in the square made it impossible to tell where the shots were coming from so he tried to dodge his horse through the scattering crowd of people and into a space between two buildings. People were panicked, running everywhere, and he was driven off to the side of the market near the Council Hall. It's high windows were brightly lit in the early darkness of the evening. If he'd had more time to think about it this would have struck him as peculiar. The Council Hall was rarely used at night. Instead, something else struck him.

There was shouting and more gunfire, but before he could pull his pistol something heavy hit him from behind. Suddenly, there was an arm around his throat and he heard a whoop behind him. A Comanche had jumped from one of the windows in the Council Hall onto the back of his horse and was trying to throw Logan off the big buckskin. Logan kicked up the horse and almost unseated his assailant, but the Comanche regained his balance and Logan knew he was there for good. Logan began to run the horse around the Market Square while the two men struggled with each other. Neither could get to a weapon, as they were holding onto each other's wrists. On the third pass around the square Logan saw Mitchell Putman step out onto the porch of a hotel. Seeing what was happening, Putman pulled out his powder flask and charged his rifle, but by the time he lifted it Logan and the Comanche were on the opposite side of the market place. None of the lamps were lit yet and it was getting very dark, but old Mitchell raised his rifle, took aim, and shot the Comanche through the head at a dead run. The Comanche fell from the back of Logan's horse while Logan struggled to get the frightened animal under control. He dismounted in order to take a closer look at the Comanche just as Mr. Putman came running up. In the time it took him to run across the Market Square he had reloaded his rifle and was charging it again.

Logan stood up from the dead man. "He's dead. Shot through the head." He looked in amazement at Mitchell Putman.

"Through the left ear I 'spect," Mitchell said, as he stood looking at Logan. "Leastwise that's where I aimed for. He had you in a pickle, son." More shots rang out. Logan and Mitchell both dropped to the ground and ran low toward to the shadow of a nearby building. They ducked into the shadow and stood peering out. "What in the hell is goin' on?" Logan asked, peering into the dark.

Mitchell Putman shook his head. "Peace talks," he said flatly.

Logan's eyes went wide and he looked surprised, then he said, "I reckon they still don't understand that killin' each other ain't the basis for peace." Mitchell paused and looked over at Logan quickly.

The shooting and shouting went on for a few minutes more. When it began to die down the two men eased out of the shadow. Logan went toward the Council Hall. He was determined not to stand by and let another travesty occur like the one that had taken place in this very same building back in '39. As he approached he expected to see more soldiers than were actually there. There was also a distinct lack of dead, wounded, or captive Comanches by comparison. A young corporal was tending several wounded soldiers and giving orders to three or four other privates. Logan asked if he needed help and the corporal stopped what he was doing and looked Logan over well. Logan was impressed. Here was a young man that was actually taking the time to use his good common sense.

After he had made his judgments he said, "Thank you sir. I could use a hand getting' this bleeding stopped." It wasn't exactly what Logan had in mind, but if it was what was needed, then it was what he would do. He pulled his kerchief from his neck and wadded it up tightly, pressing it into a four-inch long knife wound in the prostrate soldier's side. He was able to staunch the flow relatively quickly.

"What happened here Corporal?" he asked, glancing at the young man.

The corporal looked at Logan for a moment before answering.

"Some of what we thought were Buffalo Hump's people came to town four days ago saying the old injun wanted to talk peace, so we set up a meeting here for 'em. Everything started off fine, but it didn't take long to see the mistake we'd made." He moved to the next man and began cutting away the man's shirt, exposing a long wound on his back. "Damn!" he said as he probed the depth with his finger.

"Talking peace usually means somebody's gotta' stop killin' the other side. For it to really work, both sides gotta stop," Logan said, feeling anger well up inside. Fire flashed in the young Corporal's eyes.

"Mister, we were there with good intentions. It was the Comanches broke the peace," he said with anger in his voice. "Turns out none of them was Buffalo Hump's people. We don't know who it was, likely some other camp with a grudge against Buffalo Hump, or maybe even renegades." He ripped a piece of the trooper's jacket and stuffed it into the long cut. "We asked when Buffalo Hump would be coming because we didn't want to start without him and these devils all pulled knives and started stabbin' everyone around. I was able to get my pistol out and kill two. That's when they scattered." He looked at Logan again. "I got six men wounded and one dead." The Corporal stood and surveyed the line of wounded lying there then shook his head. "Dammit, but we should have kept 'em outside," he finally said with anguish in his voice.

Logan checked the wounded soldier he was working on. The bleeding had pretty much stopped.

"It's amazing how people think they can demand peace and punish those that don't agree," he said quietly. "I was here the last time they talked peace in this building. It ended similarly and the rest of the territory paid with blood for years after."

When two other privates showed up Logan turned his wounded man over to one of them and stood to leave.

"Thanks, Mister," the Corporal said. "I appreciate your help with the wounded." Logan smiled and turned back to his horse. As he crossed the street he heard a woman screaming. There were other shouts and several shots, followed by the sound of horses running off into the distance. Further away, and more faintly, there was more shouting and one more shot. Confusion reigned in Logan's field of vision. He retrieved his horse, and as he turned toward the hotel, he saw a woman run screaming into the square. She frantically ran up to a soldier. The woman was trying to tell him something, but her sobbing made it difficult to understand. As he approached, Logan thought there was something familiar about this woman, but with all that was happening around, it escaped him. He picked up a couple of words as he approached "…took her…Comanches…help…" but that was all he got. The soldier was distracted by the other wounded soldiers and was paying her little attention. Logan strode up to her, and taking her arms, looked deep into her grief stricken eyes.

"Who was taken?" he commanded. She started to go limp, but he held her up and shook her slightly. It was not his custom to treat a woman so rough, but he needed her to gather her senses. She looked shocked at first then spit it out through frightened lips,

"My daughter! They've taken my daughter!" she started to shake on her own and Logan responded by putting an arm around her. "She was on her way back from the market when we heard shooting," the woman sobbed. "I ran outside and saw her just down the street. She stopped to see what was going on and then we heard shouting. She tried to run to the house, but a Comanche came out into the street on horseback and grabbed her. He came out of nowhere and pulled her up on his horse and was gone before I could do anything." She broke down into deep sobs at this last part. Logan held her tighter for a moment. "Oh please help her, somebody help her!" she cried.

"We'll help her, ma'am, just calm down," he said reassuringly as he began to lead her to a bench on the boardwalk. "Just sit here a minute and tell me, which way did they go?"

Her shoulders shook and she was racked with sobs. He pulled her hands from her face and knelt in front of her.

With a determined face he asked again, "Ma'am! Which way did they go?" Her sobbing abated slightly as she searched this man's eyes.

"North," she finally said. "They went north out of town. Please help her!" she gasped.

Logan looked deep into her eyes again. "I'm gonna go after 'em. I'll do my best ma'am." As he turned to leave, a young soldier came running up, shouting, "Sergeant Grider! Sergeant Grider!" he snapped to attention directly in front of a Sergeant that was assembling his troops nearby and saluted.

"Report Trooper!" the Sergeant snapped.

"We've heard that there were as many as twelve or thirteen captives taken, mostly women, Sergeant," the trooper said, still at attention.

The Sergeant focused his attention on the trooper. "Go on!" This Sergeant was a soldier that tolerated no shirkers. The trooper knew he had better have all the information available before approaching or there would be hell to pay.

"Three groups of Comanches came into town from different directions while the peace talks were going on…" he started.

"Peace talks! It was a god dammed trick to catch us with our guard down!" Sergeant Grider roared.

"Yes sir!" the soldier stood a little straighter. "When the shooting started, the other groups grabbed women all over town. It appears they've headed east Sergeant!"

The sergeant stared hard at the trooper and seemed to chew on this.

"Go get Joe Painted Feather, Red Shirt, and two or three more Tonkaway trackers and get back here as fast as you can. Go!" he shouted, his face just inches from the trooper's. The trooper was gone in an instant. The Sergeant shouted orders and the troopers scattered, gathering gear and horses as they went. Logan walked toward the Sergeant.

"Sergeant, I can help," he said, stepping in front of him. The Sergeant came up short and looked up into the dark and determined eyes of this big stranger. He stepped back and looked Logan up and down.

"This is a job for the Army mister, not a farmer," he said dismissively. He started to step around Logan, but Logan would have none of it.

"My name's Logan Vandeveer. I served under Billingsley at San Jacinto and Rangered with Captain Boales and Captain Ed McCulloch for ten years. I tracked and fought more Comanches and Kiowas than you've ever seen, Sergeant, so I'm goin' after these captives. The question is am I goin' with or without you." He had stepped closer to the Sergeant as he spoke until he was almost on top of him, talking straight down into the Sergeant's face. This didn't sit well with Sergeant Grider.

When he stepped back, his hand was on his pistol. "Mister this is a job for the Army. If I so much as think you're interferin' with this troop I'll shoot you down right here," he hissed.

Logan's hand was already on his knife, and he knew at this range that he had the advantage. "Better men than you have tried. You so much as move an eyelash and you'll find out firsthand why they failed." Logan was speaking low and slow. The tension was thick enough to taste, and several troopers had stopped dead in their tracks when they saw what was happening. Just then, Mitchell Putman stepped up beside Sergeant Grider.

"I wouldn't do that if I was you Sarge. When this man says he's fought more injuns than you've seen he ain't lyin', besides he's got the drop on you with that big knife of his. Why he'll gut you and be gone before you can clear leather." Grider looked down at Logan's hand and for the first time noticed the big knife he wore. His face blanched slightly. "Don't you know who this is?" Putman asked, stepping a half step closer "Why this is the one the injuns call The Big Medicine Knife," he said, trying to break the Sergeant's concentration. "You ain't got a chance Sarge, and you won't do anybody any good by dyin' here tonight." Logan could see the doubt in Grider's eyes. Finally, he stepped back and took his hand off his pistol. He'd heard of The Big Medicine Knife and he didn't know if the stories he'd heard were true or not, but he didn't want to find out.

"This is an Army operation mister; you stay out of the way," he spat then turned and walked to where his troops were assembling with their horses.

Mitchell turned to Logan. "I ain't much good at travellin' fast anymore 'cause of my rheumatiz, but I'll go with you if you want," he offered. The tension in Logan eased noticeably.

"Thank you. I appreciate the offer, especially after seein' the shot you made tonight, but I'll have to travel fast if I've any hope of catchin' up with 'em," he said, offering his hand to Mitchell. "I thank you sir."

"No, thank you son." Mitchell stepped closer, looking hard into Logan's face. "I owe you a debt of gratitude," Mitchell said with a solemn look on his face. "I heard you was involved with Captain Boales in tryin' to rescue my children from Yellow Wolf's camp back in '39."

Logan caught his eye briefly "Yes sir, I was." He peered back out into the square.

"The way I heard it you was sneakin' up through the camp and was just about to steal the Lockhart girl back when we busted outta' the woods and botched ever'thing up," he said, with a lump in his throat. Logan glanced over and just nodded. "You was riskin' your life for my children and we don't hardly know each other. Not many men would do that."

Mitchell took Logan's hand, and as he shook it, he leaned toward Logan and said,

"I think it was Blue Duck started this whole mess." Logan jumped at the name Blue Duck. He kept holding Logan's hand and pulled him a little closer. "I'd heard there was to be some peace talks, so I came to see what the outcome would be, and when I rode into town I thought I saw him ride in between two buildings, but I couldn't be sure. I rode around a while lookin' to see if it was him, but I never saw him again." He let go of Logan's hand and stepped back, looking at Logan.

"God help 'em if it was Blue Duck that took 'em," Logan said. Without another word he swung up onto the big buckskin and started north out of town.

CHAPTER 12

INTO THE BLACK

Logan was lucky when he left San Antonio, the moon was full and bright. It was easy for someone that had tracked as many bad men as he had to follow this trail. It was obvious they weren't trying to hide it. It was almost like they wanted him to follow. This in itself caused his neck hairs to prickle. He was alert to every sound and sight, perhaps going faster than he should have, but he knew if he had any hope of retrieving any captives, he had to catch up to them before they reached the Llano Estacado, or the Staked Plains. It was the worst piece of country on god's good earth: flat, dry, hot, and certain death for anyone foolish enough to follow Blue Duck there. Yep, he would have to catch up before they got that far. He sure wished Will was with him. Will was a better tracker than he was, and Logan knew they could travel faster with two pairs of eyes and ears on alert, but Will wasn't there so it was up to him.

He pushed on, harder and harder, but didn't think he was getting closer to them. It was as if they knew every time he would pick up the pace, and in turn so would they. He rode through the night and could tell the buckskin was tiring. After all, he had ridden from sunup to sundown the day before and then, without more than a few minutes rest, had started on this chase and ridden most of the night. He would have to stop to rest or they would both be done in before they made another twenty miles. He found a heavy thicket that would hide him and the buckskin well and led the horse deep into it. He didn't want to chance getting caught off guard if it was Blue Duck leading this band. He wanted some cover and the thicket gave him plenty. The moon set just as he entered the thicket, so he had to feel for everything. He pulled his saddle and quietly rubbed the buckskin with the saddle blankets to dry the hair, at least a little, then saddled him up again, but left the cinch loose. He felt into his saddlebags and found the small bag of grain he always brought along just in case. Logan held the bag under the horse's nose and it ate hungrily. Logan had let him graze well on the trip down so he was in fairly good shape. The grain would help, but it wouldn't go far. He would have to wait until morning for water. Logan sat with his back to a tree and watched the only opening into the thicket, listening closely to the sounds of the night. There was nothing, so he and the buckskin soon dozed off.

He was dreaming of his girls when a sound woke him. He dreamed they were having a picnic and a herd of buffalo was stampeding toward them. He was startled awake and heard distinct footsteps, creeping very close by. He listened closely. Someone was creeping very slowly just outside the thicket, perhaps looking for the way in. He didn't want to get trapped, so he slowly and silently moved toward the opening. The creeping on the outside was moving the same direction. It took several full minutes of inching his way forward to reach the entrance. He stopped and listened, but heard nothing. The faint grey in the eastern sky told him he'd only slept about an hour, and as he was about to move a little further out into the morning glow, he saw the briefest of movements off to his left. It was almost as if he had thought of a movement, but he remained motionless and waited. There it was again. He hadn't imagined it. He peered through the brush into the receding darkness and could make out the shape of a man crouched about ten feet to his left. Logan couldn't make out any specifics about him, he was just a shadow. He couldn't even tell if he was Comanche, Mexican, or White, but this shadow was creeping around where Logan had slept, so he was up to no good. Logan pulled his knife from its sheath very slowly and held it alongside his leg, lest it reflect any of the new light streaking the sky. He waited as the shadow took two more slow steps toward him. He was tensed and ready to jump. Just one more step and the shadow would be close enough… wait…wait. Just then the big buckskin stomped a foot and the shadow looked over his left shoulder and away from Logan. It was what Logan needed. He sprung like a cat and had the shadow on the ground pinned by his sheer bulk, knife at his throat. It had happened so fast the shadow never had a chance and they had made little noise. With the big knife at his throat the man froze, not moving a muscle.

"If you so much as blink you'll die with your eyes shut," Logan whispered in the man's ear. Logan didn't know if the shadow understood his words, but the shadow's eyes rolled wide and there was agreement in them. They lay for a long moment and Logan listened. There wasn't another sound, so he eased his crushing bear hug and the man took a deep breath. It was getting lighter and Logan could see this was a Kiowa, but a Kiowa with a difference. He wore white men's boots and a paisley shirt with a wide collar. He was a renegade. It was true! Mitchell had seen Blue Duck. Logan's blood ran cold to think of any captives in that devil's camp.

"Do you understand my words?" Logan asked, pressing the tip of the knife against the man's throat, starting a slight trickle of blood. The Kiowa's eyes got bigger and he nodded slowly and very carefully, lest he move under the knife and cut his own throat. "Who are you?" Logan whispered, moving his weight back onto the man to reassert his dominance. "And where is Blue Duck?" The Kiowa's eyes bulged out with the added pressure on his chest. He knew he was but the span of rabbit's hair away from crossing over to meet his ancestors. This big man was not one to lie to.

"I am Raven Walks," he said, gasping. Logan pressed down harder. "Blue Duck is North," he said with the last air in his lungs. He lay still for a moment, but with no air in his lungs a look of panic came over his face. Logan eased up a bit and let him get a little air, but not much. He wanted to control this exchange completely.

"How many renegades are with him?" Logan asked. The Kiowa looked puzzled as if he didn't know what a renegade was. Logan pressed the knife in deeper and the trickle flowed easier.

The man's eyes bugged out even further and there was a look of real fear on his face. "As many as all your fingers and more," he gasped, unable to equate numbers into English. He fought to take another breath, but Logan pressed down and only allowed a little air into his lungs.

"How many captives?" Logan asked, changing position on the knife so that he could start a fresh trickle.

The Kiowa was almost blind with panic now. He wasn't sure if he would bleed to death or suffocate first. Either way he would gladly tell this big man whatever he wanted to know about Blue Duck. He didn't like Blue Duck or his renegade camp anyway. He only rode with them for the glory he had heard they shared. He had counted no coupe nor earned any glory in all the time he had ridden with them. Thieves and killers is all they were, thieves and killers with no honor.

"Less than the fingers of a hand," he gasped. His face was far past red and had begun turning purple. Tears rolled down his cheeks and he started to shake. Logan was just about to roll off and let him breathe when there was a whoop and something heavy hit him from behind. He rolled forward, and as he landed on his back, he thrust upward with his knife, feeling it bite flesh and bone. He continued the upward trust until the knife would go no further. Blood washed over his hand and arm and there was an agonized scream. He rolled to the side and threw the dying renegade onto the ground. He stood up and turned to the other Kiowa, who was still on the ground. The Kiowa raised both hands to indicate that he had no weapon and was not moving. Logan stepped backward slowly so he could see both. The one that had jumped him now lay on his back only moments from death. Logan had caught him just below the belt he carried his knife on and had cut him upward until his own knife had been stopped by one of the man's ribs. Logan had never seen a wound that big, except his own when he had fought at San Jacinto. The renegade gasped one more time, his eyes glassed over and he was gone. The Kiowa looked on in disbelief. He had never seen anyone die that way. He was completely unnerved by it. Suddenly a look of resolve washed over his face and he rolled to a crouching position.

"Don't do it!" Logan warned, but the Kiowa slowly reached down, picked up his own knife, and with a far-away look on his face, began to chant. Logan stood, every muscle tense, waiting. The chanting continued. Logan knew this Kiowa was singing his death song and it would only be a matter of moments before one of them would lie beside the dead renegade. After taking a brief moment to think about the situation, Logan stood up straight and sheathed his own knife, then held his hands out to his sides, palms forward. The Kiowa was surprised; mercy to an enemy was something he knew nothing about. His singing faltered, but he tried to continue. Logan slowly backed away, arms still out. He could see confusion on the Kiowa's face, and his singing broke. He took another step backward, and then another. The Kiowa stopped singing and slowly stood up. He felt shamed by the mercy, but also grateful. He slowly sheathed his own knife and backed away from Logan. When he had backed a good half dozen steps away, he turned and left. He didn't run, but walked quickly out of sight. Logan stood still for a moment longer, listening. There were no other sounds until the sound of a horse running off into the distance to the south. Logan quickly slipped into the thicket, and as he approached the big buckskin, the horse rolled his eyes, not liking the smell of fresh blood on him. Logan calmed him, tightened the cinch, and led him from the thicket. He mounted and turned the big horse north again. Within a mile, they came to the Guadalupe River, and while the buckskin drank, Logan cleaned the blood from his arm. He and the buckskin had gone twenty miles the day before into San Antonio and then set off right away on another trip back north that, so far, had covered

another thirty miles. He knew he couldn't keep pushing the buckskin that hard for much longer. Blue Duck
seemed to be making a beeline north toward Hamilton.
Oh, if only I could be so lucky, Logan thought. If Blue
Duck got close enough to Hamilton for Logan to run in
and get Will and the other Rangers under McCulloch,
Blue Duck's days would come to an end right there. He
crossed the Guadalupe and pushed the buckskin. He
knew a man named Milton Hye that had a ranch about
half way to Hamilton. Logan and Will had worked with
him on roundups in the past. Everybody that knew him
just called him Hye. He could trade horses there, if Blue
Duck didn't steal 'em all first. Logan didn't think that
likely. Blue Duck was moving too fast to sidetrack or do
anything else that might slow him down. He wanted to
get back onto the Llano, the big dry plateau where he
could hide and trade his captives at will, after he had
abused them.

Logan reached Hye's Ranch in the late afternoon.
The buckskin was done in and Logan had even been
forced to get off and walk him up two of the steeper
rises in the afternoon. When Milton Hye greeted him, it
wasn't as warmly as Logan would have liked. He was holding a buffalo gun and looking Logan's horse over as he
spoke.

"Afternoon, Logan," he said, standing back slightly.
He held the big rifle at the ready, his finger on the trigger. It didn't pay to get too close to someone leading a
spent horse. There was a reason they were riding hard,

and sometimes it wasn't a good reason. Even if it was, it could still be dangerous to be too close to them.

"Your ol' hoss looks done in. What brings you this far from home ridin' hard and all?" Hye asked, motioning to the horse with the barrel of the rifle and scanning the tree line for signs of movement. Logan caught the implication and stopped where he was.

"Trackin' a band of renegades, Hye. They took some captives in San Antonio last evening and I've had their trail ever since…until I broke off to come here," Logan said, standing very still.

"Ya' don't say," Hye said slowly. Then, being satisfied no one was after Logan, he stepped aside and motioned him to the hitching rail. "How many captives they get?" he asked, still scanning the tree line as Logan threw his reins over the rail and loosened the cinch.

"Not sure. The bunch I'm after got three or four, but there might be more than one bunch." He lifted the saddle from the buckskin, who gave a sigh of relief. "I'm hopin' to get close enough to 'em that I can run and get Will and some of McCulloch's Rangers up at Hamilton," he said, rubbing the grateful horse with the blanket. He turned to look at Milton Hye. He was a small man, but he had the kind of face that said, "Don't even think of trying to bullshit me." He was a man that had hacked out a three thousand acre ranch and made four cattle drives east to Arkansas fighting off Comanches, Kiowas, Mexican bandits, and cattle rustlers without losing more than a handful of cattle. Small though he was, he was made of pure iron. Logan was glad to be counted as one of his friends. There was a mutual respect between the two.

"That buckskin of yours won't be goin' no further," he said, nodding toward the horse. "Got a big black over to the barn you kin take. He's got stickin' power and he ain't slow," Hye said as he led the way to the barn. "Got him off ol' Morris in a horse race," he added with a grin.

Logan turned and saw the wily grin on Hye's face. "You didn't sucker ol' Francis into a race against that little sorrel mare of yours now, did you Hye?" he asked, grinning back at the little man. Hye just led the big black horse out of the stall and tossed the reins over a rail and the horse stopped.

"He oughtn't to brag about all the great horseflesh he's raised in his life. I just tired of hearin' it," he said, running his hands down the horse's front legs. "Shoot, this long legged black never had a chance against that little fire dancer o' mine. She took him by five lengths and wanted more. This here's a good horse, but he ain't that fast," he finished with a chuckle as he threw a fresh blanket on the black's back. Logan tossed his saddle on and cinched it tight. Milton disappeared while Logan finished. He came back with another set of saddlebags, leading the big buckskin.

"Here's some grub and grain. Hope you catch 'em." He handed the bags to Logan. "Any idea who they are?" he asked as Logan took the bags and started transferring the little bit of food, cartridges, and grain between them.

Logan looked at Hye. "It's Blue Duck and his bunch."

Hye started and acted as if he wanted to go look outside just to see if Blue Duck might be there now.

"Blue Duck! I'd heard he'd been shot by some Ranger down south of San Antonio. Can't remember the fella's name, Kyle, Cole, somethin' like that. Blue Duck caught the man squattin' behind a bush, but the feller got a shot off anyway. Never heard the outcome, just assumed he'd kilt Blue Duck." He was shaking his head. If Logan didn't have the experience with Blue Duck that he did, he might have just assumed Blue Duck to be dead too. He had heard of the run in with one of Captain Inish Skull's men, a young Ranger named Woodrow Call. One of Blue Duck's favorite strategies was to stalk around any white men on the trail and find out where they relieved themselves, then, knowing they would use the same place again, he would lie in wait and shoot them while they squatted. He had tried that with Ranger Call and got a rifle ball for his trouble. This young fella, Call, must be very good to get a shot off like that.

"Are you sure?" Hye asked.

"As sure as the threat of a slit throat can make me, I caught one of his Kiowa boys and persuaded him to tell me." He finished packing the bag and added, "Mitchell Putman thought he saw Blue Duck in San Antonio, but when he tried to find him again he couldn't, so he wasn't sure, till the shootin' started."

"I've got a couple of Vaqueros I could send with you if you want, but I'd have to go get 'em from up on the Pedernales," Milton offered.

"I appreciate that, but I can't wait. They're moving fast and I haven't a minute to lose. I'll bring this horse back to you when I can," he said, leading the big black out of the barn and retightening the cinch. He swung aboard. "You keep a sharp eye out. You can't be too careful with that devil Blue Duck around." Milton Hye just nodded and stood with his rifle in the crook of his arm. Logan kicked up the black to an easy lope and headed back to the trail. He crossed the Pedernales River and started making up some of the time he'd lost. The big black could cover some ground that was for sure. He let him run until the horse started to breathe heavy. He was amazed; they had covered close to five miles at an easy run. He slowed him to a lope and let him go for a while. A couple of miles further on, he pulled him up to a walk. It was obvious the horse wasn't done yet. He wanted the trail. Logan figured he was one of those rare horses that always wanted the trail. Horses like that were a bother when riding with other horses because they can't stand being behind, so it becomes a constant battle of wills to keep them from racing out front. He was glad to have him now though. This horse would run to Canada and back if Logan gave him his head. He wanted him fresh, and he wanted to catch Blue Duck at Hamilton, not before, so he held him back.

He stopped near Grape Creek and let the horse rest. The horse was anxious to get moving, but the sky had clouded over and looked like rain. The moon would be no help tonight. An hour after he stopped it started to rain. There is no rain like the rain in Texas. It seems to come down in buckets. Logan had tied the horse up in a thick grove of oaks. They were not as wet as they might have been other places, but with that kind of rain there was no place they could have gone to stay dry. Because of the cloud cover, it was dark in the morning, so Logan had to wait even longer to get moving than he otherwise would have. When he did get moving, he hoped Blue Duck hadn't moved in the night or turned off just before stopping. At least it wasn't raining now. An hour later, Logan was beginning to worry; he had seen no sign of Blue Duck. Just when he was about to backtrack he spotted their trail off to the west. He got back onto it and let the horse lope on the flat ground. The horse's gait was very smooth. So smooth in fact he made very little sound. It was something that surprised Logan considering the animal's size. He was very graceful. No wonder Francis Morris had so much confidence in him that he bet the horse against Hye's little sorrel mare. To look at them side by side it seemed there was no comparison, but Logan had seen the mare run. She was perhaps the fastest horse he'd ever seen, and long winded too.

Blue Duck couldn't hide his trail now, even if he had wanted to, and he was still heading toward Hamilton. Logan knew that if he lost the trail, Blue Duck would get up onto the Llano Estacado with the captives and they would be lost forever. Just before midday, the trail split, one group went to the west and one continued on north. Logan knew it was a gamble, but he felt sure Blue Duck would keep going north. He always did.

Logan figured Blue Duck would continue north until he crossed the Llano River, then follow the Colorado up to its head water before breaking for the Llano Estacado. However, in the early afternoon the trail he was following took a sharp turn to the northeast. He was going to cross the Colorado at the marshlands instead of going straight north and having to cross the Llano River, which was wide and swift. If Blue Duck crossed over and went to the north side of the Colorado, it would make it easier for Logan to get to Will and the other Rangers.

When the Colorado was behind him he kicked the horse up to a lope, figuring he was only about ten or twelve miles from Hamilton. The cloud cover had broken and the ground would dry out very quickly. He had followed them for about two miles beyond the Colorado when he caught a movement out of the corner of his eye. His pulled the big black in behind a brushy cedar and dismounted. He crawled around the tree and watched for the movement again. It was two riders coming through the cedars, but he couldn't tell any more than that. He was about to get back onto the black and reposition himself when Will rode out from under a lone oak at the edge of the clearing. Behind him rode Noah Smithwick. His luck couldn't be any better, but with Blue Duck this close, he had to be quiet and not give away his position. He cupped his hands around his mouth and gave the "tchew-wew, tchew-wew," of the purple martin. It was a bird Will knew well, and it was a call they had used before. It wasn't loud, but it was loud enough to signal Will without giving himself away.

Will froze in his tracks and Noah followed suit. He sat quietly until Logan repeated the call with an extra "wew" on the end. Will looked in his direction and Logan signaled him to come quietly. Will whispered the same to Noah, and they both dismounted, lead their horses back into the trees, and skirted the clearing over to where Logan was. All three knelt, and Logan told them briefly what had happened. He laid out his plan to ride over, get some of McCulloch's Rangers, and then deal the final blow to Blue Duck.

"Good plan," said Noah. "'Cept'n for the part about McCulloch's Rangers. They pulled out early this mornin'. Headed southwest to bring back captives that were taken west out of San Antone." Logan looked at Will and then back to Noah.

"We're with you Brother. I'd rather have a half dozen of McCulloch's roughnecks with us goin' up against Blue Duck, but it ain't to be. We gotta stop him," Will said pointedly. Logan told them about the trail and that Blue Duck was close. The other two nodded, and then all three mounted up. The sky was clear now and the moon would come out full again that night. With any luck, Blue Duck would stop for the night and they could track him to his camp.

They hadn't gone far when Noah rode quietly up beside Logan and whispered, "I know where that devil's headed." Logan pulled up and leaned closer to Noah.

"There's a cave not far from here up over Backbone Ridge. Injuns been usin' it for years. Bet this ol' grey nag that's where they's headin." Logan thought about it for a moment. He wasn't aware of the cave, but Noah had lived here longer than he and Will, so he motioned Noah to lead the way. He waited for Will and whispered the plan to him.

Noah turned north again, following the trail, and headed up over the steep ridge. If Blue Duck really did go to the cave, they would have to slow down and be very quiet going up the ridge. They topped it in an hour and dropped off the other side. It was almost sundown when Noah stopped behind a big brushy cedar. He motioned them to follow suit. Logan and Will dismounted, and all three crawled under the tree so they could look out on the other side. There was a cave entrance, but no sign of any living thing there. They sat and watched as the sun started to slip behind the horizon. Just as the top dropped out of sight, a single Comanche slipped out from under a nearby tree and went inside. Blue Duck was here…

Logan, Will, and Noah remained flat on their bellies waiting and watching for any movement. The darkness settled in around them and they could see the glimmer of a fire inside the cave. Slowly they made their way back to the other side of the big cedar. They had to move quickly, the moon would rise soon and it would make moving in on the cave much riskier. There was a good chance they would be seen anyway, but with a full moon shining, getting into the cave unseen would be impossible. They circled around to the right, since the cave opening entered on an angle from left to right. It would be harder for someone sitting back in the dark to see them. As they approached the cave mouth slowly, they could see the light of the full moon beginning to show in the sky. They stopped and made a quick plan. All three hated to waste any shots on nothing, but they needed to make the renegades scatter the fire so they could even up the odds a little. On a signal, all three fired into the left wall of the cave mouth. There was shouting and they could hear the bullets ricochet into the cave. Logan hoped they wouldn't hit any of the captives. They saw the flicker of the fire go out and darkness swept over the cave. All three men were up and running into the mouth of the cave and then hit the ground rolling to the side. There was more shouting and a rifle flashed very close to Noah. He turned, knife in hand, and drew first blood from the Kiowa that had fired the shot. The Kiowa groaned in agony as he died. Then another shot sounded from further away. It almost hit Noah, but Will was up and into the inky blackness with Logan right behind. Noah collected his wits and moved a little more slowly. Will got to where the second shot had come from. There were glowing embers scattered on the floor of the cave. They created a faint pinkish glow on the cave walls. Ten feet from where he stood Will could see a dark shape on the pink wall. He took two long strides and plunged his knife into the chest of a Mexican renegade.

Logan scanned the walls and saw several silhouettes further down. He stayed low and crept to the first. He was almost squatting, and could see the man's eyes glowing in the light of the embers. The big knife bit deep and the man grabbed at his throat puzzled by the warmth on his chest. Logan turned and drove his knife up under the arm of the second man who was taking aim at Will with a rifle. He cried out and collapsed. There was a shot, and the ball ricocheted off the wall next to Logan, followed by the sound of mumbling and running further back in the cave, then the moan of the shooter dying under Will's knife. Logan didn't know if there was another way out, and disliked the thought of going deeper into the darkness to fight hand to hand with knives. It seemed they had no choice. He led the way. They heard another groan of agony behind them. Noah was bringing up the rear and had found a renegade lurking behind, about to shoot Will in the back. He wouldn't be doing any more back-shooting. The next man they encountered was a Comanche that made the mistake of wiping sweat from his eyes. Logan caught a faint glint from his knife and grabbed him by the throat. At that moment, the moon broke over the mountain hitting the white limestone of the cave and surrounding area. The little bit of light that got back that far was faint by all accounts, but it provided enough for this Comanche to see who he faced.

He almost went limp, crying out, "Piapuha Nahuu!" But Logan stopped him from crying out anything else before moving on to the next. It was easier to make out the shapes as he moved from one to another. Twice more he encountered Comanches that called out the same words and stood as if frozen. He dispatched them quickly, moving forward. As the darkness grew more intense, Logan, Will, and Noah began moving more slowly, trying to stay as low as possible. Somewhere in the inky blackness, Logan heard a muffled whimper. It was ahead and to his left. He crept forward slowly, and as he approached where he thought the sound came from, he smelled something that gave away their position. Soap! The smell of soap, either in clothes or on someone, was coming from directly in front of him. He slowly reached out and barely touched the hem of a skirt or dress. He very carefully moved his hand to the left, but felt nothing then back to the right. He turned his head to the right and smelled the stink of filthy worn leather. Without hesitation, he came up from below and grabbed the Comanche by the throat then threw him against the wall. The knife bit Logan deep and he winced, but drove on slamming the Comanche against the wall several more times before driving the big knife through his ribs and up into his left lung. There was a gurgling then the sound of a body dropping. There was shouting and Will was in the room with another renegade in hand. Noah came in last and pandemonium broke out. These renegades had been sitting around staring into the fire for almost an hour before the three ex-Rangers came through the front. They were night blind and couldn't smell any-thing but the smoke in their nostrils. Logan, Will, and

Noah could easily smell the filthy leather and had the advantage. During the desperate hand-to-hand battle in the blackness of the cave, Logan had grabbed someone else that smelled of soap and had pushed them to the floor telling them to stay there. Twice more during the fight, renegade knives hit home. Once glancing along a rib and the next laying his shoulder open to the bone. The shouting died down and there didn't seem to be any more movement in the room. Noah made a quick survey of the walls and found no exit from this small room.

Logan crouched in the middle of the room and whispered, "Anybody in here crawl over to the sound of my voice now. We need to get out of here." At first, there was no movement or sound, and then he heard breathing and a quiet whimper. "Come on to me now. We're here to take you out. Crawl to me." There was a movement to his right and then another a little further on, and finally one to his left. In just a few seconds there were three terrified young women crouching on the floor with him.

From the blackness, Logan heard Will whisper, "Brother we need to go, now!" Logan silently agreed and took the first smooth little hand he felt and pushed it toward Noah. He pushed one to Will, then took the third himself. Staying low, they went slow and quiet. When they hit the moonlight, it was almost like walking into the light of the sun at midday. Noah stopped and crouched at the opening, surveying the night. There didn't seem to be any movement, but he figured there wouldn't be, at least until they came out. He was right; Logan and his charge had just cleared the entrance when the flash and boom came from the right and the rifle ball took Will in the lower thigh. He went down and the second shot missed him completely. Everybody started to run and Logan grabbed Will on the way by. He practically carried him along the cliff face and through the trees to their horses. He threw Will aboard his horse and one of the captives behind him then slapped the horse on the rump. He turned and stepped up onto the big black and swung the girl aboard behind himself as he kicked the horse into a dead run. The horse was sure footed and the bright moon helped them see where to go. It also showed anyone else where to shoot. Fortunately, there were few left to shoot and both had wasted their shots at the cave entrance. They headed northeast to Hamilton and didn't stop until they were at Logan's house. Logan and Noah started toward the house with the captives while Will went to get Rebecca. Logan's daughters were there with Zachary's wife, Melinda. Logan's entrance with the captives created an uproar. Logan's girls all screamed and began to cry when they saw their father, blood soaked and dirty. The captive girls were all young, filthy, and sobbing uncontrollably. Logan went to see if any had been wounded in the fight. When he got to the third girl, the one he'd carried away from the cave, she looked up at him and time stood still for a moment. There was something familiar there, but he couldn't grasp it right then. She looked deep into his eyes and thanked him, then threw her arms around his neck and sobbed harder. He held her for a moment until the sobbing lessened, then turned her over to Melinda. Rebecca burst through the door with Will hobbling behind. Both women looked the girls over to make sure there were no wounds and then turned their attention to the men, while Logan's girls ran around trying to help and holding their father's hands. Sarah, who was just five, felt she was big enough to tend her daddy all by herself and was busy mopping his dirty forehead. Aunt Melinda had to convince Sarah to move back a little and let her look at Logan. All three men had taken some kind of wound in the fight. Noah had fared best, only having been cut once and not too deep. It would be stitched up, but it wasn't as big a threat as Will or Logan's wounds. Will had one knife wound and one bullet wound, while Logan had three knife wounds, two of which were bone deep and long. He had lost a lot of blood and was feeling a little lightheaded. Melinda led him to the bed and made him lie down. Sarah hopped up onto the bed and continued to talk to him and wipe his face. Melinda slipped his boots off, and then his shirt so she could tend the wounds. She gasped when she looked at the one on his shoulder and again at the one that had slid along his ribs. Sarah sucked air through her teeth knowing the pain her daddy must be feeling. Melinda was most shocked by the one that started at his hip and stopped under his arm. The one he'd gotten at San Jacinto. Zachary had told her of it, but she'd never seen the scar. The thought of it almost took her breath away. She started cleaning the fresh wounds when suddenly another pair of hands was helping. She turned and there was the captive girl Logan had brought out.

"Please, I want to tend him. He saved my life," she said shakily. Melinda watched her for a moment then stepped back. She needed to go get her sewing kit anyway.

The girl worked with Melinda for close to two hours cleaning, stitching, and dressing Logan's wounds. Sarah sat on the bed and held his hand through it all. Eliza, Mary, and Emma hovered under foot, refusing to go away and let Aunt Melinda take care of their daddy. They were like three little blurs whenever Melinda needed something. Logan lay through it without moving a muscle. He felt very lightheaded, and several times felt as if he might faint, but he kept his head. He would occasionally look over to see how Will and Noah were doing.

Rebecca had removed Will's heavy leather chaps and pants, cleaned the bullet wound, and was ready to try and remove the bullet. Will was grinning as he lay watching her. She was concentrating so hard that she was almost oblivious to all else around her.

She noticed him staring and got a serious look on her face. "What are you grinning at William Magill?" she asked as she arranged the instruments she would need.

"You just seem so serious," He said, trying to put her at ease; It didn't seem to work.

"I'm serious because this is serious. You just wait Mr. Magill," she said as she pulled out his straight razor, "I'm about to wipe that silly grin right off your face." Will's eyes got big at the sight of the razor and the grin definitely disappeared. She offered him a short piece of leather to bite on, and at first he thought about refusing, but she flashed the straight razor again and he gladly took it.

She carefully wiped the wound and leaned forward to begin.

Will pulled the leather from his mouth. "Have I told you how much I love you lately?" he asked, laying there staring up at the ceiling. Rebecca's concentration was broken and she looked up at him to see that silly grin again. "Just wanted to make sure you know how much before you have a go at me with that razor," he said before putting the leather back between his teeth.

Rebecca inserted a small wooden dowel that Zachary had whittled for her into the wound to probe down and see how deep the bullet was. She discovered it was at least two inches into his lower thigh. It had probably hit his thighbone, but she didn't think his leg was broken. The probe didn't bother him too much, but getting the bullet out would prove to be a different story. She looked long into his eyes as if to say she was sorry for the pain she was about to cause, and Will knew exactly what she was feeling.

"Darlin', do it quick and do it clean. I'd rather you cut further than you need the first time than have to go back and cut me again. Go ahead now and cut on both sides of the hole. I'm ready," he said. Very shortly though, he realized he really wasn't ready; there is no way to be ready for that sort of thing. Rebecca made an inch long cut on the top and bottom of the hole with the grain of the muscle and felt the razor nick the bullet both times. Will was silent, but his hand shook and he began to sweat. Zachary wiped the blood and held a clean cloth tightly against the new cuts while Rebecca steeled herself to go in with her paring knife. She had bent the very tip of it into an "L" shape so she could get it under the bullet. When Zachary pulled the rag away, she quickly held the wound open, inserted the small knife, found the bullet, and tried to scoop it out. She lost it half way out and had to go back in. The second time the bullet rolled out onto the bed and Rebecca grabbed it while Zachary pressed the cloth tightly against the leg. Will went limp, except for the shaking in his hand. He was soaked with sweat already. Eliza was there to help. She wiped the sweat from his forehead and patted his face. The girls could not have loved Will more if he'd been their own father. It pained them doubly to see Logan and Uncle Will hurt so badly. Will was breathing deep and his eyes watered as Rebecca leaned over and brushed the hair back from his forehead.

Then, with love in her eyes, she said, "I'm sorry, did I make you cry?" Will sputtered and laughed aloud. She laid her head on his chest, and cried herself as he stroked her hair. Zachary got the bleeding stopped and finished cleaning the wound, then Rebecca stitched it shut and dressed it as neatly as any doctor might have. Will would recover well. Logan was up on one elbow and had watched Rebecca remove the bullet from Will's leg.

He watched as his girls moved around the room trying to tend to everybody. Mary and Emma, the youngest, had brought water to the captive girls to drink and wash up with. Emma, who had turned three in the spring, had a small cloth and tried to help whenever one of the girls would miss a spot.

"Lay back and be still!" Melinda admonished him. He lay back very tiredly as the captive girl dressed the wound on his side, and then he slipped into a deep sleep. It was partly because he'd lost a lot of blood, and partly because he was approaching forty-eight hours with only a short nap sitting up in a thicket. He was bone tired.

He slept the rest of the night and late into the morning. When finally he did wake up, it was to the sound of bustling over the cook stove and the smell of coffee boiling and bacon frying. Right then he couldn't have thought of a better way to wake up. He was starving.

He started to move and the searing hot pain in his side and shoulder made him gasp. The girl sleeping in the chair next to the bed was startled awake and jumped up, pushing him back into the bed.

"You need to lie still. You'll tear your stitches out," she said as she arranged the blanket over him. He looked at this girl and could see, now that it was light and she had been able to clean up a little, that she was a very beautiful girl, stunning in fact. There was something familiar about her, but he couldn't quite put his finger on it.

"Melinda has never bought a dress in her life. I daresay she's put stitches in me that'd hold a saddle together," he said, wincing again at the pain in his side. "I smell coffee and bacon. I hope there's plenty. I'm starvin'," he said, looking over at Rebecca who was scooping bacon from the iron skillet. She had a large mound of it already and a plate with at least a dozen fried eggs and he could see bread sliced and fried on the cook top, just the way he liked it.

"Hey let's keep it quiet, there's some of us with real wounds here and we need our sleep so's we can heal proper," Will said, rolling onto his side and pretending to go back to sleep. Rebecca finished setting out the food and walked over to where Will lay, looking down at his dirty face with genuine care in her eyes.

"Well those with 'real' wounds need to get washed up for breakfast. You're both dirty as pigs," she said, pointing the big metal spoon at him. "And you just remember, you were gonna build me a chicken coop out back, mister, so no lollygagging in bed all day, else my hens'll be laying eggs all over town." Will grinned without opening his eyes.

The girl went over to the table and fixed Logan a plate heaped with bacon and eggs and took it back to him, then returned for the bread frying on the stove and a cup of steaming coffee. She sat beside the bed and watched him eat.

"I'm sorry," he said between mouthfuls. "We've not been introduced. I'm Logan Vandeveer." He held out his hand.

The girl, still being young enough to be self-conscious, blushed slightly, "Yes I know," she said, taking his hand. Logan looked puzzled. "We've met before Mr. Vandeveer. My mother and I own a café in San Antonio. You ate there once right after the Council Hall fight."

Logan thought a moment, "Mariel? Mariel King!" he exclaimed, eyes widening in recognition. She smiled at the thought that he remembered her, and it took Logan's breath away. "Why I'd have recognized you last night in the cave if you'd smiled. I'd never forget such a beautiful smile." He said honestly. She blushed and giggled and Logan became very self-conscious of Rebecca and Will watching him.

"How did you know where I was?" she finally asked, still slightly red faced.

Logan looked at her for a moment. "I was in San Antonio in the market square when the shootin' started and your mother came in. She told me you'd been taken, though I didn't recognize her at the time."

"So, just you and Mr. Magill and Mr. Smithwick came after me?" she asked looking a little surprised.

Will chuckled. "No ma'am. Logan was alone in San Antone. He headed out to take on Blue Duck and his whole band of killers and thieves all by his lonesome." He said raising up on one elbow. "Why if he hadn't stumbled across Noah and me ridin' through the trees he'd have just gone into that cave alone, killed all the renegades, and rescued you three girls without me and Noah havin' to get shot and cut up." He was grinning again, having fun with Logan and Mariel. "Oh and by the way, did I thank you for this?" he said patting his leg gently. Logan just rolled his eyes.

Mariel looked into his eyes with a troubled look on her face. "You really set out to try and get us free all alone?" she asked, her eyes looking mistier than Logan felt comfortable with.

Finally he admitted, "The Army was headed east and your mother had said the ones that took you were goin' north. Mitchell Putman was there and said he thought he'd seen Blue Duck, but couldn't be sure, at least till the shootin' started, so I just took off." He rose up on one elbow to face Will. "By the way we need to go see if Blue Duck was one of the devils we killed in the cave before they pack off the dead ones."

Rebecca strode across the floor and pointed the metal spoon at him. "You two aren't goin' anywhere, least for a while. What if they're not gone yet? It'd be just like you two to go down there and get in another scrap before these wounds have even started to heal." She looked at Logan seriously, but with the love of a sister in her eyes, then turned and strode back across the floor.

Will was tickled. "Guess she told you, Mr. Big-time Ranger," he said with a chuckle. Rebecca spun and pointed the spoon at him with mock fire in her eyes. He stifled a chuckle, slid back down into the bed, and pulled the blankets up under his eyes.

Mariel stared at Logan while he ate his breakfast hungrily.

Logan was on his feet the next day, but Will was still bedridden. With the throbbing just getting started in his leg wound, he didn't complain, but was constantly after Rebecca to tell him what was going on outside or in town. She finally had to threaten to shoot his other leg if he didn't leave her alone so she could get her work done. At about noon, Noah came back with word that he and a troop from Ft. Croghan had gone back to the cave and pulled eleven dead renegades out. Five were Comanches, but none was Blue Duck. Logan and Will both swore. Logan asked Noah if he felt fit enough to escort Mariel back to San Antonio. He nodded, but Mariel protested and refused to go until Logan was better. He argued that, since he was up and around already, he was better. She wouldn't hear of it.

Six days later, Mrs. King arrived just as Mariel was getting ready to remove Logan's stitches. Word had been sent to her that Mariel was found and safe in Hamilton, but that she was staying to nurse the man that had saved her. Mrs. King was surprised to see Logan. She hadn't thought he had much of a chance at finding Mariel or rescuing her, especially alone. Logan tried to play the whole thing down, but Mariel, and Will, would have none of it. They told Mrs. King the whole horrific story up to the point where Mariel stayed to nurse him back to health. Will added the part about Logan probably killing most of the renegades himself before he or Noah could even get into the cave and how it was likely Logan's fault Will had been shot, though he wasn't sure how. Logan just threw his tin coffee cup at Will, who ducked it, grinning and feigning pain in his leg.

Fourteen days after the fight in the cave, Logan and Will mounted up and started northeast. They had something they felt they needed to do, against Rebecca's and both of their families' wishes. They had to go pay a visit to the Buffalo Eaters. Logan and Will had promised not to make war with *any* Comanches and yet they had done just that. They rode the trail in a leisurely manner. They enjoyed the trip and the night before they rode into The Buffalo Eater's camp, they shot two fat turkeys to present to Yellow Wolf, though they didn't know if he would eat turkey meat.

It was early morning when they arrived at the camp. Yellow Wolf had just finished washing himself in the small stream running down into the Trinity next to the camp. He had just re-oiled himself and then eaten some food when Big Medicine Knife and Smaller Brother rode into their camp. One of the warriors stationed as lookout raised the alarm with a whoop, not because there was the threat of attack, but because there was the threat of another celebration.

Two Crows heard the commotion and came down to Black Elk's lodge. This was the correct place for Logan and Will to go first. He and Yellow Wolf were both pleased to see them. Yellow Wolf plied them with questions, but Logan asked him to wait until they had spoken. Two Crows translated this for both Yellow Wolf and Black Elk. They graciously sat and waited for the big man to speak.

"I'm sorry my friends, we have broken our oath," Logan said looking from one to the other. Two Crows translated and all looked troubled and puzzled. "We found it necessary to make war with some Comanches," he said plainly. No sense trying to dress it up, what was done was done. He and Will had no idea what the Comanche thought on this might be, but they both realized that a prolonged and agonizing death could be part of it. They just didn't know. The three Comanches sat, inscrutable and mute. He went on.

"Some renegades riding with Blue Duck killed people and took white women as captives while pretending to talk peace in San Antonio." Still their expressions didn't change and they said nothing. They just waited. "My brother and I tracked them to a cave and fought them with our knives. We killed some to get back the captive women. Some were Comanches. We regret breaking our oath to you, but we could not let the captives go." He was looking straight into Yellow Wolf's eyes, but saw no hint of reaction. "We came to tell you this so you would not think us cowards to hide and let you hear of it from someone else, and to tell you we will accept whatever punishment you feel is right." Two Crows translated this and Yellow Wolf looked a little taken aback. He had not expected such honor from White Diggers, even one such as Piapuha Nahuu. The three Comanches talked among themselves in their language for a moment, and then Yellow Wolf spoke.

"We honor our sacred oaths with our lives and expect the same from others." He looked from Logan to Will and back. They waited to hear what his judgment would be. "You have sworn not to make war with any Comanche, but have killed some Comanches that rode with Blue Duck." He turned and mumbled something to Black Elk and Two Crows.

"Long has Blue Duck shamed the Comanche people. I have kept him from this camp because he is evil. He was rejected by his own father. Blue Duck has long since ceased being a Comanche." He waited for Two Crows to translate. "Any that ride with Blue Duck cannot be Comanche. Word has come to me that Blue Duck lives. This is unfortunate. He no longer can come and go when he chooses. Death awaits him at every Comanche and Kiowa camp. The Honey Eaters have spoken this also." He finished and sat looking at Logan and Will, inscrutably. Logan and Will looked at one another unsure of what to say or do.

Two Crows broke the silence. "Blue Duck is no longer Comanche, he is renegade. Any that ride with him are renegade." Logan and Will sat motionless. Two Crows looked exasperated. "You have made war with no Comanches. You are still friends to the Buffalo Eaters." The relief on Logan and Will's faces was evident, because Black Elk and Two Crows both chuckled at their discomfort. Yellow Wolf sat looking at these two unusual diggers. He wondered if their spirits were Comanche after all and they just didn't know it. He would try to find out, later.

Logan went outside, got the two turkeys, and brought them in to give Yellow Wolf. His offer was met with obvious approval.

"Yellow Wolf has been hungry for the meat of turkeys since before I rode out for the vision that told of the coming of Blue Duck," Two Crows explained. Will and Logan started as if they had been jabbed. Two Crows thought this unusual and figured he should explain more. "Because of my dreams, I sought a vision that foretold of Blue Duck. Yellow Wolf and twenty of his strongest warriors went to kill him. The direction Blue Duck would go was not shown to me. Yellow Wolf tracked the renegades and made war with them, sending all to be scorned by their ancestors. Blue Duck was not among them. Yellow Wolf has not slept well since. He feels he failed his people." Yellow Wolf sat looking expectant while Logan and Will discussed this.

"Yellow Wolf must have tracked the band that went east and I tracked the one riding north. Blue Duck traveled north. My Brother and I made war with him, but he got away in the cave. I was the one that failed, not Yellow Wolf," Logan said solemnly. Two Crows translated this to Yellow Wolf. A look of surprise came over his face.

"You fight Blue Duck in cave?" he asked. Logan nodded.

"We killed most of his renegades, but he wasn't among the dead," Logan admitted. Yellow Wolf said something to Two Crows, who got a very surprised look on his face.

Yellow Wolf motioned to Logan, obviously admonishing him to translate it.

Two Crows explained, "Yellow Wolf said that even if you have conquered death you are..." he stumbled here, looking around, obviously looking for the right word. Shortly he had it "you are...'loco'...'crazy' for following Blue Duck into a cave to kill with a knife, even with the Piapuha Nahuu, the Big Medicine Knife." He looked pleased at his translation. Logan and Will looked at each other and began to laugh. Yellow Wolf and Black Elk smiled softly and Two Crows looked confused. The celebration started that night and went until morning. Logan and Will had brought trade items and made many good trades, including a young War Bonnet filly that Logan intended to breed into some of his horse stock. They went hunting, smoked the pipe with Black Elk, and finally left two days later. The trip back was uneventful, except that they crossed some fresh sign of an unshod pony twice, but the trail was covered and they lost it. Blue Duck crossed both their minds and put them on alert. If he was there, they never saw or heard him.

CHAPTER 13

THE TRAIL DRIVE EAST

When they got back from the Buffalo Eaters' camp, Logan and Will were surprised to find Mariel King still in Hamilton. They were even more surprised to find her mother, Eleanor, there too. Mariel had refused to go back to San Antonio. She and her mother had argued, but she was adamant. This was where she would live. Mariel had just turned twenty-three years old, was still unmarried, and by her mother's own admission, the most stubborn girl that had ever lived. When her mind was made up, there was no talking her out of anything, and her mind was made up about Logan Vandeveer. Eleanor King tried to talk sense into her daughter, but that was a no go. Mariel had fallen in love with Logan more than ten years before, and thought all was lost the day he rode out of San Antonio. She had seen him several times in the following years, but she was still a young girl, too young, and she knew it. Besides he was married with children, he had no interest in another child. He was the reason she had never accepted the attentions of numerous suitors over the years. None could live up to the example set by Logan Vandeveer. Tall, muscular, handsome, adventurous, honest...she could go on and on. No, she had found a dream, faithfully held it for more than a decade, and now that she could realize the dream, she was not going anywhere. From the first night when she was brought to the house, she knew this was where she would stay. She had kindled relationships with all four of the girls and they fell in love with her as quickly as she did with them. Will, Rebecca, and their children found they also had an affinity for the girl. It was as if she were a missing family member, reunited. There seemed to be only two people that needed convincing, Eleanor and Logan. Her mother would be easy; Logan would be more of a challenge. It was something she knew in her heart that should, and would, come to pass, so she would be patient.

Four days after her arrival Eleanor realized her daughter's mind was made up. As she walked down the one small street in Hamilton, she noticed a building sitting empty. It was not an old building, there were no old buildings in Hamilton, but it was empty nonetheless. She made a few inquiries and found that a man named Tel Barker had built it to open a dry goods store, but when his wife died of pneumonia the previous winter, Mr. Barker gave up on the idea and moved back to San Antonio to be near his family. The building stood empty. Eleanor let herself inside and looked the place over. Yes, it would do. She told Mariel she was going back to San Antonio and left the next day. When she got to San Antonio four days later she went to find Mr. Barker right away. She found him in a small house on the edge of town. He was a small man with listless eyes. When Eleanor asked him about the building in Hamilton, sorrow filled the listless eyes. They talked for a while, and Eleanor found out that he had a small inheritance and had invested part of it in the building and some dry goods to stock it with, but that his wife had taken ill and died before they could open. Mr. Barker had done little since returning to San Antonio, except live on his inheritance, which was running out. Eleanor laid out her idea to him and a light seemed to go on behind his eyes as she spoke. Since she owned the building her café was in, she suggested they trade buildings. He could open his dry goods store there in San Antonio, near his family, and she would move her café to Hamilton. It was a fair trade, the deal was struck, and five days later, she sat on the seat of a hired freight wagon headed back to Hamilton with everything she owned. The building she had traded for in Hamilton had a good-sized loft in it where she could live. She figured she needn't worry about Mariel. Eleanor expected Mariel and Logan would be married before long anyway, even if Logan didn't know it yet.

Logan was puzzled as to what to do about Mariel. It wasn't proper for her to stay in his house and with seven children, there didn't seem to be room at Will and Rebecca's. It was Zachary and Melinda that offered the solution he needed. They had an extra room, and she could stay there. Zachary thought it the funniest thing ever to watch his brother squirm under the attentions of this beautiful young woman. Melinda truly liked Mariel and knew that it was only a matter of time until she was officially her sister. Mariel was embedded almost before Logan even knew it.

A week after Eleanor returned from San Antonio, Logan was getting ready to ride out to check on the roundup going on just a couple of miles away on a section of the ranch that adjoined Will's ranch. Logan had spent the week helping Eleanor get her café ready to open in the new building. He had even helped extend the loft all the way across the building giving Eleanor an entire second story. He had gotten the first batch of biscuits from the café just that morning before he headed out to the roundup. Logan was saddling his horse when Mariel came out with a bundle.

"I fixed you some fried chicken to take along in case you get hungry," she said as she put the bundle into his saddlebag. "There's some cornbread and apple pie too. You like apple pie don't you?" she asked, smiling that dazzling smile of hers. Logan had tried to resist her at first, but every time she gave him that smile, he visibly melted more and more. Now he had less than a snowball's chance in hell of resisting her.

He smiled back at her. "I surely do like apple pie, and if yours is anything like Eleanor's I'm sure it'll be better than most." She stopped and their eyes locked briefly. "I'm goin' out to see how Zachary is doing with the roundup. It'll be his first without Will or me there to help. Would you like to ride along?" he asked. Her eyes lit up, and if possible, her smile brightened even more. She dashed back into the house and was ready very quickly. As she hurried back out, Logan went to the corral and caught the War Bonnet pony he'd gotten in a trade with Yellow Wolf. Logan was beginning to see more and more strong traits in these mustangs and had started accumulating them whenever possible. This particular one was a five-year-old filly that he intended to breed within the month. She was longwinded and good on the trail, traits he wanted more of in his remuda of horses. He had her saddled quickly and they were on the trail in a matter of minutes.

To Mariel it was like a dream, riding along with the man she had loved for so long, chatting and getting to know one another. Logan enjoyed Mariel's company. She was interested in all that he was involved in and seemed to grasp ideas quickly. She was very good at listening, but also not afraid to speak. All in all, Logan and Mariel were a good match.

They got to the area where Zachary and three other hired men were branding some mavericks and sat their horses for a bit watching. The problem with branding mavericks in this country was you never knew when the maverick's mother might show up. There were few things in Texas able to un-nerve even the toughest cowman quicker than a rampaging longhorn cow bent on protecting her calf. It had happened before and made survival touch and go. Usually one person stood watch during any roundup to keep an eye out for just such a thing. Zachary and the men had been having a little trouble with the brush and pole fence, and the Vaquero that was supposed to be watching was on the ground trying to mend a hole in the fence as Logan and Mariel rode over the rise.

Zachary and the two men handling the running irons had a rangy calf down, and had just put the iron to its hide when amidst the bawling came the crash and bellow of a big cow from the scrub brush nearby. The lookout was on the opposite side of the pen from Zachary, so he didn't have any chance at all of stopping her. Sometimes they would ride between the rampaging longhorns and the men on the ground and lead them back out onto the prairie and lose them in the trees, giving anyone caught on the ground a chance to find cover. Occasionally the animal gave them no choice but to try to find the tiny brain with a bullet. Even when they did shoot straight, sometimes it took more than one shot. On one occasion, it took six shots to bring down an old cow bent on making Logan into a mushy spot under hoof.

Logan had packed rifles on both saddles, he always did. You could never tell when you'd need the extra rifle and he carried the newest revolver to come into the area, the .44 caliber Colt Walker Revolver. It had a long barrel, held six shots (though only a fool would load the chamber the hammer sat on while riding through the brush), and packed a real wallop. He wore it on his right hip because he wore the big knife on his left, and always would.

When the wild-eyed cow crashed through the brush, bellowing and looking for a target to fix her anger on, Zachary was the first she saw. Without missing a step, she turned and ran full speed toward him. He was at least a hundred yards from the nearest tree, which probably wouldn't have saved him even if he could get there in time. He made the dash anyway looking back over his shoulder hoping he might sidestep her and let her run on by. Her six-foot wide horn spread was pretty much a guarantee he wasn't going to pull that off. Logan reached down and pulled the old muzzleloader from the scabbard, checked to see that the percussion cap was still in place, and threw it to his shoulder. Mariel's horse bumped his slightly, but he got the old cow in his sights and was about to pull the trigger when he saw Mariel bolt toward Zachary.

He hesitated just a split second and then fired. The bullet hit home, but hit just under the right horn. It stunned the big rangy cow and she stumbled, making Logan think that she might just go down. She bellowed, shook her head, then found her feet and was up and running again, although not quite as fast. When Logan realized this he reached for his new Colt... he looked down and it was gone. He had a hammer loop that kept the gun in the holster...but it was gone. Just then, he heard the first boom of the big .44. He looked up. Mariel was riding full speed on a collision course with the cow and had his pistol in hand. She fired twice more and Logan could hear the 'whump-whump' of the big slugs hitting the cow, but he couldn't tell where. She only had two more shots and as the range was shrinking, she was now in grave danger. Mariel was kicking the little pony, which was running for all she was worth, and Logan saw her raise the pistol again. She fired and the old cow bellowed, shaking her head. Staggering, blood flew from her nostrils and she bellowed again, but kept Zachary fixed with her blind rage. Mariel veered off toward Zachary, who was still running for the tree. Mariel cut in front of the cow, which seemed to be slowing slightly, but was still moving fast. The little pony was wild eyed at having the bellowing cow behind her. Mariel screamed at Zachary, who looked back and saw what she was doing. He didn't slow down, but readied himself. He'd only get one chance to live or die. As the little pony closed the distance to within fifty feet of Zachary, Mariel turned in the saddle, raised the big pistol, and fired her last shot. It was now or never. She didn't wait to see if she hit or not, she just turned back and when she was beside Zachary, ducked the sure-footed little horse to the left and cut right in front of him. He grabbed at the saddle horn and missed, but got it the second time and swung up behind her. As the little horse took the added weight on her back, she stretched out and ran for her life. Mariel and Zachary heard the thud behind them and both turned in time to see the old cow plant her chin in the dirt and begin to tumble. She went end over end once, and rolled over sideways twice, before skidding to a stop. Dust filled the air. Zachary gasped for breath as Mariel eased the brave little horse down to a walk, turning her back toward the brush pen. The little horse was still wild-eyed and veered wide around the old cow lying motionless in a swirl of dust. As Logan met them there, the other men came running up talking a mile a minute. They had never seen anything like that, and from a woman no less. Mariel stopped the little horse, and after Zachary slid off, she got down and loosened the cinch, then petted the horse, talking softly and rubbing her face and ears.

"That was the most dangerous thing I've seen all week," Logan said, stepping off his horse and taking the pistol from her waistband, anger flashed in his eyes. His anger dissipated quickly when he looked into Mariel's beautiful face. "But by God I'm glad you did it now that it's over." Then, turning to Zachary, he added, "Little brother, next time you better run faster 'cause I'm not lettin' her risk her life to save your hide again." As he finished, he turned, put his arms around Mariel, and kissed her. She seemed to melt into him, and after what seemed a very long time for a kiss, the ranch hands actually got a little embarrassed. They began to shuffle around with their hands in their pockets shaking their heads. Zachary snapped them out of it. "OK boys! We got cattle to brand. Stop standin' around watching my big brother smooch on Mariel," he said, grinning from ear to ear. Logan and Mariel suddenly became aware of the others and separated themselves, though they didn't let go completely. Both were embarrassed, but stood with an arm around one another.

As he walked by, Zachary stopped, put his arms around Mariel, and hugged her tightly, saying, "Thank you, Sister. I wouldn't have made it if it weren't for you. I owe you my life." He looked deep into her eyes. Mariel wasn't used to such attention, and part of her wanted to run away, but a much bigger part wanted to stay right there next to the man she loved, forever.

Logan and Mariel talked all the way back to the house. Logan no longer felt uncomfortable around her, he finally realized what it was that had made him feel that way in the first place. It was his feelings for her. He realized that deep down he had felt the attraction to her from the first night when he brought her to the house and she had practically carried him through the door. He thought he was rescuing her, but in reality she was rescuing him. He would no longer feel lost, as if missing a part of himself. He would no longer wish for the comfort of a good woman, a life partner. Logan knew they would be together from that moment on. Mariel had known it for a long time.

Logan and Mariel didn't court long, and when they announced that they were getting married, Logan's girls squealed with delight, sweeping Mariel away to question her extensively. Logan was relieved the girls took to Mariel. He was afraid they would not be able to tolerate another woman in the house after their mother had died.

They were married a month later, and Mariel moved into the house. Logan was once again happy and felt complete.

The happiness that rained down on the Vandeveers and Magills seemed as though it would last forever, but fate is a fickle thing. In November of 1852, Will decided to take Rebecca and the children into the new Capitol of Texas that was called Austin. There really wasn't much reason to go, but Will thought it would be nice for them to get away for a few days and see the fastest growing town in Texas. It was said there were a thousand people living in this newly laid out town, so they packed up the wagon and left at first light on the 17th of November. They headed east, following the San Gabriel River on the south bank all the way from Hamilton. After about twenty miles, the girls started to complain. They were tired of riding in the wagon. They wanted to stop and camp about two hours before sunset. The country was flat and there were wide openings between the thickets of brush and trees. Will figured they could get one more hour in before stopping to make camp, maybe make another four or five miles. They finally stopped at a point almost due north of Austin and made camp. The younger children romped and played around the area while Will and the older boys, James, William Jr., and Samuel set up the camp, then went hunting. James shot a nice fat tom turkey, and

Will cut it up and roasted it for their supper. After dark, they all sat around the fire and listened to Will tell stories about their grandmother and grandfather. He also told them some stories about their uncle Logan when he was a boy, and about their trip out to Texas from Casey County, Kentucky. Some of the stories they had heard, some not. They liked to hear them all.

The small man was up at first light and on the move. Nathan Barnard was not the type to handle hardship well and traveling light made him grouchy. Nathan and his brother Ralphie had been on their own since Nathan was fifteen and Ralphie was twelve. Their father was a mean man and a drunk, so when he drank he became the meanest of drunks. One day the old man picked up a shovel and hit Ralphie in the side of the head with it, then stole a horse and rode out of town. Ralphie was in a coma for a week and when he woke up it didn't take long to realize that he was not the same boy. The old man had been caught on the stolen horse in the next town and hung the following day.

They hadn't eaten the night before because Ralphie had spooked the only game they had seen all day, a skinny little whitetail spike. Ralphie was constantly after Nathan to let him shoot the big Springfield rifle Nathan had found lying in a ditch when they were in San Antonio a few years back. They had been looking for ranch work when trouble had broken out with some Comanches. Several people were killed. One man was shot through with an arrow right before their eyes. His big Springfield rifle fell into a weed-choked ditch. Nathan had cared for the man while Ralphie went for help. The man died before help got there. Nathan went back to the ditch that night and recovered the rifle, after all the man was dead. He and Ralphie left San Antonio that night.

Nathan had warned Ralphie to stay away from the rifle, but Ralphie pestered him almost daily. Finally, Nathan had let him shoot it, thinking the kick and noise would scare him enough that he wouldn't want to shoot it again. Ralphie loved the noise and squealed with delight every time Nathan shot it. Today was no different from any other day, except Ralphie started in on the gun earlier than most. Nathan put up with it for the better part of the morning, and then out of exasperation gave in. He sent Ralphie out with two big white rocks and told him to put them on top of an old cedar log near the camp. With the targets set, Nathan loaded the old musket and explained to Ralphie how to sight and shoot. Ralphie was so excited he almost peed in his pants. Nathan held the musket until Ralphie finished peeing, buttoned his pants, and took the gun back. He aimed just as Nathan told him, then took a deep breath and was trying to blow it out slow, but got too excited and jerked the trigger. The shot went wild and Nathan swore. Shooting at rocks was wasteful enough, but hitting nothing was worse. Ralphie begged for another chance and finally Nathan gave in. Ralphie was so excited that it took Nathan a full five minutes to get the gun reloaded, get Ralphie calmed down enough to go over the instructions with him again, and then hand the gun over to him. Ralphie aimed carefully, took a deep breath, let it out slowly, and this time squeezed the trigger. One of the big rocks jumped and spun a quarter turn. Ralphie squealed with delight. Nathan took the big musket and reloaded it just in case they came across another whitetail or maybe a turkey.

◐◑

Will, Rebecca, and the children were up, had eaten breakfast, and were ready to roll by sunup. The children were excited, as children often are in the morning. Will figured by noon they would have become bored and would probably sleep in the back of the wagon.

They had been on the trail again most of the morning, and Will figured they'd stop in another hour or so at a nice little picnic area he knew of beside Running Brushy Creek, when they heard a shot off in the distance. Will pulled the mules up and they all sat listening and looking around. At this time in Texas you could never be too careful. One shot was all there was and that usually meant someone was hunting. The shot sounded pretty far off, so Will slapped the mules on their rumps with the reins and they moved on. A few minutes later, there was another shot that sounded as far away as the first. Without stopping again, Will dismissed it thinking it was the hunter just finishing off a deer. Rebecca leaned her head on his shoulder and slept. The weather was warm, the ground was flat, and the wagon ride was pretty smooth. Will hoped all the children would sleep for a while.

When he got to the picnic spot he had been thinking about, he pulled up the wagon and set the brake. The children were up and out of the wagon in a flash. Will moved his shoulder to wake Rebecca, but she slept on.

"Hey, wake up," he said as he reached around with his other hand to shake her. "We got hungry young 'uns that'r fixin' to eat all the fish..." as he turned she slid down from the wagon seat and he noticed the blood staining the front of her dress. "Rebecca!" he said, shaking her. "Rebecca!!" he jumped from the wagon, and lifting her out, noticed for the first time the red streak running down through her blond hair. He laid her on the ground and turned her head to look. There was a jagged cut just behind her temple. "REBECCA!!" he screamed into her face. The children began to crowd around and all started to scream and cry. Will held her to him rocking slowly back and forth. He sobbed openly, something he had never done before. This frightened the children as much as seeing their mother bloody and dead.

Will cleaned her face and hair at the little stream and then wrapped her snugly in a blanket. He drove on into Austin and went straight to the Ranger barracks to report what had happened. Will told Captain Blackwell that he was going on to Bastrop and asked if he could send word to Logan. Blackwell dispatched several troopers right then, one to take word to Logan, and two others to search the area for whoever might be responsible. Will drove slowly through Austin and on to Bastrop. Rebecca had loved Bastrop and had told Will she wanted to be buried there. There was a small pecan grove near the house they had lived in where she used to go and sit when she needed to get away and think. It was here that Will would lay her to rest. Logan and all his family arrived in Bastrop two days later. Rebecca was buried at sunset that same day. It was her favorite time of day.

The months following Rebecca','s death were sad beyond belief. The two Rangers caught up with Nathan and Ralphie Barnard, but it was decided the whole thing was an accident and they were released. They weren't bad men, they just happened to be unlucky men.

◉◉

During the next two years, Logan accomplished many things. He completed the church he had started, built a Post Office called the Burnet Courthouse, and became the first Post Master of Burnet County. He also built a school and called it the Collegiate School, then hired Oxford University graduate William H. Dixon to teach French,

Latin, geography, history, philosophy, mathematics, and elocution to the children of Burnet County.

In 1854, he began to build the first stone building in Hamilton. It was a two-story structure that was used as a mercantile and Masonic Lodge. This took the better part of a year to complete because the stone was quarried some twenty-five miles to the south and had to be hauled in by a freight wagon with a team of mules.

During this time, Will received word from his brother James in Kentucky and went back for a short visit. There he met and courted Elizabeth Alice Hedrick. They were married in December and left for Texas at the end of February 1855.

In May of the same year, Logan was visited by one Lucien "Lolo" Mansion.

Lolo Mansion was a very wealthy tobacco and cigar dealer in New Orleans. Lolo was also a relatively well-known poet, at least locally. Mansion wanted five hundred head of cattle delivered to New Orleans. The Orgain Brothers had told him about Logan and his ability to get cattle delivered quickly and on time. Driving a herd of longhorns was a very difficult thing to do over flat open ground with lots of help, but it was another thing entirely to try to drive them around and through the rivers and bayous of Louisiana. The herd would have to be driven north to avoid the largest swamp in the country and then turned south somewhere above Baton Rouge. It was a daunting proposition, but Logan was up for it, as this could be the beginning of a very large contract for him and Will. New Orleans was, after all, one of the largest and most industrious cities in America. He could easily foresee driving many thousands of cattle there in the future.

He, Will, and Zachary worked for ten days with the hired hands to roundup that many of the rebellious longhorns. During this roundup, Logan noticed that many of the cattle weren't quite as wary as they normally were, and jokingly accused Zachary of trying to tame the lot of them. Logan had hired J.C. Bradley as the foreman for the roundup and drive to New Orleans. Bradley, being an experienced cattleman, was also familiar with the area between Hamilton and New Orleans. Since Will's new wife Elizabeth was expecting and due to deliver in late September or early October, he and Logan had agreed that he shouldn't go along on this one. Zachary would take his place instead.

Being just shy of six hundred miles from New Orleans, J.C. figured it would take them better than two full months to get there and about a month back. So, on July 21, 1855, with five hundred twelve head rounded up, penned and ready to go, Logan, Zachary, J.C. Bradley, and seven other hired hands hit the trail for New Orleans and certain wealth. Logan had promised to be back inside a hundred days with enough money to build a new house. Mariel was tearful and worried, but she trusted Logan and kissed him goodbye at the brush pen. She rode along with the herd for about five miles before finally waving goodbye and turning back to the little house.

CHAPTER 14

THE LETTER

The summer had been a dry one that year, some even called it a draught. It hadn't rained for more than a hundred eighty days. Will was up early that morning in the first week of November. There was a change in the weather coming. He could feel it in all his old scars and wounds. He sat on the porch drinking coffee as usual and watched the sunrise. It was blood red, and a slight breeze fluttered across the yard. Elizabeth had delivered their son George just a month earlier and hadn't slept well the night before. Will decided to let her sleep, so he had another cup of coffee. After his coffee, he went into the kitchen and started rattling skillets and pans around, more to get her moving than to actually cook anything, but at least he had to appear to be taking a stab at it. Elizabeth waddled out of the bedroom, hair tousled. She shuffled across the floor, and as she put her arms around him, she gave him a quick punch in the ribs. He feigned injury and tried to pretend he was busy cooking something, although not a skillet was even warm yet. She took over and he went to the other two bedrooms of the house and rousted the children. The younger ones squealed when he ran into the room, and threatened to eat them instead of eggs and bacon. The older ones were used to his routine and were already up getting dressed. His oldest daughter Mary was changing the baby, George. After breakfast, he went out to see how the hired hands were doing with the cattle. They were shorthanded, and Logan was so certain of a continuing contract that they had decided to keep the roundup going. Perhaps they could do a quick turn around when he got back and run a few hundred head more over to New Orleans. Logan was already more than two weeks later than he had expected, so Will wasn't so sure about a fast turnaround. Will figured at least the cattle would get used to being around men and horses and not be so wild. The prairie was in such bad shape from the drought that he was thinking of just waiting until Logan got back. This morning was different. There was something in the air.

Around midday he rode back to the house to check on Elizabeth and to get something to eat. After he ate some stew that Elizabeth had cooked for him, he went on over to Logan's to see how Mariel was doing. He hadn't seen her that day, which was unusual. She was normally over to check on Elizabeth early in the day. The two had become friends quickly. Their friendship reminded him of younger days when Rebecca and Lucinda would take care of each other while he and Logan were out chasing down renegades or bandits. He smiled and felt younger at that moment.

As he rode toward Logan and Mariel's house, he could see her sitting in a rocker that Logan had traded a full-grown steer for so she could rock on the porch. Today she wasn't rocking. He smiled and gave her a little wave, but she sat and stared out across the yard toward the open prairie.

He dismounted. "Hey there," he said, walking around the back of his horse. "I feel a change in the air…," then he noticed the tears in her eyes. She was wearing a blue dress and the front was wet from tears. His eye was drawn to the letter she held in her shaking hand. "Mariel, honey, what is it?" he asked as he hurried up onto the porch. Just then the door opened and Logan's father William stepped out with a cup of hot tea trembling in his hand and tears in his eyes. He looked from one to the other. Mariel jumped to her feet, and buried her face in Will's chest, screaming and sobbing until she couldn't stand, then fell to the floor. Will scooped her up and put her back in the rocker then turned to Logan's father, whose chin was quivering. He was unable to speak. Will bent down and picked up the letter. It was from a C. O. Dugue addressed to Mr. William Vandeveer. Will began to read it, but he didn't really absorb what it said because his eye was quickly drawn to the middle of the letter where he read;

"...Mr. Logan Vanderver and Mr. Zachary P. Vanderver departed this life some weeks ago in the Parish of Plaquemines leaving in this State in the Parish of Jefferson some moveable effects valued at $6,000 for each..."

Will stood in shock, unable to think. His vision seemed to darken around the edges and his ears began to ring as he reached out and grabbed one of the porch posts to steady himself. The letter fluttered unnoticed to the ground. Logan and Zachary had both died in New Orleans of yellow fever contracted at the end of the drive through the swamps of Louisiana.

Two weeks later, Will left the house early in the morning and rode to the northeast for five days. He rode into the Buffalo Eaters' camp with a heavy heart and didn't stay long. There was a whoop of jubilation when he rode in and a moan of sorrow when he told Yellow Wolf and Two Crows of Logan's death. Logan and Will had been welcomed into this clan's camp and were considered friends, if not brothers. To learn of the death of the one many felt could not be killed caused much anguish and concern for their future. Will didn't stay long. He gave Yellow Wolf a bundle wrapped in oiled canvas and rode out of the camp. Logan was mourned as though one of them.

Two days later, Yellow Wolf rode out to a small grove of pecan trees where he often went to relax and reflect on his life. Here he built a mound, placed many sacred objects of shell, bone, and feathers in patterns his ancestors had used, and their ancestors before them, to honor a great spirit. Such was the honor here. He worked on it slowly, and just as he was finishing, Two Crows rode up. He dismounted, and as he and Yellow Wolf sang the songs that honored the passing of great warriors, Yellow Wolf removed the Piapuha Nahuu, the Big Medicine Knife that had been carried by their friend the great warrior, from the oiled canvas, placing it in the center of the mound. Now it would watch over the camp of the Buffalo Eaters, and maybe all Comanches.

THE END

AFTERWORD

Logan Vandeveer was only 40 years old when he died. Many historians in Texas believe that if Logan had lived just another ten or twenty years, he would have become one of the most prominent citizens of Texas, possibly even Governor. Logan was buried in Plaquemines Parish, Louisiana where he remains to this day.

William Magill went on to serve as a Captain in The Home Guards during the Civil War. He and Elizabeth had ten more children, the last of which was born just three years before his death at the age of sixty-five. He and Elizabeth remained married until Will's death in 1878, while sitting in a rocker on his porch in Hamilton (however the name had been changed to Burnet by then). He was buried in Burnet near his home. Elizabeth and at least nine of his seventeen children were later buried near him.

It is unknown what became of Mariel (King) Vandeveer. No record exists of her before her rescue by Logan, or after his death.

Yellow Wolf and Buffalo Hump were both respected leaders of different Comanche camps. Both were considered great warriors.

13045438R00187

Made in the USA
Charleston, SC
13 June 2012